Morganne,
My book cover is so
much better with your
face in the mirror's reflection.
Thank you for letting me
use a photo of you.
I hope you enjoy the book!
Barbara Brooke

Glimmers
Barbara Brooke

Chapter One

G liding along metal hangers, my hand lightly brushes over lush designer fabric. Moving slowly, I shift the clothing apart. Each piece has a personality of its own and each clamors for my attention. My heartbeat quickens and my hunt shifts gears. A treasure is hidden in here somewhere. I can feel it.

A cashmere sweater falls into my arms. I hold it to my chest in deep embrace, caressing its velvety sleeves. But when I look in the mirror, I see its color is just too dull against my complexion, and right now, that's the last thing I need.

I catch a glint in the mirror and glance over my shoulder. A golden mannequin stands there with attitude, wearing what must be the cutest pair of jeans I've ever seen. I rush over, and some-what rudely, strip the jeans off the plastic goddess. With bated breath, I peek at the size . . . yes! I hug them tightly and continue on my expedition.

And suddenly, there they are: suede fold-over ankle boots. I pick them up and gently turn them over in my hands. The leather is smooth and supple; its color is rich and warm. There are only a few signs of wear on the soles, but they really are in great shape. These are true designer boots all the way from the eighties.

But what if they don't fit? Don't even think that way, Paige, they must, they just have to. After all, they will go perfectly with my new favorite jeans. Ever so carefully, I slide my foot down into the tan colored boot. I push a little further, and my toes barely graze the tip. The fit is absolutely perfect! Now, if only I had somewhere to wear them. No, I will wear them: to the grocery store, PTA meetings, and maybe even for Hailey's bridal shower . . . or maybe not. I mean, who wears boots to a bridal shower?

~ * * * ~

Suddenly, a familiar sound drifts from the backseat of my minivan, "I am not a baby!" From a blurry distance, my daughter's voice manages to find me. And just like that, my most recent shopping daydream is over.

"You are too!" Liam shouts back.

"I am not!" Elle exclaims.

I peer into my rearview mirror and see the reddened faces of my children.

I sigh and ask the dreaded question, "What's going on back there?"

"Liam said I was too old to wear a kitty on my t-shirt. He said the other kids would think I was a baby!" Elle says, pointing toward the Hello Kitty graphic on her shirt.

"Liam, that little kitty is all the rage on the kindergarten playground," I say, trying to lessen the tension in the car.

"The girls in *my* class wear shirts with guitars and cool stuff on them," he replies.

"Well, you are also two years older than Elle. If she's happy with her clothes, then that's all that matters," I say.

Liam rolls his eyes before looking out the window. I can barely hear him mutter, "I was only trying to help."

Elle rests back in her seat, and a smile spreads across her sweet heart-shaped face. I know I must've said something right. I take another moment and stare at her reflection. Since the day she was born, Elle has resembled my husband: golden-blonde hair, bright blue eyes, and a smile to brighten my day. Today, she looks a little different. Is it possible she is beginning to resemble me? Her hair has darkened, and her waves are straightening . . . hmm, maybe.

Liam, on the other hand, looks remarkably like me. Except, his hair is golden, (like his father's), his complexion is fair (like his father's). All right, Liam still resembles Elliott, but he *does* have my chocolate brown eyes.

~ * * * ~

Sunshine Elementary School appears ahead . . . time to be herded like cattle. A person adorned in an orange vest whistles and motions for all of the cars, minivans, and SUV's to merge into the right turn lane. I pull up to my assigned spot, and my kids hop out of the car.

"See ya," mumbles Liam, leaving with a little wave behind his back.

"Okay my little man, see you later! I love you and will give you big hugs later!" I say very quietly to myself.

Elle's a different story; she still allows me to dote on her with great affection. I receive a large hug goodbye, before she heads for her class.

First mission accomplished. Next, pick up a few groceries . . . sigh.

~ * * * ~

"What to cook for dinner, what to cook for dinner," I agonize on my drive home from the supermarket.

Even after purchasing a cart overflowing with food, I'm still not sure what to throw together. If I'm being honest here, I dread coming up with meal ideas. I know in my heart, my feeble attempt in the kitchen will most likely fail in a major way. And although I loathe the process, I believe I owe it to my family to prepare something home cooked and healthy.

Over the years, my husband Elliott has endured countless subpar meals . . . poor man. I suspect our lack of company at the dinner table is due to the fact dinners at the MacKenzie household are typically served burnt, dry, or tasteless. It's very frustrating, to say the least.

My cell phone rings, and I rummage through my purse. Let's face it; I already know it will be one of three people: Elliott, my little sis Hailey, or Mom. Who will it be this time? After finding the phone, I look at the screen . . . and it's Hailey.

"Hey!" I say into the receiver.

"Good-morning, Paige," she chimes. "So what's on your agenda for today?"

I laugh a little in response. "Why do you even bother asking? You know it's going to be the same answer: drive kids to school, grocery shop, clean house . . . and help my little sister plan her wedding."

"Sounds fun, especially the last part," she sighs before adding, "I like the article you sent on art inspired centerpieces."

"Well?"

"Well, what?"

"Which do you like the best? Which do you want to use?" I ask eagerly.

"I like them all. I can't choose. Why don't you pick one?"

"Hailey, you're the bride, and the wedding is only two months away! Speaking of which, have you sent out the invitations?"

"I've been so busy with my designs for Julian . . . my new client. Maybe you and I can work together on the invitations tomorrow night?"

"Sure! It will give me an excuse to wear my new jeans and boots!"

"Paige, it's just me. Don't dress up on my account."

"Hailey, I need to dress up on your account. In fact, if I don't make up reasons to wear my new cloths then they'll just sit at the bottom of my closet, collecting dust. Actually, I'm wearing my new boots today—just for the grocery store."

"Have you been hitting the consignment shops, again?" questions Hailey, and I know she's smiling on the other end.

"I did a couple weeks ago. Unfortunately, I don't have time to shop much. I miss the old days when I was able to shop *and* have a social life. Don't get me wrong, I adore Elliott and the kids. It's just sometimes, I wish I could escape for a little while, explore different places, and meet new and interesting people. Just once, I'd like to spend a few hours in someone else's shoes," I say dreamily.

"Paige, that's what books are for. In fact, I have a fantastic one at home; remind me to give it to you."

"Right," I sigh. "Listen, I have to go. These groceries aren't going to unload themselves."

"Talk to you later!"

"Later," I say, and toss my phone back into my purse.

After flinging my bags of groceries onto a counter, I begin to shuffle and sort them. Hmm, where did this shrimp come from? I never buy shrimp! I shrug my shoulders and throw the bag into the sink. I come across another strange item, paprika. Did I end up with someone else's cart? I search and find something I recognize, frozen mini-pancakes—these are definitely my bags. I reach for the paprika and stare. What sort of dish would call for paprika? Hmm . . . and just like that, I am inspired! Tonight, I am going to be creative!

I grab an onion and dice it! After wiping the tears from my eyes, I wander over to my prep area, both arms overflowing with ingredients.

"What the . . . " I groan. Something has just popped under my "new" suede boot. Without even looking down, I know what has just squished and smeared across the floor. It's something small and round; a little burst of liquid has broken free of its skin. I bend down and check. A veritable army of purple grapes cover my wooden floor; most are still whole, but one is squished flat.

"Nice!" I lament and sit on one of the high-top stools. I lean over and clean off the purple-red goo. Thank goodness the stain's limited to the sole of my boot and hasn't ruined the upper portion. I rub a rag over the messy substance, and the back of my finger grazes my boot's surface. It's both smooth and soft.

All of a sudden, something strange occurs. My vision is clearer. I look around my kitchen and everything appears sharp. I'm immersed in high definition! This is kind of cool! Wait, what's going on here?

I stand, and the room starts to shift. My hand clutches the counter, and the area around me begins to swirl. Its circulating motion revolves faster and faster, making me dizzy. I squeeze my eyes shut. This isn't right, something is terribly wrong! In an effort to steady myself, I concentrate on my breathing...one, two, three...all right, this isn't working! Finally, when the room feels like it may have stopped spinning, I reopen my eyes.

I'm in the kitchen, but not in *my* kitchen anymore. Where am I? The cabinets are replaced by dark Formica. The walls are plastered with beige wallpaper overflowing with images of fruit and birds. And . . . is that an avocado green stove? I haven't seen one of those in decades. I'm standing on gray linoleum. *My* boots, now those I recognize.

Hmm, what's that? Something smells yummy in here. I wonder what's simmering on that green stove. I inhale deeply and pick apart the scrumptious fragrance. Ooh, I can smell a sautéed onion, along with stewed tomatoes and bell peppers. Strange, this isn't *my* nose; it belongs to someone else.

All right, I must have slipped and hit my head. Surely, I'm hallucinating and this is just an illusion. Strange, I am aware of someone else's thoughts and feel the motion of her body. Yes, it must be a female. I can hear her boots crossing the floor. No, I mean *my* boots! This has to be a dream.

Frantically, I search for a reflective surface. This is difficult, because I have little control. I can't move! Thank goodness, she's looking for a mirror . . . hold on. How do I know this?

Long delicate fingers reach for a cabinet door. It opens and attached inside is a round mirror. Wow. I'm not me. I mean, this is not me. I don't have strawberry-blonde hair, light freckles, and a soft pouty mouth . . . and I'm definitely not a teenager.

Delilah's Story, June 1988
Lewisburg, West Virginia

"I'm not sure what you're makin', but it sure does smell good."

"Dad, when are you gonna learn to stop sneaking up on people?" I admonish, turning away from the mirror.

My dad smiles, and his weathered face tells a tale all on its own—he has spent his entire life working hard outdoors, while raising a daughter all on his own. His salt and pepper hair is matted to his forehead, beads of sweat cling to his skin, and his white t-shirt and jeans are smudged with dirt from the day.

He peers down into the bubbling pot. "I can't wait to have a bowl of whatever you're cookin'."

"It's called crawfish etouffee. I found it in the gourmet cookbook you just gave me," I explain excitedly. "I had trouble finding crawfish, so I substituted them for shrimp."

"Well, I'm lookin' forward to tryin' something new from my little girl. One thing I just don't get; why is it when everyone else around these parts makes mashed potatoes and gravy, my Delilah comes up with a strange new dish?"

"I suppose I take after the man who raised me . . . always ready to try something new. In fact, I noticed there's a recipe in here named for you, 'Sheppard's Pie.' I'm assuming that's why you bought this cookbook for me."

"Hmm, that's funny. I didn't realize that was in there," he says, but I can tell he's fibbing. "I suppose since it's in there, you're just gonna have to practice makin' it. I expect it will be a huge success at your future restaurant."

"I expect *all* my meals will be a huge success," I tease. "I'll have the shrimp etouffee ready for your supper."

"I feel bad eatin' a meal you've put together, when you aren't here enjoying it with me," he says, looking me sincerely in the eyes.

"Don't worry about me. I'll just have to taste this meal for myself before I run off to work. Since it's my first day at The Greenbrier Resort, I want to make a good impression. Besides, you know I plan on earning lots of money this summer to help pay for culinary school." I pat him on the shoulder. "Now go, get back to work."

"Yeah, I suppose the cows won't feed themselves. I best be gettin' off." He heads toward the door and places his cowboy hat on his head. "Now, I'm serious, when you get to work I want you to march straight over to your boss and tell him what you're all about. Why, you're the best cook south of the Mason Dixon Line."

"Thanks Dad, but the truth is I'm just lucky to have a job."

"Now Delilah, what you have there's a God given talent. The only person who doesn't believe in you is you," he says, his voice stern.

"I'll talk to my boss about working towards a position in the kitchen. But, can I at least start the job before I go blabbing my mouth off to him?"

"Well, alrighty then. I'll see ya later." He tips his hat and walks out the door.

Chapter Two

I fill the saucepan with ingredients from my shrimp etouffee recipe. It's spicy and bold, yet celery adds crisp and refreshing coolness. After tasting it, I'm pleased with the outcome.

I look over at the clock . . . . Oh for heaven's sake, I need to get ready for work!

I finish cleaning the dishes and rush to my bedroom. My uniform hangs in my closet, pressed and ready for wear: a black skirt, white dress shirt, and black vest. I sit on the edge of my bed and remove my tan ankle boots. I stare adoringly at them for a brief moment, remembering how I had saved up all last summer just to pay for them. It was the first time in my life I splurged on something after seeing it in a magazine.

I search under the bed for my uncomfortable, black, work pumps. After hitting my head on the white bed frame, I sit and stare around my room. I am surrounded by faces from my favorite bands: U2, Madonna, and REM. My pink phone sits on my wicker nightstand and tape cassettes are sprawled out over the shaggy carpet.

Just then, I hear my friend's car horn, blaring through my open window. I literally fly around my bed, knocking my quilt to the floor. After leaping over piles of clothes, I stop in front of the tall whicker mirror. Quickly, I dab on more petal-pink lipstick and plaster my hair with Aqua Net spray. I spritz on some perfume, reminding me of fresh orange blossoms.

I'm finally ready and head out the door.

My friend Lydia waves to me from behind the driver's seat, "Hey sugar, are ya ready to roll?"

"Ready as I'll ever be. Thanks again for helping me get this summer job. I'll work real hard at it," I say, hopping into her car. My foot nudges something balled up on the floor. It's Lydia's "Class of 1988" t-shirt, in a heaping mess. "You oughta show more respect to our senior class," I say and toss the shirt onto the backseat.

"Aw, who cares about that grubby old shirt? I'm ready to leave high school behind and hit the big time!" Lydia says enthusiastically.

I smile in agreement, feeling lighthearted just thinking about all the fun we're gonna have this summer. After all, Lydia's my best friend and we always have a great time together. We grew up knowing each other our whole lives and feel more like sisters than friends.

Lydia reaches over and turns up the music. The radio's playing *The Loco-Motion* by Kylie Minogue. We pay little attention to the beauty around us, as we sing and bob our heads from side-to-side. The drive's familiar, since we both grew up here. The road cuts right through the small town of Lewisburg before weaving around mountains.

After we round the corner, Lydia parks her car in the employee lot. My stomach flips and flops. I must remind myself this isn't the first job I've had. In fact, I worked all year at the local diner, but The Greenbrier is entirely different. I'm intimidated by the grandeur of the resort. Lydia told me all about her experience working there last summer. She isn't the sort to leave out any details, either. She raked in a lot of cash. And that's just one reason why I'm here. Truthfully, I can't wait to watch and learn from the resort's award winning chefs.

"You'll do fine. Just smile at the guests and they'll smile back. They're only human, just the same as you and me, remember that," Lydia says.

"They aren't the same as you and me. They're bigger than we are. They come here from big cities. I've never even left this area of West Virginia. The only big city I've ever seen was on TV." I look down at my plain old work pumps.

"Sugar, you'll do just fine. Why, you're flawless at anything you set your mind to doin'. And don't you forget what Mr. Frank told ya about workin' hard. I believe him when he said you'd end up helping in the kitchen. Now stop this nonsense, will ya?" Lydia laces her arm through mine and together we take our first steps of summer.

We enter the resort through a back entrance and walk down a large tunnel. It leads us into the kitchen, where we're greeted by our boss, Mr. Frank.

"Good evening ladies, welcome," he says, and his mustache stretches distractingly into a thin line. "You're just in time for my little speech." We join the rest of the wait staff and try to appear interested in whatever Mr. Frank has to say. "Remember, The Greenbrier Resort is an established vacation destination for influential families. We are fortunate to have such an important historical attraction so close to our homes. Never forget, while you work to make a living, you also represent our hometown." He then proceeds to brief us on how the night ought to run. "Tonight's probably the most important of them all. You can only make a first impression one time." He raises a finger, as if we don't clearly understand.

We receive an updated sheet of paper with our guests' names and we're told to memorize them.

Lydia whispers, "It wouldn't hurt for you to learn some information about the guests, as well. You know, like where they're from and what they like to do for fun. Stuff like that. We're on. Let's go meet and greet."

The wait staff enters the main dining room in perfectly synchronized, almost choreographed, movements.

"Breathtaking," I whisper.

Ornate chandeliers, with dangling crystals and emeralds, hang over circular tables. In the center of each table is a beautiful vase of fresh flowers, along with some candles, and gorgeous emerald-green water glasses. The guests are already seated.

Nervously, I gulp and approach my first table. There, in front of me, sits a group of eight sophisticated looking people. Jewels and fancy gowns bedazzle the women and the men wear tailored suits. One by one, they stop mid-sentence and offer me their drink orders. Strangely enough, I am able to push aside my nerves, and the night flies by in a complete blur.

~ * * * ~

By the time all the guests have cleared the room, Lydia and I find ourselves sitting at one of the tables.

"Thanks Lydia, I can't believe I made it through the night without a single major accident. I mean, I'm surprised I didn't trip over my feet and spill a drink on someone."

Lydia waves a dismissive hand. "You did great, kiddo. See, you worried for nothin'. Are you ready to celebrate?"

"Celebrate? What do you have in mind?" I know my friend too well not to feel both thrilled and nervous.

"You brought a change of clothes, right?" Lydia looks at me questionably. I nod eagerly, and she smiles in her mischievous way. "Good, then you just leave the rest to me. It's only 10:00, and we're only young once."

With that, we leave The Greenbrier behind, ready to find ourselves a good time.

~ * * * ~

As Lydia drives her car toward town, I jump into the backseat and transform my appearance. I put on my favorite floral pink sundress, add a jean jacket, and then slip on my tan boots. Since I've practiced it many times before, changing in the car is easy. After returning to the front seat, I check my hair and lipstick in the mirror.

"When do you plan on telling me where we're heading?" I ask anxiously.

"Some of the gang's gonna be at Max's Bar. I figured we'd start there," she says and pulls over to the side of the road. "Are you ready to take the wheel? I need to get out of this uniform and make myself over. I'm anxious to see if Bradley will be there. He's so fine, just thinking about him makes my toes curl."

Lydia's toes are constantly curling for one guy or another. I, on the other hand, don't have much time for romance. My life is full enough. I'm happy and have other ideas for *my* future; one that doesn't include any of the men I know. Thank you very much.

After jumping into the passenger seat, Lydia exclaims, "Let's tear it up!"

She has successfully changed into a black and white striped shirt and a pair of high red pumps. I'm not surprised to see her stone washed jeans. They're her favorite; she has often told me how proud she is of the Guess logo on the back. Lydia has frosted blonde hair that stands high above her head. Although I think she wears too much eye shadow and hot-pink lipstick, she's definitely pretty.

My excitement's high after having such an awesome night at my new job. With my close friend leading the way, I'm ready to make the first night of summer a memorable one.

Not long after entering the familiar bar, Lydia squeals, "Bradley's here! Let's go over there and chat it up!"

"I'll meet you in a minute. I'm gonna have the jukebox play our favorite song," I say with a smile.

"Okay. Wish me luck with Bradley!" Lydia says and scurries off to where her latest crush is playing darts.

Max's bar is busier than usual. I know just about everyone here. In fact, most of us started kindergarten together. As I push my way through the crowd, I smile and hug many of my old friends.

Against the back wall, right next to the pool table, sits *my* jukebox. Coins fall into the music machine, and it plays *my* song. I close my eyes and hum lightly, allowing Tom Petty's lyrics to flow through me . . . *American Girl*.

"This is a great song choice." Some guy says, interfering with my song, but I don't look up. I'm trying to ignore him, when he adds, "I was getting tired of listening to big hair bands and heavy metal. For a brief second, I considered changing the music, but I'm glad you beat me to it," he says, and I open my eyes to see who is brave enough to interrupt. Wow, I'm unable to respond and simply stare, dumbstruck. It takes an uncomfortable minute before I realize this is the point at which I'm supposed to insert a witty comment...

My eyes slowly trail up his tall well-built frame, and I just know my cheeks are turning pink. I must say something. Finally, I am able to ask, "So why didn't you?"

"I figured this crowd wouldn't appreciate it if I took the liberty of changing the music to U2 or INXS," he says with a smile, showing his sparkling white teeth.

Will I ever breathe again? I can't be making a very good impression here. I must force myself to inhale and act cool. All right, here goes nothing. "Those guys aren't so bad. You're right though, since you're an outsider, it's probably best not to shake things up in here. Unless, of course, you're the sort to go *looking* for a little trouble."

"I'm just in here trying to have a good time. I'm definitely not looking for any trouble with those guys." The stranger looks around the bar and leans in closer. Quietly he adds, "Have you noticed how massive some of them are?"

"You'd never know their workout and diet consists of tipping cows and drinking beer," I say, smiling brightly. "They're a great group of guys though, big teddy bears. I've known most of them all my life."

"Well, I hope one of them doesn't pulverize me for talking to his woman."

"Why, are you worried? I bet you could take any one of them in a fight, if you had to."

"I don't know about that. Just for kicks, I'd rather not push my luck," he says, peering over his shoulder.

"You won't have to look over your shoulder, while talking to me, that is. These guys are more like my brothers than anything else."

"I'm not sure that's a whole lot better. Brothers tend to be pretty protective of their little sisters."

"I guess you'll just have to see if I'm worth the risk," I say, the words falling out of my mouth far too easily.

"I have a feeling you are, and I'm willing to take my chances." When he smiles again, I'm pulled into a trance. He leans in closer, lowers his voice and says, "It will be even better if I don't get pulverized in the process."

"Just make sure you keep your hands where everyone can see them, and you'll be just fine," I tease.

"Understood," he says and places both hands in the air. "By the way, I'm William Berringer."

"Delilah Jones. You know, you look pretty silly with your arms raised like that. I guess you can lower them."

"It's nice to meet you, Delilah," William says, as his arms fall to his sides.

I like hearing my name roll off William's lips. He holds a certain air about him, a mixture of quiet confidence and sophistication. It's obvious he isn't from anywhere around here.

"What brings you to our quaint little town? Are you visiting someone?" I ask.

"I'm on vacation with my family. We've been coming here for the past few years. My parents normally stay all summer, but I'm usually only here for a week or so."

"Not enough to keep you around very long, huh?"

"Maybe I haven't found anyone friendly enough to show me the town properly."

"Is that so?" I say and look down.

"What do you think? Can I take you out sometime? Perhaps you could show me around?"

"That'd be great!" I say a little too enthusiastically.

"What are you doing tomorrow?"

"I have to work, but I'm free Sunday."

"Perfect."

I size him up, again. Yeah, he definitely has style. William's sculpted dark-brown hair looks cool. I like his blue jeans and buttoned down shirt. How cute, he even rolls up his sleeves. And I bet if the bar didn't smell overwhelmingly like stale beer, I'd fall in love with his cologne.

Chapter Three

William and I continue with our playful banter for hours. After awhile, I realize I've been slurping on an empty glass of cola, but who cares! I'm really digging this guy!

"Your drink is empty," William says.

"Yes," I say in return.

"I must apologize for not having it filled. Don't worry though, my manners have returned. Please, let me buy you another drink," he offers sweetly.

"Thanks."

"All right, I'll only be a minute. Why don't you surprise me with a few more songs? I have a feeling I'll like whatever you choose," he says and hands me five dollars.

"I can cover it, there's no need to give me money."

"My ears will be forever indebted to you."

Reluctantly, I take his money and watch him walk to the bar. Hmm, his backside looks equally as good as the front. In fact, the way his jeans mold to his . . . . All right, I need to focus on choosing some music.

I'm studying the playlist, when an all too familiar voice echoes, "What are you doing?"

I don't have to look up to know it is Lydia. She quickly gains my attention after squeezing my arm. Wow, she looks darn right rattled.

"I'm picking out some music. Geez Louise, Lydia, what do you think I'm doing?" I say and roll my eyes.

"I'm sorry, but you can't hang out with him," urges Lydia. "He's one of The Greenbrier guests, one of *my* guests. You're gonna get yourself fired if you start hangin' around him!"

"Darn, I thought there was something familiar about him. It figures I'd fall for someone who's off limits," I say with a sigh. "Hey, we've been talking for hours, and you're just now warning me!"

"Delilah, this is the first time I've been able to get you alone. He's been hovering over you all night."

"He has, hasn't he?"

"Sugar, you need to wipe that silly smile off your face. This is serious. You can't fall for him."

"Maybe I could date him and not tell anyone. It's not like they ask me about my personal life at the time clock."

"I'm sorry, sugar, but you're gonna have to let him go. You know how small this town is when it comes to knowin' everybody's business. Just forget about this one." She shrugs her shoulders and adds, "Maybe at summer's end, you can pick things up."

"No, you're right. Besides, his teeth are a little too polished for me anyway," I say, trying to look brave.

As if on cue, William shows up with our drinks. He and Lydia exchange polite smiles and hellos.

"Good luck," she whispers into my ear and wanders away.

"I guess you found me out," William says, gently placing the drink in my hand. "Look, I didn't say anything because I guessed it might be a problem."

"You think? I could lose my job," I say, trying not to look up at his gorgeous face. Why do his eyes have to be a delicious shade of golden brown?

"All right, confession time . . . I saw you at dinner."

"What?" I say, and a mixture of hot and cold runs through my body. "You knew I worked at the resort. We've been talking for hours, and you didn't bother to mention you were a guest there."

"You made quite an impression on me. I wanted to get to know you. What's the big deal? So what if you work at the same place where I'm a guest? It shouldn't matter."

"I'm sorry, but I don't want to lose my job. It's been fun talking with you though," I say, focusing on a crushed peanut shell on the floor.

"If that's how you feel, I'll respect your decision, even if it is for the wrong reason."

"Thanks for understanding. I wish things could've been different," I say with false confidence.

"Just so you know I'm actually not put off that easily. We'll see each other again. In fact, I believe we both have obligations to be in the main dining hall tomorrow evening." He leans in closer, and I can feel his hushed words on my neck, "I'm not giving up easily. Like I said before, I believe you're worth it." After pulling back, he winks and disappears into the crowd.

I smile, realizing it's too late for me. I'm hooked. Secretly, I hope he does pursue me, even if it is a bad idea. I watch him walk away and from the corner of my eye, I can see Lydia heading my way.

"Hell's bells, it looks like our good time tonight was just cut short. I'll go say good night to Bradley. Give me a sec, okay?" Lydia says, putting her arm around me.

~ * * * ~

Surely some good music will cure me. I turn on Lydia's car radio and playing is a stupid sappy song. I turn it off. Heck, I wish I could pull the stinkin' radio out of the dash and toss it out the window. Maybe that would make me feel better.

"Hey, I like that song," Lydia says, while driving me home.

"Sorry, I just need a little peace and quiet."

"Whatever you say."

Neither of us speaks a word. And for that I am grateful.

All right, enough silence. I can't stand it anymore!

"So, what's the scoop on Mr. William Berringer, anyway?" I ask.

"You sure you want to know 'bout him?" Lydia takes a sideways glance at me before spilling the beans. "Well, his family lives in the D.C. area . . . you know, the Capitol?"

"Really, I didn't realize D.C. was the Capitol," I say, and for good measure throw in, "Duh."

"Look, I realize you're mad, but don't take it out on me! If you're gonna act like a big baby about it, then you can go and find out about him from someone else."

"Sorry, I don't seem to have much control over what I'm sayin' tonight."

"Alrighty then, I guess since you just had your heart squished like a bug, I'll let it go. So anyway, his father's a big-wig politician, and his mother floats around high society circles, recruiting for her favorite charity of the moment. From what I gather, William goes to college. For the past few years, they've been comin' here every summer. Only William doesn't usually stick around very long. Guess he'd rather party it up with his frat buddies on campus or somethin'. Can't say I blame him. I'd rather do the same."

"Hmm, thanks for the lowdown," I say and continue staring blankly out the car window.

"Anytime, sugar . . . and Delilah, you did the right thing."

"That's good to hear, because it sure doesn't feel like I did."

~ * * * ~

Early the next morning, sunlight blasts through the mini-blinds, and I am immediately reminded of my unfortunate encounter with William Berringer.

"Shoot," I murmur, throwing back the covers. "I'm tougher than that. I can handle anything. This girl's not gonna be kicked down that easily."

I *will* get William Berringer out of my thoughts. I must remind myself of that over and over.

I wish I could slow down time or stop it all together. I'm not looking forward to working today. I don't want to see William Berringer. The thought of it makes me sick.

~ * * * ~

Before I know it, I'm standing in the resort's kitchen, waiting to greet my tables. I can't pull my attention away from the door. On the other side sits William. I am so nervous I could scream!

"Let's go, Delilah. Time's up," Lydia says and pats me on the shoulder.

The crew embarks on their usual rounds. I avoid looking in the direction of *his* table. I'm successful at this for about one whole minute. Gee, this is gonna be tougher than I thought. What if I just sneak a little peek? Surely, he won't notice.

"This is a complete and utter nightmare," I mumble to myself.

Maybe, I was too rash. Maybe, I shouldn't have canceled my date with William; maybe, I should give him a chance and not worry about my silly old job. Besides, by not dating him, it makes my working conditions extremely uncomfortable.

What am I thinking? I can't date him and that is that! I will pretend William isn't here.

I can't stand it anymore! I'll briefly look his way. He probably won't even notice. Casually, I peer over with a sideways glance. Wait just a minute! Who is that?

23

Some girl is laughing and edging her seat closer to William's. Unfortunately, she's pretty, too. Her hair looks annoyingly silky and smooth. Plus she's blonde. What a complete nightmare! She's the sort of girl who wears pearls and pink cardigan sets. I don't like her, not one single bit.

What's he up to, anyway? Well, he can't have us both! How dare he toy with my emotions! I can't believe I was so charmed by him and didn't see him for what he truly was! "What a jerk," I say through gritted teeth and turn my back.

Although I'm filled with (I'll admit it) jealously, I'm determined to exhibit grace around my guests. I know I'll get through this. In fact, I'll just turn up my nose and pretend he doesn't even exist.

I mean, I realize he doesn't belong to me; far from it, but I can't believe he's sitting with another girl right in front of me! As far as I'm concerned, he's the rudest person on the planet! I feel so stupid for ever falling for him in the first place. What was I thinking? I should have been able to see through his fake lines and lack of sincerity.

"Her name's Camilla," Lydia says quietly. "She comes here every summer with her family, only she doesn't leave, she stays the entire time! She's just itching to find herself a rich husband, and it looks like she's got her claws into William!"

"William doesn't owe me anything. He's free to do what he wants. Besides, we only just met last night."

"Right, you keep tellin' yourself that. Well then, we best be gettin' our butts back to work," Lydia says eloquently.

~ * * * ~

After the room's been cleared, Lydia and I sit at our favorite table. I can't wait to rehash tonight's turn of events. It feels great to complain about William and that tart he's seeing. In fact, I'm gonna purge all my frustrations—release all my negative thoughts and emotions—cast them out into the far reaches of the universe!

"And for another thing, that little hussy he was with . . ." I'm midsentence, when I realize Lydia isn't looking at me anymore. She's staring over my shoulder and telling me to hush. "What's the matter with you? He's right behind me, isn't he?"

Lydia nods and I slowly turn my head. How embarrassing. William's standing right behind me. I wonder how much he just heard. You know what? Quite frankly, I don't really care.

"Can we talk?" he asks.

Lydia leaps out of her seat, excusing herself with some lame reason to run into the kitchen. I'm left alone to fend for myself.

"May I sit with you?" he asks, but I don't respond. In fact, I'm just gonna ignore him, all together. He takes the liberty of sitting right beside me. I'm not sure how much time passes, as I am picking at my nails. Finally, he speaks, "Did I do something to offend you? You've been acting like you're mad at me."

"I'm not sure what you're talking about. I'm perfectly fine," I say.

"Does that mean we're still on for our date?"

"Not a sunflower's chance in hell sweetheart." I'm not sure where I got that one, but it feels pretty darn good saying it. "You'll just have to ask little Ms. Debutant to show you around town. By the looks of her, I expect she'd like that very much."

I wait, expecting William to become angry with my candid remarks. However, he begins to laugh. This is a little unsettling.

"Why Delilah, is that a little green monster I see? You can't possibly be jealous of her."

"How dare you suggest such a thing? I couldn't care less what you do!" I raise my head, in an effort to look uninterested.

"For your information, I've known Camilla my entire life. We were childhood friends. Our parents have known each other since before I was born."

As his words sink in, I blush and feel a little foolish.

"Well, it looks to me like she has other intentions towards you."

"Maybe she does." He shrugs his shoulders, before adding, "She acts that way with every guy I know. No one takes her seriously. Besides, she's more like a little sister to me."

"I'm not sure that's a whole lot better. After all, big brothers tend to be pretty fond of their little sisters."

"I believe the word I used last night was protective, not fond. If you're going to quote me, you should at least do it correctly."

"Whatever, same difference," I say, while glaring at him. "What is it you want from me? Can't you just leave well enough alone?"

"I had a great time last night; we connected. I don't want this to be over with before I even have the chance to take you on a proper date. Delilah, I've done nothing wrong. Give me a chance."

"It's not gonna work out this time. I'm sorry," I say and rise out of my chair.

He stands before me, hovering a little too close.

"I'll pick you up tomorrow at 11:00 AM," he says and his smile brightens.

"You're awfully determined aren't you?"

"I find in life I have to be, if I'm to get what I want. Yes, I'm very determined. Look, how about we keep our date for tomorrow? We can see if this is worth pursuing. If you're still uncomfortable, then I'll back off. What do you say about that?"

"This is a bad idea, but you win," I say and walk away, flinging my hands up in the air. "Besides, I'm not gonna tell you where I live. Good luck finding me."

Although I sound smug, I'm guessing nothing I say can throw him. He'll find my home and be there to pick me up in the morning, just like he said. I can feel my spirits lift. I don't say another word, and although it takes effort, I leave him standing alone in the main dining hall.

Chapter Four

I t's morning, and William will be here soon! I spring out
of bed! My heart's overflowing with excited anticipation!
Within seconds, I'm racing for the kitchen. I can't wait to
put together our picnic lunch. Thank goodness, I started planning
our meal last night. Although, I don't want it to look like I tried
too hard, I want something that sings *romance.*

Which blanket should I pack? This one with pink flowers is
adorable. No, I need something more masculine. Perfect, I'll use
the one with oversized fish all over it! I mean, who doesn't like
to fish? Now, my nicest silverware rolled up in a blue napkin, and
this white ribbon will look so cute tied around it. Glasses, glasses
. . . these will work. Maybe I should tie a little bow around their
stems. No, that would be overdoing it.

I'm so glad Shep gave me this set of storage containers for my
birthday. It didn't hurt that a few weeks ago, I left a catalogue
on the counter—opened to just the right page. I wasn't surprised
Shep bought the powder-blue bowls for me, only that he gave
them to me a whole month before my eighteenth birthday.

I close my eyes and imagine the picnic spread I'm gonna put together. This is gonna be the best lunch William has ever had.

I want to look good, too, without letting on like I'm trying too hard. I find my pink t-shirt, with a large neckline that hangs nicely off one shoulder. A brown skirt adds a touch of elegance, but still looks casual. I put on my tan ankle boots before checking the mirror. My feet move from side-to-side, and I have to admit the outfit's flattering.

The hands on the clock are moving at a snail's pace. After running around working on small tasks, I look back at the clock . . . it's only 10:42. I can't believe only twelve minutes have gone by! Dramatically, I fall onto Shep's favorite chair and flip through his book. At last, I hear the sound of tires coming up the driveway.

Anxiously, I grab the basket and leap for the door. After flinging it open, I look down and straighten my skirt. Casually, I glance up, but what I see isn't good. It's not William; it's Shep coming home for lunch. The idea of introducing my father to my date is mortifying!

"Dad, what cha doin'?" I ask.

"What was that?" he subtly reminds me of my grammatical mistake, as he often does.

"Hey Daddy, what are you doing?" I correct.

"I thought it'd be nice to have lunch with my little girl," he says, as he unloads some objects from the back of his truck. After getting a glimpse of me, he freezes mid-stream. "Now, there's a pretty woman. What's the occasion?"

I reach into the depths of my mind to come up with a good reason for my appearance. I've come up with nothing. Not one single good reason. I guess it's best to tell him the truth, "I'm going to lunch with a new friend."

"Would this friend be of the male persuasion?" My father's a clever one, I'll give him that.

"Yes, he would. It's nothing serious, though. In fact, you could just leave now and not even have to meet him."

"And pass up the opportunity to embarrass my daughter? Nah, I'll stay put right here. I'd like to meet any boy who can manage a date with Delilah. No offense, but rumor around town is it's nearly impossible to get a date with Delilah Jones."

"Funny, Dad," I say and even though I try to get rid of him, deep down, I know that will never happen. Why is he beaming like that? Great, he's gonna humiliate me. I'm sure he's wondering if he ought to clean his shotgun in front of William, just for effect. "Dad, please don't embarrass me."

"Don't you worry; I'll make myself scarce once I've met the boy."

The sound of crushed gravel reaches us. In unison, we look down the lane at the black car heading in our direction.

Shep leans toward me and asks, "Nice ride. Where'd you meet this fella?"

"I'll tell you all about it later," I whisper, as Shep is still gazing admiringly at the fancy car.

William exits and confidently approaches my dad. He extends his hand towards

Shep, and says, "Hello sir, I'm William Berringer."

"I'm Sheppard Jones, Delilah's dad, it sure is nice to meet you," Shep says, shaking William's hand. My dad peers down at me with a look of mischief on his face. I pray he won't choose this moment to tease me.

"Delilah and I have planned a date for today, with your consent, of course," William says sweetly, and now, I can't shake this silly grin off my face.

"Why certainly! You two have fun!" Shep exclaims, sounding a little too enthusiastic for my taste.

"All right Dad, I'll see you later. Remember, I have the day off. So I don't know when I'll be home. Don't worry about me, okay?" I kiss him on the cheek and whisper, "Thanks."

"It's nice to meet you," William says to my dad.

"Have a great time," Shep adds.

"Thanks, Dad!" I say, and as William holds the car door for me, I slide onto the seat.

My palms are sweaty, and my feet shift around each other. I look down at the leather interior and run my hand over its surface. It's soft…this is calming. After studying the seat a little further it dawns on me, I've never been in a car this luxurious before.

William takes his place in the driver's side and gazes briefly in my direction. "So, Ms. Delilah, what do you have planned for us today?"

My stomach is in my throat, but I think I can manage to sound composed. "That'll have to be a surprise. I'll let you know which way to go."

"I'm glad you've decided to go out with me," he says with a sweet smile, and I'm not about to admit it out loud, but I'm glad too.

"At the end of the drive, take a right," I say and stare at my long driveway.

After heading down the double lane road, I instruct him to turn left past my favorite cattle and horse farm. We drive through a covered bridge and then up along the base of a mountain. We swerve along a few switchbacks, and I have him pull over near a large maple tree. Like many trees in this area, it is centuries old and has an ancient spirit. Birds play in its branches and leaves dance with the breeze. I close my eyes and inhale deeply, filling my lungs with sweet aroma from wild flowers and fresh green grass. When I reopen my eyes, I see dragonflies zip through the air, and . . . William Berringer is staring at me. Why isn't he looking at the valley, rolling hills, and sheep?

"I'll say one thing is true for West Virginia, it's overflowing with beauty," he says.

"Ah-hem, right," I say, busily setting up the perfect picnic— anything to avoid William's intense stare.

After a few minutes, I realize there's nothing more I can do. The food, desert, blue and white dishes, flower centerpiece, and fish blanket look perfect. I peer up to watch William's reaction.

"Lunch is ready. I hope you like it," I say, softly clapping my hands together once.

William kneels down on the blanket and gawks. "Are you kidding? Everything looks great. No offense, but I didn't expect you to make more than PB&J sandwiches. You really outdid yourself."

"It's nothing, really. I just whipped all of this up this morning."

"You must have woken up pretty early."

"A little," I say with a smile and scoop up some pasta with olives and feta cheese, placing it on his plate. I add a spring-mix salad along with my homemade salad dressing: dill, olive oil, garlic . . . . I leave the French bread, cheese, ham, and grapes on a wooden platter. I figure we can just nibble from it.

"This looks delicious." He takes a bite of pasta and grins. "Where did you find this fish blanket?"

"It's great, isn't it?" I begin before realizing he is looking at it questioningly. "Don't you like it?"

"It's interesting."

"I figured you'd appreciate the blue fish, since you're a guy and all guys like to fish, right?"

"I guess," he says and shrugs his shoulders.

"You don't like to fish?"

"I'm not sure; I've never been," he says casually. "Why are you looking at me like that?"

"You mean to tell me, your father never took you out fishing?" I say with my eyes still large.

"We never got around to it. What's the big deal?"

"I'll tell you what, I'm gonna take you fishing, and you can see for yourself."

"It sounds like we've just planned another date," he says with a grin. "All right, show me the magical and mysterious world of fishing."

"You may tease now, but you'll see how rewarding it is."

"I'm sure I will," he says before tasting the salad. I wait nervously for his reaction. He grins and quickly takes another bite.

"Would you like some lemonade?" I ask overeagerly and reach for his glass.

"Let me guess, you squeezed the lemons yourself."

"But of course!"

"I like how you made ice-cubes around lemon slices."

I pass him a glass, and for the briefest moment, our fingers touch. Did I just feel a ripple of electricity? I look away, trying not to blush.

Thank goodness, he says something right away, "This tastes amazing. You know, I'm surprised you haven't opened your own restaurant."

"I hope to, one day, but you have to start somewhere, right? My boss told me, after a few weeks of proving myself I'll be able to help more in the kitchen!" I say excitedly and pop a grape into my mouth.

"Do you have to go to school to become a chef?"

"This is a serious profession. I'm gonna go to culinary school and then do some training with a great chef. And one day, I'll open my own restaurant," I say enthusiastically.

"Where would you like to open your first restaurant?"

"Well, I suppose somewhere more tropical, maybe near a beach in Florida. And my second restaurant will be right here," I say with a smile.

"You want to return and open one here? I thought you were ready to run off to explore distant places. Why do you want to come back?"

"I want to make a name for myself in a bigger city, and I will travel to foreign lands. And maybe after I open up my first restaurant, I'll come back. The people I love are here, and they deserve an opportunity to have great food just like everyone else. You know…just because you live in a small town doesn't mean you can't appreciate exotic food."

I wait for William's reaction. What does he think about what I've just said? Will he laugh at my crazy ideas? Maybe he'll understand. But what if he doesn't? I can't hang around with someone who doesn't support my dreams.

William continues shoveling in mouthfuls of pasta, as I wait and wait.

Finally, he clears his throat and says, "I'm sure you will accomplish all of that. But before you open your restaurant, I think you should travel the world. Live off the land. See how other people live. Try strange and exotic cuisine."

"Is that your dream, William Berringer?"

"I must admit, I would like to travel for a while. But once I have that out of my system, I'd like to design buildings."

"You want to be an architect?"

"Yes, I do. My father still believes I'll follow in his footsteps by becoming a politician. But that's not for me."

"Well, the way I see it, you have to follow *your* own path and only *your* heart can show you the way. In fact, I'm sure your parents will be proud of you, just so as long as you work hard and find your own kind of success."

William shifts his gaze away from the valley and focuses on me. "And who cares if I destroy the dreams of both my parents in the process," he says, and I'm not sure whether or not he's serious.

"William, I think becoming an architect is a great idea. You'll create buildings people will live, work, shop, and eat in. The possibilities are endless! I realize I don't know you very well, but I believe you'll be happy with whatever you choose to do, as long as you follow your heart."

A smile stretches his gorgeous lips. "I believe I will too," he agrees. "So, what do you say, do you want to visit foreign lands with me?"

Again, I'm not sure whether or not he's serious. So I scramble for something with which to busy my trembling hands. I wish my heart wouldn't beat so fast, and my head wouldn't feel so light. I peer over at William. He doesn't seem fazed at all about what he just said to me. He's pulling apart his bread and stuffing his face with it.

All right, he must have been kidding. I won't think about his invitation again, at least for the rest of the evening . . . or maybe for the next few seconds. I really don't know how to respond. Okay, I have an idea. I reach inside my picnic basket. From it, I retrieve my absolute favorite dessert and remember *this* is my passion.

"I've almost forgotten the best part of the meal! Now close your eyes!" I declare. "I've been workin' on this new recipe. I plan on entering it in the State Fair at summer's end. I'll feed you a bite, and then you'll have to honestly tell me what you think."

I slice through the moist chocolate cake, sliding a knife down through alternating layers of peanut-butter and fudge. After the piece gently falls onto my pretty blue plate, I am ready to share a spoonful of decadence with William.

"All right, open your mouth," I say, while carefully slipping a little taste of heaven into his mouth.

His closes his eyes. I'm having trouble reading whether or not he likes it. He takes his time chewing; torturing me in the process. What does he think? Does he just like it or love it?

Finally, he opens his eyes and smiles. "This has to be the best thing I've ever tasted. What do you call it?"

"Whew, I'm so relieved. I was scared to death of what your reaction might be. Actually, I'm having trouble with the name. Do you have any ideas? It has to be something catchy if I'm to win a prize."

"I'm guessing it has peanut butter, chocolate fudge, and there's something crunchy, sort of cakey, too. It tastes unbelievable. I'm sure you could call it Crunchy-Munchy and win. Maybe if I had some more, I would be better able to help you with a name."

I serve him a plate of dessert and enjoy one for myself. It really is good. In fact, I could eat it all day long.

~ * * * ~

Time is flying by way too fast. I have just shared my vision of my future restaurant with William, telling him that naming it is easy. I will call it *Desirez'*, which means desire, as in 'what do you desire' in French. I heard the word somewhere and it has stayed with me. I think it shows the passion I have for food.

Desirez' will serve French cuisine with an American flair, and as I explain this to William, he understands, or at least he acts like he does. I mean, like, he is really concentrating on the ground, nodding his head. When he finally does say something, I am impressed how he brings *Desirez'* to life, describing the incredibly innovative architectural touches he would add.

~ * * * ~

Our afternoon date is almost over. Twilight is here and the valley below sparkles with pin points of light.

We've been in a heated discussion about how to cheat the Rubik's Cube, but I abruptly change the subject, "Lightening bugs are one of my top five things I enjoy about summer."

"I've forgotten how some of the more simple things in life can be the most memorable," he says, and his eyes focus on the flashes of light bouncing over grassy slopes.

Although I don't want our date to end, I'm aware it's almost over, but William's first to say the words, "It's probably time to head back. The last thing I would want is your father coming after me for keeping you away too long."

"Don't worry about ol' Shep. He's just thrilled to have me out on a date. Though, I'm sure I'll be interrogated when I get home. He'll want to know everything," I say and immediately realize I've given away too much information.

"Does he quiz you after *all* your dates?"

"He hasn't exactly had much opportunity." Great, I can't believe I just revealed this about my pathetic dating life. I try salvaging my dignity by adding, "We live in a small town. I wasn't kidding when I said most of the guys in town are like my brothers. We've grown up together; it's kind of weird to imagine dating any of them."

"Well, I hope you tell your father about how much you enjoyed your day with me."

How cute, William looks so hopeful!

"We'll just have to wait and see," I say while batting my flirty lashes. "Our date isn't over, yet."

"No, I suppose it isn't."

He stands up from the blanket and reaches his hand down to help me. I take it and manage to land on my feet. We watch as the stars fill the sky, and I am frozen to the spot. William slides his arm around my waist. Whew, I'm not sure how they got in there, but lightning bugs are buzzing around the inside of my entire body.

How exactly is this date gonna end?

"Wow, look at the lightning bugs over there," I say nervously, turning away from him.

But suddenly, his gentle hand turns me around. I'm facing him now, but I can't look him in the eyes. I am such a complete nerd. Now, he's encircling both his arms around my back, and as he pulls me closer, a tingle runs down to my toes.

"Delilah, I was just wondering . . ." he whispers, allowing his lips to travel from my ear to my mouth, and his kiss is sweet as a sugar plum. A shiver dances up and down my spine. I try not to jump. Wait, what was he about to say?

Although I am trembling, I wrap my arms around his neck and tighten my embrace. I believe my feet have left the ground. I am floating in air . . . until he backs away, and I return to earth.

"I better take you home," he says, appearing rattled and running his hand nervously through his dark hair.

I don't know how to respond. I want to pout like a baby and say I don't need to go home! I want to remain in this moment for the rest of my life! A feeling of desperation has swept through me, but all I can do is nod and head for the car.

The ride home goes by too quickly. Unfortunately, there's no denying it, the night has come to an end. I know I'll have trouble falling asleep tonight. I'll be thinking about William.

"Thanks for the picnic. Can I see you tomorrow?" he asks.

"Sure, I have to leave for work around 4:30," I say and am reminded of the rules of my workplace. "Do you mind not telling anyone about us seeing each other? I don't want to get fired." Suddenly I hate my new job.

He leans over and brushes his lips lightly over mine. "Don't worry, your little secret's safe with me. I wouldn't want for you to be fired. Dinner's much more interesting now that I can watch you scramble around the dining room."

"Aren't you the funny one? We'll see how much you enjoy dinner, especially after

I accidently spill a drink on your lap," I tease and playfully swat his arm.

He moves out of the car and around to my side. I'm not exactly used to men opening the door for me. I like it.

"All right, I guess I'll try real hard to not spill a drink on your lap," I say.

Why isn't he saying anything? And why is he staring at me like that?

At last, he kisses me briefly before saying, "Sorry, I can't seem to control myself around you."

I smile before strutting towards my front porch. Just before I reach for the door, I turn around and say in my most sultry voice, "Goodnight, William."

"Goodnight, Delilah," he says and watches as I enter my house.

Chapter Five

I'm gonna be late for work. It's a race against the clock, and piles of clothes fling over my shoulder as I search for my black skirt and hose. Truthfully, my room is a complete mess.

William Berringer . . . I can't concentrate on anything else. Maybe I should call in sick to work and if I do, William could come over and spend the afternoon with me. We'll sip fresh lemonade on the front porch and then…what am I thinking! I know this is a bad idea. I need to hurry.

My uniform hangs on me in a rumpled mess. I look pathetic. It'll be all right, I'll see him at the resort.

Oh no, there's Lydia's car horn. She can't be here already. I hurry to my bedroom window and greet her with a wave.

After another couple minutes, I dash for her car. "Sorry I'm late. I lost track of time," I say, hopping onto my seat.

"Just don't make a habit out of it," Lydia says teasingly. "So, you gonna be okay seeing William at dinner tonight?"

"Sure thing, jellybean."

If she knew the truth, she'd see I'm better than okay! I'm thrilled at the mere thought of being in the same room with

William! I wonder how long I'll be able to keep my mouth shut around Lydia. What I really want to do is tell the whole world about my feelings!

Lydia and I barely make it to work on time. The wait staff has just entered the main dining room with their standard graceful flow. We follow, acting as though we have been here all along.

I look towards William's table. There he is, staring my way with a pleased grin on his face. Over the course of the evening, we make a game out of giving each other seductive winks and smiles. But at the end of my shift, I'm saddened when I realize he's gone.

I round my vacant tables and notice that sitting there, on one of them, is a small piece of paper. It's folded into the shape of a rose. I look over my shoulder. Good, nobody's around.

Cautiously, I open the note: "Urgent, meet me on your front porch at 11:00 tonight."

It's from William! What could possibly be so important?

~ * * * ~

Thank goodness, Lydia rushes me home. What a great friend, I don't even have to tell her why I'm in such a hurry. As soon as she pulls up the gravel drive, I bolt, barely even saying goodbye.

Lydia puts her head out the window and hollers, "You feelin' all right?"

"I'm fine, darlin'! Don't you worry about me! See you tomorrow!" I yell, as I swiftly enter my house.

Shep must've gone to bed. Thank goodness.

Quickly, I change into jeans and a pink tank top with spaghetti straps. The outfit feels casual but sexy. Look out William Berringer.

I run to the front porch and wait and wait. What could be so urgent? Why does he need to see me tonight? Anxiously, I pace the entire length of my porch. At last, I see the glow from his headlights appear.

William's here. A shiver rushes down my spine. He smiles, and my feet can't remain bound any longer. I rush over! But before I reach him, he puts up his hand for me to halt, and I stop midstream. What's going on here?

All of a sudden, he pulls the other hand out from behind his back…aw, roses! Even through the darkness, I can see that half are white and the other six are each a different color, reminding me of a cupcake covered with white icing and colorful sprinkles.

With a large stride, he moves closer to me. As soon as we are mere inches away, he barely touches his lips to mine. His face is still ever so close. If I were to simply lean forward, just a little, then maybe he would kiss me . . . but he doesn't. I think he's into torture, but then he hands me the first bunch of flowers I've ever received.

"They're beautiful. Where'd you find them?" I say, gently running my fingers along each petal.

"It wasn't easy, but I knew you were worth the effort." He wraps his arms around my waist and holds me closer.

My face nuzzles into his shirt and I inhale deeply, taking in his scent. The little bit of cologne he wears still holds faintly on his skin.

"By the way, what's up with your message?" I whisper, and he looks blank, as if he has absolutely no idea what I'm talking about. "You wrote that you had something urgent to tell me . . . in the note?"

"Oh, that?" He looks down, as if embarrassed. "I just wanted to see you."

"Oh, well, just don't go making a habit out of scaring me half to death," I say playfully, while nervously chewing my lower lip.

"I guess I didn't think it through very well. I wrote the note in a hurry. You have no idea how long it took me to fold it up into a rose. Lydia almost busted me when I was putting it on your table," he says, and right at this moment, I am lost in his gorgeous eyes, knowing he can see through into my very soul.

Mmmm, these flowers smell so sweet. William is so sweet.

"Would you like to sit on the front porch, for a spell?" I finally ask.

"Actually, I had better go back before my parents start questioning me about where I'm spending all of my time."

"Oh, I suppose you haven't mentioned me to them."

"I am on strict orders from a certain someone to keep this relationship confidential. Remember?"

"Well, keep up the good work then," I say playfully.

I can't believe it! He hasn't told his parents about me. I mean, I've told Shep everything, well almost everything, about William. Even though I asked him not to tell anyone about us, I figured he'd at least tell his parents.

All of a sudden, the excitement of our secret and forbidden romance isn't as electrifying.

"Sweet dreams, princess," he whispers and places his hand under my chin before gently lifting my head.

"Goodnight, William."

I need to remind myself of the reason he's even here tonight—just to bring flowers! The corners of my lips curve up, and I lean in closer. After all, how else am I supposed to show him I want for him to kiss me? He holds me tighter. I melt. This is the single best moment of my life.

When suddenly, the flowers fall from my hand and drop to the ground with a thud. We look down at the rumpled pile of flowers and hushed laughter erupts between us.

"Goodnight, Delilah," he says with an amused grin.

"I'll see you tomorrow, William. Thanks for the roses," I say and wander toward my front door. Before walking through, I look back and whisper, "Good night." And I blow a flirty kiss into the air.

He brought me roses! He brought me roses! I can't believe he actually brought me roses! There's a pink colored vase under my kitchen sink—my flowers will look perfect in it. I pour water into the glass vase and snip the ends of my roses. Ah, they smell so good.

~ * * * ~

41

The next morning, light pours into my room, and I am immediately reminded William will be here soon. There, on my dressing table, sits my beautiful bouquet of roses. William is so sweet. Just look what he did for me last night.

I have the whole day off. In just one hour, he will be here, and then we will go fly fishing. Secretly, I can't wait to see him out of his refined comfort zone. Come to think of it, if I'm gonna look good, I better get a move on.

Within minutes, I hear the sound of *his* car, and my heart does a little flip-flop. I can't wait to see him! But before I open the door, I pause so I can straighten my beige short-sleeved shirt and cut-off jean shorts. After taking in a large gulp of air, I step out onto the front porch.

Even in his somewhat "scrubby" clothes, William is breathtaking.

Before leaving, William and I load up our arms with the essentials for our journey: fly rods, net, blanket, and picnic basket. Our journey begins just outside my home. The trail weaves us around trees and along the stream, eventually leading us to a small grassy area near the water's edge. I put down our things and watch as the wind rustles through leaves. A grin washes over my face. I am at peace.

"What're you thinking?" William asks, as I pick out the perfect lure for the season and attach them to the lines.

"I think I'm gonna catch way more trout than you."

"Haven't you ever heard of beginners luck? I believe that could happen today."

"We'll have to see about that, now won't we? Don't think just because you're a guy, fishing is gonna come naturally."

"I definitely don't think it will come naturally."

We head into the water, and William whines a little before following me into the cool depths of the stream. While handing him the fly rod, I offer some good tips on how to fly fish. Our lines strike the water, and it only takes a few tries before William catches his first trout. I can't help but laugh at the way he squirms like a little girl. He's putting on a tough guy act, but I can tell he doesn't want to touch the wiggling fish.

"You are such a wimp! You're gonna have to man up, if you're gonna hang with me!" I exclaim between fits of laughter.

After taking the fish off the hook, he allows the tiny little trout to swim away.

I can't stop myself from wondering out loud, "How is it, you've managed your whole life without ever having handled a live fish?"

"I was never certain of that myself . . . up until now," he says and heads for land. "I think I'll hang back here awhile and enjoy the view."

"I'm sorry for teasing. Come on, stay with me. I'll tell you what, if you catch another fish, I'll take it off the hook for you."

"I'll tell you what, how about we relax on this blanket, and I'll let you snuggle up to me?" he says, and I giggle.

"You know, this water is awfully cold," I agree.

The blanket is soft, and a breeze rolls over my body. William places his head close to mine. I can barely hear his breathing over the murmur of the stream.

"So this is what it's all about?" he questions.

"What's about?"

"I've heard the expression 'Lazy days of summer,' but have never experienced one."

"How do you like it?" I ask, lacing my fingers through his.

"I don't ever want it to end."

~ * * * ~

June turns into July and July into August, and well, the lazy days of summer continue rolling along. William and I spend most of our free time together. The truth is I can't stand being away from him for even a minute.

Although I dread the end of this glorious summer, I can't help but look forward to the upcoming State Fair's bakeoff competition. Like every other summer before, most of the town's talkin' about it: the livestock competition, rides, food, crafts, concerts . . . and well, I could go on all day long. The excitement is contagious, at least to me.

"I don't understand what the big deal is. It's just a fair," William confides to me, one sun-drenched afternoon.

"It's only the biggest thing to come to our area! People from all over the state come here! It makes me feel like a kid just thinking about it!" I realize I probably sound like a child, too. Poor William, ever since I drove past the fair grounds and saw the rides already in place, I have been babbling on and on about it.

"Does this mean you'll finally allow me to take you out in public? I mean, all summer you've been so concerned about losing your job."

"I guess it's time to relax, a little. Tell you what, I'm gonna take you to the fair and show you the time of your life. And I'll bet you'll learn to love it, as much as I do."

Chapter Six

I t's time! The State Fair is finally open! I'm so excited, I can't sit still! William has been laughing at me, but I'll show him how great the fair is! In fact, I plan on leaving there with a blue ribbon from the bakeoff competition! My dessert, newly called 'Bite of Delight,' will be a hit sensation. The grand prize is $75.00; plus, my recipe could be published in an actual cookbook! Maybe, they'll even put a photo of me holding my prize-winning dessert! I can see it now. I'll wear an apron and smile with an expression of sophistication! They'll probably want a clever quote from the award winner! I better come up with one, just in case.

Anxiously, I stare out the window of William's car: through the town, past all of the store front windows, and our drive is taking way too long. I can't wait to get to the fair, especially now that I'm about to let everyone see me with William.

Earlier today, I spilled the beans to Lydia about William being my boyfriend. What a relief. I couldn't believe it when she told me she figured as much all along. I guess I'm not such a good liar after all.

William and I are still driving through town. I'm so anxious I could burst. William, on the other hand, is cool as a cucumber.

I recline my seat and sigh lightly. I'm studying the contours of William's face. And since he's paying little attention to me, I allow my gaze to trail down to his chest. I'm fantasizing about running my hand over his well-defined muscles. I want to lightly brush kisses along the side of his neck and bury my nose into his hair. He always smells sooo amazing.

William turns his head towards me and looks at me questioningly. He must've heard my breathing become heavier. Rapidly, I pretend to focus on something outside my window.

The fair has arrived, along with droves of people. I look forward to riding the rides, treating myself to hoards of carnival food, and petting the livestock. Later, William and I will cuddle up while listening to the music from a live concert.

We enter through the gates, and I become childlike in my frenzy of excitement! Neon lights flash and the scent of fried delicacies drift towards me, calling to me, reminding me of Sea Sirens. As we wander past food vendors and carnival games, my nostrils flare, leading me toward the unmistakable aroma of corndogs frying in oil, popcorn popping, and burnt sugar swirling into clouds of cotton candy.

The trouble is where to start? Rides come into view on our right, but down just a little further are tons of crafts. I make an impulsive decision and quicken my pace.

"What are we going to do first?" William asks, but he isn't looking at me. He's staring longingly at the funnel cake stand.

"We are on our way to see the livestock. It's better to go in the morning, before the manure heats up."

"What about the rides? I suspect you're the sort of girl to look for some thrills."

"I prefer to go on the rides at night, when they light up! It's much more exciting that way!" I reach for his hand and tug, attempting to quicken his pace.

I drag William past most of the food. After we round the corner, I stop in front of a sign, advertising fresh-made doughnuts.

"You just have to try these. They're to die for! They're fresh from the fryer and will melt in your mouth!"

We approach the stand and make our first purchase. Eagerly, William stuffs a doughnut into his mouth. He then makes a funny sounding muffled grunt and tries to speak, "Mmmm, this is definitely to die for."

We round another corner and are surrounded by large tractor trailers. As William continues devouring his doughnuts, I focus on our path ahead. Not too far now, I can already see a sign for bunnies.

Suddenly, my body stiffens. I can't go any further.

"Are you all right?" William asks.

"Just over there is one of my old friends. Don't look right at him, but he's the big guy over there. Well, I suppose it's time to introduce you two."

A large guy with blonde hair races towards me. His name's Charlie. Before knocking into me, he lifts me into the air and swings me around!

"Well, lookie who I have here! It's my long lost friend, Delilah Jones!" Charlie announces and sets me back on the ground. "Shoot, I thought you ran away from home or somethin'! Girl, where've you been all summer long?"

"Why, do you mean to say you missed little ol' me? You know I've been working at the resort," I respond with the most charm I can muster.

"It's funny you mention that, 'cuz you know I spend a lot of time with your pal Lydia, who also happens to work there. Only she finds the time to hang out with us." Suddenly, he turns toward William. "I suppose you're the reason our little girl here disappeared?"

I respond before William has a chance to, "Charlie, this is William."

Charlie extends his hand, while still giving William the once over. "Looks like you kept her out of trouble. It's good to meet ya," Charlie offers.

"It wasn't easy, but here she is," William says, while shaking Charlie's hand.

Charlie laughs and looks back at me. "Why Delilah, I like this boy. You should've brought him around to some of our parties.

You know all the ones you missed? It ain't like her to miss a party or miss joining the gang in floating down the river, with coolers in tow. You two missed out on some great summer fun."

"I missed you guys, too. But William and I had some summer fun of our own," I say while gazing up at William.

"Well, I don't get it. Why not bring him around?" Charlie asks, looking confused.

"She probably just wanted to keep me a secret from you guys. All along I've suspected, she wants to leave her options open, you know, for when I return home," William says.

Charlie laughs and pats him on the shoulder. "I can't say I blame her for that. Delilah, don't be such a stranger. It was weird seeing Lydia runnin' around without you. You two are like peas in a pod. I figured you'd gotten yourselves in a fight or somethin'."

"I'll keep that in mind next time around," I say.

"Good to hear. It's nice to see Delilah's finally found herself a boyfriend. Take good care of her." Charlie leans a little closer to William, adding in a lowered voice, "I don't want to have to come after you, now." And with that, Charlie nods and walks away. After taking a few steps, he turns around. "By the way, I'm one of the judges in this year's bakeoff. I can't wait to try your new dessert. What's it called again, 'Delight in a Bite' or somethin'?"

"It's called 'Bite of Delight'," I correct. "I didn't realize you were a judge. Isn't it a conflict of interest for us to be talking?"

"Nah, if that was the case, I'd have no one to talk to all day," Charlie says and turns to leave.

William slides his arm around my waist and looks down with a grin. "See, that wasn't so bad. We just have to do it a few hundred more times and all will be well."

"Charlie's a dear friend of mine. I feel sort of bad knowin' I abandoned all of my friends this summer."

"I think they'll understand. Friends usually do, and they'll stick around," William says and squeezes me tighter. "Besides, you've shown me the time of my life. Doesn't that count for anything?"

"I can't believe I let this stupid job push me into hiding you. We could have done so much more if I hadn't been afraid of what would happen at work."

"Well, we can hang around your friends next summer," he says and leans his forehead to mine.

"Well, if you promise to behave then I guess I can take you to a party," I say and loop my arm through his. "Right this way, Mr. Berringer, we have some animals to see."

~ * * * ~

Evening is here, and most of the day has revolved around William's stomach. Honestly, I've never seen anyone eat so much in my life.

"I suggest you ease up there, or you're gonna feel sick when we start on the rides," I say, adding hopefully, "If you want to try more food, we could always return another day."

"We'll just have to do that."

Vibrant reds, yellows, greens, and blues illuminate the rides. Rock music is blaring and strobe lights are flashing. I can't wait to ride the coaster; I know it'll be both thrilling and fun.

After finishing off a lamb gyro, William asks, "Are you having a good time?"

"Are you kidding?" I wave my first place ribbon in his face and say, "This makes my whole summer of working in the kitchen worthwhile. Can you believe it? My desert won first place!"

"You know, you're kind of like a little 'Bite of Delight,' yourself," he says while nibbling on my neck and pulling me closer.

All of a sudden, a man's voice catches William's attention. It's getting closer, "William, William! Over here!"

A shadow slowly falls across William's face. Quietly, he says, "Brace yourself; you're about to meet my parents."

A bolt shoots through my stomach and my insides wrench. I may have wanted to meet his parents before, but I've changed my mind. I don't want to anymore!

49

"Good evening, Father, Mother," William addresses them, and for the first time, I am face-to-face with Mr. and Mrs. Berringer.

"It's good to see you out, son," his father says. "I suppose now I know why I haven't seen much of you this summer."

William introduces me to his parents. They shake my hand graciously and we exchange polite greetings.

"You look familiar, Delilah. Have we met, before?" William's father asks. "Perhaps you are staying at The Greenbrier?"

William places his arm carefully around my waist and answers for me, "Actually, she works at the resort."

"Of course, I have seen you," his mother says. "How could anyone miss you? What, with your gorgeous strawberry-blonde hair."

Although the woman is saying one thing, her frigid expression says something entirely different. I don't take her for the sort of woman to be cruel to your face. Instead, I believe she would prefer to stab you in the back. I wonder what she'll say about me.

William quickly redirects the conversation, "Mother, I'm surprised to see you and Father here. I wouldn't think the fair would interest you two."

"Normally we wouldn't entertain the idea of a fair," says Mr. Berringer. "However, some of the other guests spoke highly of the event. We had to see it for ourselves. Besides, there is little else to do in this small town."

"Actually Father, Delilah has shown me how much there is to do here. Perhaps we should take you out with us, sometime," William says.

Mrs. Berringer adds smoothly, "William, you should bring your young lady *friend* by to see us before we return home. You realize, Delilah, we are leaving in just two short weeks. Sad really, but I suppose summer has to end at some point." The corners of her mouth pull back slightly, showing the faintest impression of a smile.

William rests his hand on his mother's shoulder and says, "Enjoy the rest of your evening. I'll be back later tonight. Don't wait up for me."

"It is nice to meet you," Mrs. Berringer says, shaking my hand and an uncomfortable chill flows through my veins. "You are truly lovely."

"Thanks, it's nice to meet you, too," I mirror her sentiment and fake smile.

William walks in an opposite direction as his parents. I simply follow. Right now, I'm just too stunned to do anything else.

William's the first to break through the tension. "That went well."

I say nothing. I've lost my voice for the moment . . . maybe forever.

We stay at the fair for a little while longer, but I can't find any joy in it. My happiness has literally been sucked out of me. The world around me feels different, wrong somehow. Perhaps William and I are wrong, somehow.

The air is thick, and it takes a while before I can speak. When I finally do, my voice quivers, "William, could you take me home? I'm not feeling so well."

"The concert starts in fifteen minutes. Are you sure you want to miss it?"

"I'm sure," I mumble.

I can't look at him, so I stare at my boots instead . . . all the way to the parking lot.

"Sorry," I whisper.

He opens my door, but before I can enter the car, he blocks my way.

"You know Delilah, my parents act like that with everyone. Please don't take anything they say personally."

"It's difficult not to. Especially, when on some level, I know they're right."

"They're right about what?" William says somewhat agitatedly.

"It's pretty obvious about what they thought about me. Don't tell me you didn't notice."

"So you have the ability to read minds?"

"You know as well as I do, what they'll say to you later."

"What exactly will that be?" he questions.

I bite my lip and hold back from saying something I'll regret. And although I attempt to look away, I know he has seen my eyes and the tears they hold. Finally, I am able to say, "That I'm not good enough for you."

"Delilah, you are more than good enough for me. You're everything I could ever hope for in someone." William places his hands on either side of my face and gently raises it. He positions his mouth next to my ear. "I'm in love with you. Haven't you noticed? Who cares what my parents may or may not think?"

My mouth hangs open, as if waiting to catch flies. Night after night, I have dreamt of hearing him say these words. Why is it so impossible to feel anything at this moment?

He's waiting for me to respond, but a lump has formed in my throat, and I remain quiet.

"Delilah, you don't have to say anything now. Just know, I care deeply for you, and my intentions have never been to hurt you. Can you please believe in me? I don't have to live by my parents' wishes. They have no influence over my decisions." He places his forehead to mine and looks deeply into my eyes. "I'll be with the person of my choosing, not theirs."

For some reason, I become angry, and suddenly, I see him as a hypocrite. My temper gets the best of me, and I speak without thinking. "I'm curious, William, have they already chosen someone for you? Perhaps that girl, what was her name? Camilla? I'm sure they would be proud if you were seeing her!"

His lips tighten, and the lines across his forehead deepen. He doesn't say anything . . . not one single thing. With his shoulders slouched, he walks to the driver's side of the car. Silently, he sits behind the steering wheel.

This ride is lasting forever. I can't believe I said those things about Camilla. Truthfully, I know William hasn't been hanging around with her. There's no point saying anything about it now. Maybe I can fix this mess in the morning.

Suddenly, reality hits and knocks the wind right out of me. My throat squeezes shut, as if I'm being choked by invisible hands. Dramatically, I reach for the door handle. William's not paying any attention to me; he's staring at the road and seems to be a million miles away. I'm right next to him, suffocating to death, and he doesn't even notice!

I lean my seat back and close my eyes. One, two, three . . . I can't relax! I'll imagine all the colors of the rainbow: red, orange . . . green, no yellow, then green . . . this isn't working either. What am I going to do? I should probably keep quiet for the rest of the night. If I say anything now, I'll only make matters worse.

Up ahead, light from my porch illuminate the darkness. In just a few short seconds, I'll leave William's fancy car and enter my safe harbor.

As soon as the car comes to a halt, I leap from my seat. I run for my front door, determined to leave my feelings behind. I can't believe it! William's letting me go. Why is he just sitting there? Did I really expect for him to stop me? His tires are rolling backwards! He's actually leaving! Wait a minute, I can't allow the night to end like this! I run for him, shouting for him to stop . . . and finally, he does.

I reach the car. He rolls down his window, but doesn't say a word.

"I don't know what's wrong with me. Don't go," I plead.

"I need some time. Can I just see you later?" Darkness has fallen across his face, and he looks different.

"Please don't leave like this!" I shake my head, as tears stream down my face.

"We'll talk tomorrow, I promise."

"Okay," I say meekly, and he begins to drive away.

In desperation, I try to stop him! Only, he isn't slowing! I freeze in the center of my driveway. I shout into the night air, "I love you!" and I wait.

After what seems like an eternity, he stops and gets out of the car. His stare penetrates deep into my soul.

"I love you, too," he declares.

William pulls me into his arms, and I can feel his heart beating, pounding through his chest. He releases me from our embrace. I tilt my head back, hoping for a kiss…he complies, but his lips are tight and void of emotion.

"Goodnight, Delilah," he says solemnly.

"I'll see you tomorrow, then?" I say, and I could just kick myself for sounding so completely pathetic.

Again, he hugs me. Only, I'm not so keen on how this feels. I am reminded of how it feels to say goodbye, not goodnight. I'm thinking like a crazy person. Tomorrow, we'll talk and everything will be right as rain. Although it's difficult, I let him go.

"See you tomorrow," he says and heads for his car.

I watch as he leaves and finally, the lights from his car disappear.

"It's gonna be a long night," I whisper and look up at the stars.

Maybe I should wish on the biggest one. It may sound silly, but the way I see it, it couldn't hurt. So I search the heavens for the brightest and most beautiful star, and I wish with all of my heart . . . with all of my heart.

Chapter Seven

Gloomy shadows are cast across my bedroom walls. Desperately, I toss and turn, yearning for comfort and sleep. No matter what I do, my mind won't calm down. The thought of losing William is devastating. We've shared some of the best times of my life. I've never met anyone like him and most likely never will again.

For the first time, I taste heartache—it stings.

I can't take anymore of this. I get out of bed, grab my robe, and fling it around my body. I know what will make me feel better.

A light glows from above the stove, reminding me of a lighthouse. Perhaps it will help steer me through this torrential storm. I wander to the fridge and pull out an armful of ingredients. The only thing missing is shrimp.

"This may work," I say, staring at a can of crabmeat.

All summer long, I've spent endless hours trying to perfect the shrimp etouffee recipe. Every time, I can tell there's something missing. My father thinks I've lost my mind. He keeps telling me I'm wasting my time, that it is already perfection, and maybe it's time to 'move on.' I simply let him know it will turn out to be one of my best dishes.

Gradually, I am absorbed. My hands enjoy the texture of peppers, dicing them into tiny squares. My senses are heightened through delicious aromas from the broth and spices. I should play some jazz music and wear a few green and purple strands of beads, New Orleans style. Come to think about it, I need to visit New Orleans. I could learn how to make something fun and zesty.

When my creation is finished, I tantalize my taste buds with succulent flavors from my ~~shrimp~~ crab etouffee. And again, I am aware I still haven't gotten it right. I did use crabmeat instead of shrimp, but that's not the problem. The flavor of the broth is just sub-par, lacking somehow.

After a few hours of cooking therapy, I've relaxed enough to go back to bed. And sometime in the early hours of morning, I am able to drift off to sleep.

~ * * * ~

Although the morning sun has washed away the foreboding shadows, there's little comfort in the brightness of the day. My stomach is twisted into knots, and I'm not sure I'll ever be able to untie them. I don't want to get out of bed. Maybe I'll pull the covers over my head and stay here all day.

I close my eyes and it is William I see.

"Ugh!" I grunt in irritation, as I am forced to leave my bed and face the day.

~ * * * ~

I keep myself busy with meaningless tasks. The phone still hasn't rung. With each passing second, I fall into deeper despair. I could call him, but that would be a mistake. William told me he'd see me later. I just wish I knew when.

By the end of the day, there's still no sign of William, and I have to get ready for work. I stare in the mirror. Although I've used tons of makeup, dark circles are still visible.

Lydia's here for me, just as she always has been. I stagger to her car, gravel crushing under my working pumps.

"Geez Louise, you look awful. What happened?" Lydia asks.

As soon as I see her, my emotions surge and I cry. Lydia hugs me close, running her hand over my hair.

"Don't worry, sugar. You'll get through this," she whispers soothingly.

After a few minutes, my tears subside. I already feel stronger than before. Without another word, we head over to the resort.

~ * * * ~

Management at The Greenbrier strongly discourages for anyone to spy on guests. Fortunately for me, Lydia doesn't mind breaking a few rules tonight. Every minute or so, she puts her head out the door and peeks in the direction of William's table. I realize we're acting childishly, but as I watch her run back and forth from the swinging door, I perk up a little bit.

"Well, I see his folks sitting over there, but William's still missing." Lydia shrugs her shoulders. "Probably, just running a bit late is all."

The time has come for us to greet the tables. We enter the main dining area, and I immediately look for William . . . but he isn't there. William's mother is, however, and she is staring at me. It's an icy stare, and hairs on the back of my neck stand up. I smile, but honestly there's little point. After sighing, I make my way around my tables.

A few minutes pass like this, when I finally realize Mrs. Berringer's no longer at her seat. Air from my lungs seep out, and my muscles relax. But, all of a sudden, Cynthia Berringer is standing at my side, and an entirely new shiver passes over me! Lightly, she rests her boney fingers on my arm. They feel like icicles, thin and frosty.

"Excuse me, Delilah, would you be so kinds as to help me with something? It will only take a moment," says Mrs. Berringer, who still hasn't released my arm.

"Of course Mrs. Berringer," I say and escort the woman away from my tables. Finally, William's mother releases her firm grip and walks by my side.

"Delilah, may I have a word with you?" she asks.

Although she is smiling, it lacks sincerity. I stop walking, plant my shoes firmly to the tile floor, and stare at her.

"What can I do for you?" I inquire.

"I hope you don't mind if I speak candidly?" Mrs. Berringer says in a tone both soothing and polite. She starts to say something. I can hear her, but I'm not really listening. I wonder how many other helpless victims have been able to see through her façade. I look down and stare at the black and white tiles beneath my pumps. The floor's shiny and arranged in a checkerboard pattern. I can almost see my reflection.

"Very well then, since you won't answer my question, I will let you in on a little secret. As a mother, I have concerns about the well-being of my son. Since our arrival, I have noticed a change in him."

The woman's words swirl around the vacant hallway, but I barely hear. Another few seconds go by. She's probably waiting for me to be a part of this discussion, but I remain mute. I mean, how am I supposed to react to this woman? I want this moment to end and I wish she'd finish her little speech already. I still don't grasp the point of this private conversation. What does she want from me?

Finally, more words seep from Mrs. Berringer's paper thin lips, and I tune into them, "You seem like a very pleasant girl. I honestly don't wish to see you hurt. However, I believe it would be best if you let him go."

"I don't understand," I say.

"As a concerned parent, I can't sit back and watch as the two of you make a 'mistake' and have to spend the rest of your lives paying for it."

What did this woman just say? Did she just imply . . .

Before I am able to respond, she continues, "My hope is, if you truly care for William, you will see it in your heart to allow him to live out his dream."

"Would that be your dream or his?" Oops! I bite my lip.

"Mr. Berringer and I hold our son's best interest as a priority. You have only known him a few short months, whereas we have raised and nurtured him his whole life."

"I may have only spent two months with your son, but I believe I've gotten to know him very well. Perhaps, in some ways, I may even know him better than you do. I know he dreams about designing buildings with the inspiration of the great cathedrals and the cutting edge vision of Frank Lloyd Wright." I take in a deep gulp of air and continue giving her examples from William and my frequent discussions. At last, I finally pause for breath and say, "I also know he wants you to be proud of him."

"I see this conversation isn't going anywhere. This must be extremely uncomfortable for you. I am truly sorry I have imposed."

She begins to walk away, but I grab her arm. "Wait a minute! I realize you see me as a small town girl with little ambition. But for your information, my dream is to become a great chef and own an entire chain of phenomenal restaurants! You probably didn't know that about me . . . and William believes in me," I say loudly, and a tear slowly trickles down my cheek.

"Hopefully, you can find it in your heart to do what is right. Thank you for being so gracious with your time. I won't bring up this subject with you again. Good evening, Delilah."

I release Mrs. Berringer from my grasp and she swiftly returns to the dining hall. I am left behind, feeling dejected and confused.

I try to see my relationship with William from his mother's perspective. Although I hate her, I think I understand her . . . a little.

Before returning to my tables, I wipe away my tears and lift my head. I am not going to look over at Mrs. Berringer. I can't believe she had the nerve to insinuate that William and I might make a 'mistake' and *she'd* wind up taking care of it. How dare she say such a horrible thing! I still can't wrap my mind around how someone could be so, so . . . rude!

Oh no, I just looked over at William's table and there he is, right next to his mother! What am I supposed to do? The kitchen! I race as fast as I can through the swinging door. I made it out of there, just in time. My breathing is shallow and my head is light. I must be hyperventilating! To steady myself, I grasp for the table. Thank goodness, Lydia has found me.

"Take a deep breath. There you go. Do you need some fresh air or somethin'?" Lydia says, but her mouth moves too fast. I can't understand what she's trying to say. Lydia loops my arm over her shoulder and helps me outside. She sits me in a chair and fans my face. The steady flow of air feels nice.

"I've never seen you like this, before. Sugar, you look white as a ghost. What happened to you out there?" she asks in a raised voice.

After composing myself, I tell her about my conversation with Mrs. Berringer. Lydia's face turns a shade of red like I've never before seen.

"How dare that woman treat you like that! Who does she think she is, anyway? Why, you're the best thing that boy could ever hope for! Humph!" Lydia rants on like this for another minute.

"Thanks, you're a great friend," I say and hug her. "I'll be fine. Let's get back in there before we both get fired."

I must put my emotions on hold and go numb. I will move around like a zombie and no one will even notice.

Just to grind salt into my wounds, Camilla is now sitting at William's table. She is such a tart, and his mother is a royal pain. Worse, my shift won't be over for another hour.

"Geez Louise, won't this evening ever end?" I mumble under my breath.

~ * * * ~

This night has truly been one from hell. I don't think it could possibly get any worse. I stand corrected—it can.

Lydia rushes over to me and whispers, "You might want to speed it up a bit. 'Cuz here *he* comes, now."

Great, just what this unbearable night needs—a nice little visit from William. I really don't want to face him, but I know I can do this. I wait a second before spinning around.

"Delilah, can we talk?" he asks faintly.

"I just wish we didn't have to. I wonder if it would be easier to leave things be," I say, sounding both weary and deflated.

"I'm sorry for all of this. You were right about my parents. And you do realize I had nothing to do with Camilla being at our table. That was yet another one of my parents' brilliant ideas," William says. He wears a familiar smile, but his face looks different . . . hollow.

"Parents generally are full of brilliant ideas, aren't they?"

"*My* parents always have been," he pauses, and my heart goes out to him. His anguish's written plainly across his face. "As meddlesome as they are, their intentions are good. They don't know any other way."

"I thought I'd see you before work. I hoped we would straighten out this mess. Now I'm not so sure if that's even possible."

"I had every intention of coming over. Instead, I had to endure a long discussion with my parents. I did manage to tell them about switching my major," he says with a twinkle.

"I know all about that. It didn't go over very well for you, did it?" I ask, but he looks confused by this. So I further explain, "Your mother informed me of your little discussion, today."

"My mother? When did you two talk?"

"Just before you arrived at dinner, we had a nice little chat," I say, half-heartedly.

William's hand rubs roughly across his forehead. "Then, for that I apologize, as well. I had no idea she could sink that low. What did she say?"

"I think you already have an idea. Besides, it doesn't really matter."

"It does matter. I'd like to know what she said to you," he says, his voice strained.

"Look, she's just concerned. She seems to be under the impression I've been a bad influence on you."

"Delilah, I understand you've had a rough day. Having my mother speak to you like that is unacceptable. I can promise, she will never do it again," he says and places his forehead to mine. "I should've come by your house today. Obviously, I chose a bad time to talk with my parents."

"It doesn't matter anymore. Goodbye, William."

His eyes widen, and I can see sorrow behind them.

"What're you doing? Please tell me you aren't going to allow her to scare you out of my life."

I step back, using the space as a shield. "The truth is . . . our relationship was over before it even started."

"That's ridiculous! There's absolutely no reason we shouldn't be together! The next few years may be difficult with both of us being away at school. But we can work it out."

"It could never work. What're you doing with a small town girl like me, anyway? Your mother's probably right about one thing. You are too good for me. We were both caught up in the thrill of summer. It's only a matter of time before we enter back into the real world and realize we don't belong together."

"I can tell you this much, I believe we can survive in it, together, but not if you aren't even willing to try. I'll tell you what, why don't we just say goodnight. We can sleep on it and talk tomorrow."

"All right, goodnight then," I agree, but the truth is . . . I doubt I'll ever see him again.

I turn away, but he reaches for my hand and wraps his arms tightly around my waist. I want to fade away into his embrace, and for a fleeting second, I allow myself to enjoy the moment.

"No matter what happens, I will always love you," he says before releasing me.

Tears swell in my eyes. I know I can't hold them off any longer; I want to run for the door.

"I need to leave," I say meekly.

At last, he loosens his hold. Swiftly, I slide out of his arms and back away. He doesn't stop me. And although my back is now facing him, I know he is watching me go. Before slipping through the door, I look back and mouth the words, "I love you, too."

~ * * * ~

My body has gone numb. I don't recall walking to Lydia's car, and the ride home is a distant memory. I'm exhausted and yearn for sleep. Instead, I find myself fiddling around in my kitchen. I pull out pots and pans and scatter them across the counter. I reach for spices and lighten the fridge of some of its contents.

My hands know what to do; they start by washing and then chopping veggies. I toss peppers, onions, garlic, and celery into a pot with butter. Ah, that familiar sizzle and popping sound. I add a handful of flour to make my roux. When it is the consistency and color of peanut butter, I pour in diced tomatoes and broth. I add spices to the mixture—a pinch here, a spoonful there.

After an hour of preparing my dish, I take a bite . . . and it tastes good, but something important is still missing. I've altered the ingredients and amount of broth and tomatoes. I just can't seem to get it right.

"Oh well," I sigh.

Just before I clean up my mess, I realize what's missing. I leap over to a cabinet and search. Back there, sits a lonely bottle of paprika. I throw in a spoonful and stir. I taste the etouffee . . . and my face lights up with delight! I jump around the room, punching my hands into the air!

"I've finally done it!" I squeal and fall into a chair.

I can't wait for Shep to try *this* for lunch tomorrow. He has been teasing me all summer long about my crazy behavior, preparing the same meal over and over. Now he'll see why I've anguished over this for a couple of months. It's absolutely delicious! Probably the best thing I've ever prepared!

For a minute, I forget all about William and his mother. I forget about how my heart has been run through the grinder. I forget about how cruel life can be at times. For now, I'm Delilah, a chef who's about to own the best restaurant the world has ever seen.

After packing up the food and cleaning up my mess. I stumble back to my room and change for bed. Ah, comfort. Instantaneously, two things happen; my head hits the pillow and I drift into a deep sleep.

~ * * * ~

It's noon before I even bother looking at the clock. Eventually, I pull my weary body out of bed and head for the shower. The gentle spray of water massages into my aching muscles. It's the little things that'll bring me back to life.

I'm concerned. William, most likely, will come by soon. I want to stay clear of him. I must get out of my house. I must go somewhere where William won't be able to find me.

Lydia will be here any minute, and I'll let her know we have to leave—right away. Thank goodness, she agrees with my plan and takes me to a place where we used to play as children. It's both peaceful and safe. Our dads built a fort here for us years ago. I can't believe Lydia and I still fit inside its rickety wooden walls.

A breeze finds its way between cracks in the boards. I close my eyes and allow the cool air to caress my face. Ah, flowers and fresh grass.

Few words pass between Lydia and me. Sometimes, it's better to relax in the serenity of silence . . . for a few seconds anyway. It doesn't take long for Lydia to ask the burning question, "So you gonna avoid him?"

"I can't face William. He can be awfully convincing, and I don't want to be talked into changing my mind," I say, but Lydia doesn't look convinced.

"Are you really sure that's what you want?"

"No. I *know* that isn't what I want. It's what's best, though. The more time that goes by, the deeper in love I fall. I need to protect myself."

"All right, you know I support you. In fact, I'm gonna get your next couple shifts covered for you. Even, if I have to work your tables myself. The boss-man will understand; don't you worry about a thing, jellybean."

"Thanks, but I don't want to put you through the trouble. I'll be able to work my shifts."

"Not if I have anything to say about it! You're gonna just have to let me do somethin' for you. Unless you want to walk yourself all the way to The Greenbrier, you better stay home and take care of yourself."

I giggle at the thought of trudging to work in pumps. A smile finally comes to my face. Lydia's the best. I appreciate her more than words can ever express.

"All right, you win, but only cover two days for me. I don't want to stay away for too long," I say and peer out the crooked window. "Hopefully, by then he'll be long gone."

~ * * * ~

Being housebound makes me stir-crazy, and later the next evening, I want to explode. Perhaps staying home from work isn't such a brilliant idea. I'm anxious to talk to Lydia. I wonder if she has seen William, yet.

Shep is sitting in his favorite chair, watching me pace the floor. "You're gonna wear a hole in that rug if you don't hold still."

Just yesterday, I spilled everything to him. This is new territory for us. I don't think he has any idea how to console me, but he has listened and given me many heartfelt hugs. I'm satisfied.

The phone rings. Shep and I look at each other. It's time for the Lydia report.

In an acrobatic feat, I dive across the room and chime into the receiver, "All right, Lydia, tell me everything!"

"William was wonderin' where you were. He asked about you several times," Lydia informs.

"Well, what'd you tell him?" I ask, and I'm just dying to jump through the phone.

"Nothin', which made it worse, I think. By the end of the night, he left me alone though. I think he got the picture."

"Thanks, I'll see you tomorrow," I say and hang up the phone.

~ * * * ~

A couple days later, I finally return to work. When I arrive, I discover William is gone . . . literally gone. According to Lydia, he returned to his home in D.C. Unfortunately, his parents stay at the resort for the remainder of the week. I'm sure they're here to keep an eye on me.

I must remain positive and concentrate on my future. More than ever, I am determined to make my dream come true. Heck, I'll be too busy creating a new world for myself to ever bother with falling in love again.

I wasn't kidding when I told William I wanted to open a restaurant right here in Lewisburg, West Virginia. But first, I have something I must accomplish, like tackling a bigger city and making a name for myself. Maybe I'll go somewhere tropical. I can see myself strolling along sandy beaches, while dreaming up recipes for my restaurant. One day, *Desirez'* will be a huge success!

For now, I'll just spend the remaining part of summer standing by the jukebox, holding a handful of quarters, and playing my favorite song, *American Girl*. I finally understand the last few lines. When I close my eyes, I pretend William is with me. I whisper along with the lyrics, "And for one desperate moment there, he crept back in her memory. God it's so painful, something that's so close and still so far out of reach." And when the song ends, I place more quarters into the box. I wait for the music, and when it plays, I hum along with Tom Petty, over and over again.

Paige, Monday Afternoon
Kitchen Counter

My hands are white, chalk-white, and clutching the countertops in *my* kitchen. Frantically, I look around and discover I have returned. I shake my head, trying to clear the fog. From the hallway, I can hear my husband; he's coming this way.

"Wow, it smells amazing in here. What are you cooking?" Elliott inquires, leaning over to kiss me on the cheek.

I stare at him blankly, while trying to process what has just occurred.

"Are you feeling all right?" he asks, gently placing a hand on my back.

No, I'm not all right! I'm freaking out! What just happened? Where was I?

Okay, I'll nod and sit on a chair. I am able to do this successfully, but Elliott is quickly by my side. "Paige, you have tears running down your face. What happened?"

It's difficult to say, since I have no idea!

"I'm fine. I was . . . chopping onions," I whisper. "How long have I been gone?"

"Gone? Paige, did you go somewhere?" he questions, sounding really worried.

I glance down at my watch. How is that possible? Only thirty minutes have gone by. I gaze up at the simmering pot. Did I just cook something?

"You're home from work early," I finally realize.

"Yes, do you need for me to pick up the kids?"

"That would probably be a good idea. I feel kind of strange," I say and look up at his concerned face. "You know, I must be exhausted. My mind's just playing some strange tricks on me."

"What kind of tricks? What are you talking about, Paige?"

"Geez Louise Elliott, you'd think I was standing here in a straitjacket the way you're staring at me. Really darlin', it's nothing to worry about."

"Did you just call me darlin'?"

"Yeah, I suppose I did," I say, not really sure what else to say. "Would you like to try my latest creation?"

"All right, I'll try it," he says, strolling over to the stovetop. "In fact, I'd love to try it!"

"Okay, you don't have to pretend anymore. Just wait and see."

I push past him, quickly adding some paprika and a splash of Tabasco. After stirring, I taste it and smile with recognition. Ah, Delilah would be proud. Elliott reaches for a spoon and with little hesitation tastes it.

"So, what do you call this dish? It's fantastic!" he exclaims with his mouth still full.

"Shrimp etouffee," I say, wearing a grin.

Chapter Eight

I sigh, trying to remember what I'm supposed to do next. Since my strange hallucination, time for me is completely skewed. Before leaving my house this morning, I had to look at the calendar just to remind myself today is Tuesday.

I feel as if I have lived an entire lifetime in the small town of Lewisburg, West Virginia. Delilah's thoughts and feelings have been indelibly imprinted upon me. How is it possible for my mind to have fabricated such an intricately woven story? If I've never been to West Virginia, then why do I suddenly feel homesick for it?

Last night, I shared with Elliott a small portion about my recent visit with Delilah. Ever since, I've had difficulty convincing him I am all right. He is continually checking in with me about my mental health, asking me questions like, 'How are you feeling now, dear?' Maybe I shouldn't have told him about Delilah. Honestly, he needs to back off a little. He is starting to get on my nerves.

I have just dropped my kids off at school, when my phone sings, *Don't Worry Be Happy*. The tune indicates Elliott is calling. As a joke, he programmed the melody into my phone, and every time he calls, I can't help but look up and shake my head.

"Good morning," I sing into the phone.

"Good morning. What are yooouuu doing?" Sometimes Elliott inflects his voice in this way.

"I'm heading toward the craft store; I need to pick up some things for Hailey's bridal shower."

"What does the bride-to-be have on the agenda for you today?"

"Actually, my phone has been eerily quiet. I'm just waiting for it to ring so I can hear Bridezilla's next request."

"Did you just call your little sister Bridezilla?" he says with a chuckle.

"Believe me, over the past few months, she has more than earned that title."

"I can't say I disagree. She makes you do *everything* for her," he pauses, "Speaking of which, we should have her and Derek over Friday night. We need to have a Pictionary rematch."

"Honey, you need to give it up. You guys will never beat us girls. Besides, have you forgotten about the couple's shower we're throwing this Friday night?"

"Oh…that's right. I guess I need to pass out those invitations you gave me."

"You still haven't passed out the invitations? Please, please do not forget to do that today, and make sure all of your and Derek's work buddies mark the date on their calendars. It's only a few days away."

"Sounds exciting—I can't wait."

"Why does that comment reek of sarcasm? You know, it is going to be fun. It'll be more of a party than a shower. Just wait until you see all of the decorations I'm about to buy."

"Don't go too crazy with the fluffy stuff."

"Honey, I don't do fluffy. Besides, I need to be able to do fun things like this every once in a while."

"What is that supposed to mean? Does this have anything to do with your little 'Delilah' episode last night?"

"First of all, it wasn't an episode. Actually, it was fun. And you know, it would be nice if we had a little fun of our own—get away for an evening, enjoy a quiet dinner by candlelight, with violins harmonizing in the background," I sigh, luxuriating in the imagery I've just conjured.

"Then, that's exactly what we'll do," he says. "I can't do it tonight, but I am free for lunch. Would you care to join me?"

"Of course, I'd love to go for lunch."

"Great, meet me at Silver Spoon Café in about two hours?"

"Sure, see you then," I say, "Bye, love ya."

"Love you too. Bye," Elliott says before hanging up.

I can't wipe this silly smile off my face. Elliott just made my day. We barely ever have lunch together. Something always seems to get in the way.

Forget about going to the craft store, I have a lunch date to get ready for. Abruptly, I turn the car around and rush home. I need to properly freshen up.

~ * * * ~

I am putting on my favorite new/used pair of jeans and a chocolate brown shirt, that ever so slightly falls off one shoulder, when suddenly, I hear my/Delilah's boots calling to me; their song comes from the floor in my closet. I cannot resist the whisper of their melody—I must answer.

Desperately, I work out my ponytail lump. My flat iron should do the trick. A few products later, and my hair falls gracefully around my shoulders. The mirror seems to give me a nod of approval, so I venture off to meet my husband.

~ * * * ~

71

Silver Spoon Café is a favorite of ours. The food is light, with yummy sandwiches, gourmet soups, and unique salads. The restaurant has a nice outdoor eating area, surrounded by beautiful tropical plants. An added bonus: the absence of TV's. I know I can eat in peace and not worry about whether or not I'll catch my husband looking over my head, watching some sport's clip of the day.

Elliott has already arrived. There he is, sitting at one of the white cast iron tables. I pause under the carved teak archway and take in the scene. Sometimes, I like to pretend it's our first date. I want to enjoy a moment and see Elliott with a renewed freshness. Right now, he's dressed in his standard work apparel: a long-sleeved buttoned-down shirt with khaki pants.

My husband is one of those rare men who comes across as both rugged and nerdy, the perfect combination of Indiana Jones and Clark Kent. Not only is he handsome, he's smart (an engineer by trade). Yes, he drives me crazy half the time, but I still find him attractive. And I remember, over the years, he has remained my best friend.

His eyes twinkle and his grin spreads across his entire face. He must be up to something. Immediately, I become suspicious and can't wait to find out what he's up to.

"This is a nice surprise. What's the occasion?" I ask, as my curiosity rises.

"Now, can't a husband have lunch with his wife and not have an ulterior motive?" He smiles sheepishly and adds, "All right, you've got me."

He pushes a brochure across the table. A photo of a beachside cottage decorates the cover.

My eyebrows scrunch together questioningly, and I inquire, "What's up with this?"

"I was thinking about what you said this morning, and you're right. We need to spend some time away together. I saw this advertisement and thought perhaps . . ." he starts to explain, but my phone rings and cuts him off midsentence. Our conversation is just getting interesting, too.

"You're not going to answer that *now* are you?" he asks, while I rumble around in my purse.

"It could be the kids' school or something else important. It'll only take a second. Ah, here it is," I say, grabbing my phone.

"Let me guess, your mother or your sister?"

"Sister, do you mind? It won't take long." At this, he rolls his eyes and sits back in his chair. I blow him a little kiss and answer the phone. "Good morning."

"Good morning to you. How is my wonderful big sis doing?" Hailey inquires.

"What can I do for you?"

"Funny you should ask," she responds, and I sit back in my chair, mirroring my husband. "The jewelry store just called. It would seem that my ring is ready, and I need to have it back on my finger before Derek starts wondering why I'm not wearing it."

"You haven't been wearing your engagement ring? Why not?"

"Don't ask me stupid questions. It's with the jeweler. Listen, I'm completely swamped. Could you swing by there, and pick it up for me, please?"

"When?" I mutter.

"As soon as possible would be great. I'll owe you for life."

"All right, after lunch I'll swing over there," I say, adding in a half-joking manner, "And with all I do for you, you already owe me for life."

"Great. You're the best. Bye!" She flutters off the phone.

When I look at my husband, he is sighing, loudly, and wearing an exaggerated expression of boredom. I cast him a silly smile, showing lots of teeth.

"Thanks for waiting. I'm not really sure why I even answer her calls. I suppose I'm just a glutton for punishment or something," I say and lift the brochure. "Well, now you have my undivided attention. What's up with the cottage?"

"I was thinking you and I should take a mini-vacation; have a weekend full of pure romance and passion. Just us, no kids allowed," he says and removes his glasses to demonstrate his point by raising his eyebrows up and down.

"Really, when? I am so there!"

"In two weeks. It'll be a good time to leave work behind and focus on nothing but us."

"Sounds perfect, but this doesn't have anything to do with my telling you about Delilah, does it?"

"Well, I have to admit you have caused me some concern. It's obvious you need to get away…we need to spend some time together, *alone*."

"That's cute."

"What's cute?"

"You're trying to fix my *problem* by taking me on a trip," I reveal. "Believe me; I'm thrilled about this . . . . I just hope you want to go for the right reason."

"And what reason would I have other than wanting to spend some time alone with my wife?"

"I just want to make sure you're not trying to 'fix' me," I say and anxiously wait for his response.

The corners of his mouth turn upward, and he says, "I would like nothing more than to spend some time with you. I'm only sorry it took your having delusions to help me realize that."

"Elliott, it was not a delusion. I really saw those things, and I'm going to figure out a way to prove it. In fact, later tonight, you and I can research information about Delilah on the computer."

"All right, but until then, let's just focus on the trip," he says and extends his hand across the table to hold mine.

"Who's going to be brave enough to watch the kids?"

"I've already spoken with your mother, and she has agreed to stay over with them."

"The kids have never slept a full night without one of us right down the hall. I hope they don't wake Mom in the middle of the night," I say, but as I imagine a night away, I want to jump out of my chair. Elliott watches my reaction and seems pleased by it. Good thing too, since I almost ruined a sweet moment by answering my sister's call. Mental note to never do that again.

Throughout lunch, we excitedly plan our upcoming vacation. I feel charged by our discussion and have enjoyed the meal immensely. In fact, I'm thinking we should do this more often.

When it's time to leave our little bubble of happiness, I frown. Elliott walks with me to my minivan, and as I'm about to hop inside, he grabs my waist and pulls me close to his chest. I gasp, but slowly lean in closer and wrap my arms around him. I nestle my head against his chest and listen to him breathe.

"We need to spend more time alone. Love you," he says, and I can feel his words trail down my cheek in a soft whisper. I'm surprised by his romantic gesture *and* by my body's reaction. This is different from our normal 'routine' of moving about like robots, mimicking each others' actions. This is fresh and wonderful. In fact, I find myself melt a little.

When we part, I'm a little light headed. He releases me, and I begin to slide behind the steering wheel, a silly smile is on my face. Before I can sit, however, I feel a sudden *WHOMP* on my rear! I literally jump into the air! When I turn, I see Elliott is laughing.

"Couldn't help myself, just got carried away by the moment." He smiles and walks away. "Have fun trying on jewelry!" he hollers and jumps into his car.

~ * * * ~

Funny thing, not even the traffic bothers me, as I think about our upcoming beach vacation. I can't wait! It's been a long time since I've felt any sort of heightened anticipation about anything.

And then it occurs to me, and I mumble, "Great, it looks like I better go shopping for a new swim suit."

Don't get me wrong, I love shopping for clothes. I just absolutely detest trying on bathing suits. What a nightmare! Although I consider myself healthy looking, I find there's nothing worse than standing in front of a full length mirror, pale skinned, in a suit that doesn't fit right. Those awful fluorescent lights enhance every imperfection. I always feel like a giant marshmallow stuffed into a rubber band. Not a pretty visual.

The radio's playing Squeeze's *Tempted by a Fruit of Another*. I love eighties music. Although I've heard this song a million times, I don't think I've ever paid attention to the lyrics. Still, I hum along with the tune.

When my phone rings, I can see it's my sister calling . . . again.

"Are you there yet?" she asks abruptly.

"I'm on my way."

"Great, I really appreciate it. I realize I should have taken care of this sooner. It just slipped my mind. You know, I've been tied up at work and stuff. Speaking of which, guess who's going to be the interior designer for the new boutique on Park Ave?" she asks, sounding giddy.

"Hmm, let's see . . . Hailey Smith?"

"Right, the owner didn't stand a chance once I led her into my office and . . ." Hailey begins, but I am quick to cut her off.

"And she fell dumbstruck by the flashy design of your office interiors, and the breathtaking view from your window overlooking downtown Orlando."

"All right, so I've told a similar story once or twice before. What can I say, it works every time."

"Hailey, I have a feeling it takes a little more than having an incredible office view to land a client. I mean, you're a very talented designer. Your prospective clients would have to be crazy not to hire you," I say, not really sure where this sudden inspiration came from. And even though I'm speaking the truth, why am I paying her a compliment? Lately, she has been such a pain.

"You're just saying that because you're my sister," she says humbly.

"Actually, I have to say that despite the fact you're my sister," I throw in for good measure.

"Thanks, so anyway," she says, and then continues to flutter on about events at work. She's especially excited about her interior designs for a hot new restaurant scheduled to open downtown, very soon.

After rambling on and on about her work and newest client, she finally changes the subject, "Are we still going to work on the wedding invitations tonight? I'll bring a bottle of wine, and we can chat."

"I'm looking forward to it, darlin'."

"Did you, in some strange twangy tone, just call me darlin'?"

"I guess so. Why, what's so wrong with darlin'?"

"I don't know. It's just that you sound different. Oh well, no biggie."

"All right, I'll call you after I pick up the ring."

"Thanks so much! Oh and Paige, one more thing," she says and I brace myself, "since we wear the same ring size, could you try it on for me? I've had so much trouble having it fitted correctly. I mean, it should *easily* come off my finger *without* soap."

"Good bye," I say and hang up.

Maid of honor is the equivalent to a bride's personal servant. I am constantly running errands for Hailey, and now I have to try on her engagement ring.

~ * * * ~

I approach the shiny doors of the jewelry store, and as soon as I am inside, find myself surrounded by breathtaking jewels . . . and I am bedazzled. I peer into a glass display case, gleaming with sparkling items, when a blonde woman approaches. Her name's Hilary, or at least that's what she has written on her name tag.

"How may I help you today?" she asks, while casually flipping her perky hair behind her shoulder.

"I'm here to pick up a ring for Hailey Smith. I'm Paige MacKenzie," I say, smiling in return.

"Of course, she mentioned you might be the one to pick it up. I'll only be a moment. May I offer you some coffee while you wait?"

"No, thank you."

"Let me know if there is anything else I can help you with." Hilary's polite smile slowly fades as she moves away.

I'm left alone, surrounded by display cases. Look at that bracelet! And what a deal! How much time until my wedding anniversary? Ooh, it's only a few short months away! This jewelry is really unique. I must remember to drop subtle hints and descriptions later. After all, I'm sure Elliott will need some ideas for our big eleven year wedding anniversary.

Hilary returns with the ring, holding it in the palm of her hand. Gracefully, she places it on a black velvet pad.

"This diamond is gorgeous, isn't it? Your sister is a very lucky woman," she notes, still gazing down.

Although I'm mesmerized by its splendor, I'm surprised this ring is so traditional. Hailey is not a traditional sort of girl. I imagine her wearing a ring with a modern twist. This looks more like a ring *I* would choose for myself.

"Hailey asked if I would try it on for size," I say, feeling awkward.

"Of course, please do."

It slides easily onto my finger. A perfect fit. Light, from overhead, penetrates into the stone and a glow sparkles from inside. Each color appears so crisp and precise, and I am further drawn into the rainbow. Wow, this diamond is absolutely stunning! I've never seen anything like it before. When I look up to ask Hilary if they have another gem similar to this one, I realize she also appears super-clear.

In fact, *everything* is crystal clear: the display case, jewelry, even the people are ultra-defined! The room around me is distorting. Everything is spinning out of control! My temples throb. I squeeze my eyes shut and desperately reach for the glass counter!

Around and around, faster and faster! When suddenly, it stops! I open my eyes and look down. I am mortified at seeing my hands, not on the glass counter, but in a kitchen sink! The ring is still on my finger, but I'm trying to slip it off.

"The soap isn't working! Get off my finger!" the words come out of my mouth, but this isn't me.

Wait a minute, I recognize this voice! It's Hailey! Just as with Delilah, I am trapped. Only this time, I am hostage to all of the thoughts and emotions of my sister!

"Are you still trying to take off that ring?" *he* asks.

Hailey lifts her head and glances over her shoulder. Wait, this isn't Derek. Sitting, relaxed, on a black sofa is a very handsome stranger. A playful grin spreads across his tanned features. The expression on his face . . . total adoration.

Chapter Nine

Hailey's Story, one week ago
Orlando, FL

Although I'm annoyed by this seemingly permanent fixture on my finger, I soften upon seeing *him*.

"Why are you wasting so much time over there, when you could be closer to me over here?" he says, while running his strong hand over the couch's leather surface.

"I don't feel right about wearing Derek's ring. At least, not while we're together, Julian." I turn off the water and saunter in his direction.

"Maybe it's time to return the ring all together," Julian says.

"Look, I'm going to cancel the wedding. I'm just waiting for the right moment."

"And what 'moment' might that be? Hailey, we've been seeing each other for over two months."

"And they have been the best two months of my life."

"Then break it off with Derek."

"It's not that easy. Derek is a good man, and I'm not exactly looking forward to ruining his life!" I admonish and hang down my head.

"Don't you think maybe you're overacting a little? I'll admit you're an incredible person, but I seriously doubt you'll ruin his life."

"All right, perhaps ruin is *too* strong a word, but I still don't want to see Derek upset. I don't even like to think about it," I say, sticking out my lower lip. "Besides, what would my mom and Paige think if I just called off the wedding? They're always accusing me of starting something and not following through. Besides, I've made so many stupid mistakes. I don't even trust my own judgment anymore."

"Do you consider us a mistake?"

"You weren't a mistake, you were an accident! I didn't plan on falling for you! In fact, I didn't plan any of this! I wouldn't have agreed to marry Derek, in the first place, had I known there was a Julian Medina waiting out there for me."

"So, what are you saying? Please don't tell me you were *settling* for Derek, and I'm just an accident? That's pretty harsh, Hailey."

"What's that supposed to mean?"

Julian laughs before saying, "First, I've never seen you settle for anything. You always strive for perfection. That's what makes you such a good designer, and just one of the many reasons I fell in love with you. And second, we're not an accident . . . it was fate."

My smile has returned. After reaching him, I climb up onto his lap, striking a sexy pose. I lean forward, and my long hair falls over my shoulder.

"Why don't we just cut the chit-chat and enjoy what little time we have together?" I suggest, as my hands roam over the familiar definition of Julian's perfectly sculpted chest. Blood surges throughout my body. I can hear it reach my ears. "I'll give you a massage, deep tissue. I'm sure with a little candle light and soft music I could ease away some of your tension."

"You're pretty amazing, you know that?" he says and runs his hands along the sides of my body, slowly inching up my shirt. "You have no idea what you do to me. The way you make me feel."

"You have a funny way of showing it. What, with that ridiculous rule of yours," I remind him.

"It may seem ridiculous to you, but it's important to me, when I'm sleeping with a woman, there isn't another man in the picture. Besides, it's the only bargaining chip I've got."

"You do realize I'm not sleeping with Derek," I say and watch as Julian recoils. "Sorry. You probably don't want to think about that."

"You're very perceptive."

I'm running my fingers through his hair, when a chiming sound comes from my purse. I pull away from Julian and stare in the direction of the invasive noise. But Julian holds me closer and trails sweet kisses down my neck.

"You don't have to answer," he mumbles softly.

It is extremely difficult to peel away from him, and I stress the word *extremely*. Once I am safely a few feet away, I say, "Yes, I do. I'm sorry."

I stumble over to the kitchen and grab my cell.

"It's him, isn't it?" Julian asks irritably.

"Yes, but I'm not sure why he's calling; we're not supposed to meet for another hour."

This scene has played out before. Julian scowls, stands up, and storms out of the room. With regret, I watch him leave. All the while, the phone in my hand continues on its quest for an answer. For a second, I debate whether or not I should take the call. As usual, my guilt about Derek overrules everything else.

"Hi," I say, answering my cell.

"Hey, listen, I'm running late. This deal has me swamped and I'll need a couple more hours. Can we meet at your condo around ten?" Derek rattles off quickly.

"Sure. I'll see you there. Bye," I say and calmly turn off the phone.

Julian reenters the room. He won't make eye contact with me, instead he looks everywhere I'm not . . . perhaps he's searching for answers.

"I'm so sorry, Julian," I say, reaching for him.

Julian doesn't respond. His hands are placed firmly at his sides. He hangs back his head and stares at the ceiling.

"I don't have to meet with Derek until later, so I have more time. You and I could continue where we left off," I say, but he doesn't respond. I wait another second before adding, "I'll take that as a no . . . and I guess that's my cue to leave." I say and grab my purse.

"No, don't go," he says before I reach the door.

I look back and see he is approaching. Swiftly, I meet him half-way and try to seduce him with my smoldering eyes. He grins, while wrapping his arms around my waist.

"So, does this mean we can pick up where we left off . . . on the sofa?" I ask hopefully.

"Funny thing, suddenly I'm not in the mood. I'll tell you what, why don't we just go and grab a bite to eat?"

I'm disappointed, but I'm not giving up. My fingers curl around the ends of Julian's hair, and I pull him closer.

"No really, it's not going to happen right now," he says and pulls back.

Begrudgingly, I nod and back away. He reaches for his shirt and begins to fasten the buttons. Darn it, I had only just managed to have him remove that blasted thing, too.

After he is dressed, he motions towards the door. "Ready?"

I'm still sulking, but I manage to make my way to his car. Julian opens my door, and I fall onto my seat. I'm still upset about how things turned out here. We shouldn't go out, we should dine in. I'm so frustrated, I could scream!

Julian seems to be in high spirits. He's actually whistling; how annoying. For someone who had just acted so distraught over Derek's little phone call, Julian seems to feel pretty darn good.

"Humph!" I grumble and fold my arms over my chest.

"What's up?" he asks, while hopping onto his seat.

"Nothing," I reply icily.

"Remember, there's no pouting in the convertible."

"I'm not pouting," I murmur.

"All right, let's have dinner and maybe we can pick up where we left off."

"We'll see, by then *I* may not be in the mood."

"Hailey, it's me you're talking to. You're always in the mood."

"Aren't you the funny one?"

"I find it can help ease an awkward situation," he says.

"Been in many awkward situations, have you?"

"They seem to crop up more and more frequently."

Julian's car is almost as sexy as he is. I love riding with the convertible top down. The air is crisp, the stars are out, and the wind is blowing away my cares. By the time we arrive at *Amura's*, I'm actually hungry (for more than Julian) and am looking forward to a delicious meal, while sipping a cocktail.

The sushi bar is buzzing with activity. How unfortunate. Luckily, we're seated rather fast. A hostess leads us past various couples, flipping chopsticks and sipping on their Saki.

Ooh, I like that colorful glass fixture over there. It looks really cool. Red swirls, I love red swirls. I'm trying to memorize every line, every detail of the piece, when my attention is pulled away by a loud *whoosh* coming from the kitchen! Flames erupt and shoot out colorful sparks. Chefs are busy preparing food on the back grill. I'm caught up with the activity, when all of a sudden I bump into someone…literally.

"Oops! Sorry, I wasn't paying attention," I say, and when the woman turns around, I realize I know her! It's Wanda from work, and she has the biggest mouth! Great, now everyone at the office will know I'm having dinner with Julian! My life is over.

Okay, just calm down and act natural. I smile brightly and say, "Wanda, hi!"

Julian is standing at my side. I watch, as Wanda takes in every inch of him. This is so awkward. What am I going to do?

Finally, Julian extends his hand towards Wanda and says, "I'm Julian Medina."

"Julian, this is Wanda. She works with me," I say.

"Yes, Julian, I have heard of you. It's nice to meet you," Wanda says and looks at me. "Hailey, where's Derek?"

"He had to work late tonight. You know how it goes." I fumble to get the words out. This is awful. I think I'm going to pass out.

Just then, in a tone both relaxed and seemingly effortless, Julian intercedes, "I must say how happy I am with all of the work your team has done for my restaurant. In fact, Hailey was just about to go over some new designs with me. Would you care to join us?"

All of a sudden, Wanda's eyes don't appear as narrow. In fact, she waves a hand dismissively and informs us she is officially off the clock, but we should enjoy our meal, anyway.

Whew!

Julian and I are seated in a nice booth against a far wall. He reaches across the table for my hand. Instinctively, I pull away and peer around to see if anyone is watching.

"You don't have to do that, you know," he says with a sigh.

"Do you realize how close that was back there? Wanda might as well have her own gossip column in the work newsletter. She's the worst!" After scanning the restaurant and realizing no one is even glancing our way, I relax. At last, my attention returns to Julian. "By the way, thanks for saving me from her. You were really smooth."

"No problem," he says with a smile both bright and sparkly. In fact, Julian is always bright and sparkly. I adore him. He leans back into the booth. "Hailey, you're going to have to face Derek and cut the ropes…" Julian says and continues on and on with his 'dump Derek speech.'

I listen and watch his mouth move, but honestly, I've heard this so many times before. In fact, I already know what he'll say next. My mind trails away from his words, and I notice the glass partitions separating the tables. An interesting pattern is etched across the opaque glasswork.

I'm taking mental notes of the designs, when Julian snaps, "Hailey, have you even heard a word I've just said?"

"Yes, I mean no, not really. Honestly, we've gone over this before. I'm just not sure how to break off the engagement. I need more time to think it through."

"You were sitting right in front of me, but your mind was a million miles away."

"Maybe."

"All right, let's just leave it for now. I'm not going anywhere. So, change of subject. What sort of new design plan do you have rolling around in that pretty little head of yours?"

"I have a fantastic idea for some added touches of color to put in your restaurant."

"So, come on, let me hear it," he says and lounges back. He actually cares about my ideas. He's actually interested in my thoughts. He's right, we do belong together.

I will always wait for you...
just don't take too long.

Love always,
Julian

Chapter Ten

"I don't want to go home," I say and glare at my parked car.

"You could very easily stay," Julian reminds me. "Look, I know breaking up with Derek will be difficult for you, and I'm a selfish jerk. But you can't blame me for wanting to spend more time with the woman I love," Julian says, pulling me into an embrace. I lean further into his body and inhale, wishing more than anything I didn't have to leave.

"I love you," I whisper.

A jolt passes through Julian, and he pulls back, staring directly into my eyes. "You finally said it."

"Said what?"

"Come on, I want to hear you say *it* again."

"Don't be ridiculous. I'm not doing any such thing. Besides, I've said I love you a million times."

"Hailey, I think I would remember if you had."

"Well, I have. And I shouldn't have to say it all the time. You know how I feel. I mean, you know *everything* about me."

"It would still be nice to watch your lips actually form the words."

"Julian, I love you, and we'll make this work; just give me a little more time."

"I'll take that," he says with a smile.

"Thanks. I better head home now," I say, as he kisses me goodbye. "I'll see you tomorrow night?"

"I'll be waiting . . . as always," he says, placing a finger to his lips and then to mine.

It's difficult, but I leave Julian and head for my home.

~ * * * ~

I'll never forget the day I first set eyes on Julian. He had only just moved here from South Florida, where he was manager and part-owner of the hottest restaurant in Palm Beach. He was going to open a sister restaurant right in the heart of Orlando.

Guess who he hired to create the interior designs for his new restaurant? That's right, me! And that was through a phone interview. We hadn't even met in person, yet. I remember looking forward to his calls. Oh, how I enjoyed the sound of his voice. We would have the most delicious, maybe a little inappropriate, phone conversations. And he may have been a little overly flirtatious, but I liked it.

After a few weeks of this, my assistant and I arranged a meeting with Julian. In all honesty, I didn't really have a good reason to meet with him face-to-face. I could have answered his questions over the phone, but I was just dying to see *this* particular client in person.

On that day, my assistant and I found Julian as he was circling the unfinished bar area. He stood amidst a complete mess, raking his hand through his dark hair . . . luscious. Immediately, I felt sorry for the guy; he looked so frustrated. I wanted to help him any way I could.

"Good afternoon, Mr. Medina," I said from a few feet away. "Mr. Medina…Hello, I'm Hailey Smith, and this is my assistant, Stacey Potter."

He finally turned around, and why was he just standing there like that, staring at the two of us, wearing a very strange expression? One thing was for certain, I was immediately drawn to him. He didn't even have to speak. I was already completely hooked. Thank goodness, I was wearing a sexy dress. Every so often I would twirl just a little and wait for his reaction. I was well aware of how the fabric skimmed over my body. Actually, I really shouldn't have worn a sexy dress. What was I thinking?

Another second passed before Julian responded, "Of course, of course, thank you for coming. I have a million questions for you."

Finally, he removed his hands from his hair, crossing them at his chest. He was a perfect stranger, yet I had the urge to comfort him. I collected myself and tried not to drool.

I lifted my shoulders and tried to sound professional, "Is there somewhere we can sit and talk? I need a surface to lay out my plans."

Julian looked around the dirty room. What a complete disaster; it was as if a bomb had landed right in the center of his restaurant.

Finally, Julian motioned across the room. "There's a spot, I just need to clean it up."

He rushed over to a make-shift table, and we followed his dust ridden trail. I tried to keep from laughing, as I watched him scurry to a back room, only to remerge with a few pathetic looking paper towels. He was so cute.

I handed Julian my sketches, trying desperately to sound confident, "Now, I've reviewed the photos of your sister restaurant. I am very impressed by the innovative thinking that went into the plans. People just weren't designing spaces like that back in the nineties. Your architect is quite visionary!" I said, trying to suppress some of my excitement.

"Thank you. I'm sure you are aware of the impact the surrounding design can have on our guests. It is imperative they enjoy themselves as they eat," Julian said in an overly business-like manner.

"Of course, and I have incorporated all of the important details from the original site. I was inspired by the initial plans and added a few features. I hope you don't mind."

His expression pulled back into one of complete shock. "No, not at all. Please proceed," he said, motioning his hand toward the sketches.

After reviewing my ideas for the restaurant's interior, Julian appeared to relax. He also seemed to match my excitement over the new alterations. In fact, he surprised me by making some astute observations. I must say, I was very impressed by him in the end.

"You have no idea how you just helped me," he said, as he walked me to the door. "Thank you for coming to see me on such short notice."

"That's what I'm here for. Please feel free to call me with any questions you may have." And I hoped he would call, very soon.

"I will do that. How long will it be before we meet again?" he said, and I could feel a blush rise to my cheeks.

My professional exterior was fading away fast! I began to fidget with my dress.

"It will most likely be a week or so before I'll have your designs complete. I'll call you . . . um, so I can schedule a time for you to see them," I said.

"I'll look forward to our next meeting," he said.

What I thought was going to be a polite handshake, immediately changed, when he lightly brushed his lips over the back of my hand. A strange electric current passed between us. What was that? I've never felt anything like that before. He pulled away, and I continued staring down at my hand. It was glowing, my hand was glowing. Well, not really, but at that moment, that's what I saw. But I'm engaged to Derek.

Cautiously, I refocused my attention back to Julian's face and muttered, "Goodbye."

From somewhere else, I heard someone say, "Hailey, are you ready to head back?" I looked to my left, and there was my assistant, Stacey. Had she been there all along? Why was she wearing a devilish grin?

Before leaving, she and Julian gave each other a polite hand shake and said goodbye. We were cool as we left, but as soon as we reached the sidewalk, we giggled like little girls.

"All right Stacey, he's cute, but we still need to keep this professional."

"Cute, more like hot! And I don't think he wants to keep things professional. Did you notice the way he looked at you? I think he was imagining you without that flirty little dress," Stacey said and laughed. "For a second back there, I thought I'd have to douse the two of you with water."

"Obviously, he doesn't realize I'm already taken."

"Obviously, he doesn't really care," she said, narrowing her stare and tilting her head. "What are you going to do about that?"

"I'm not going to do a thing! I'm perfectly happy with Derek! Our wedding is in four months!" I exclaimed and watched as Stacey rolled her eyes. "What's that supposed to mean?"

"Nothing, it's just . . . I haven't seen you act like that around Derek before."

"Mr. Medina happens to be our client. So he ruffled my feathers a bit. It's not a big deal," I said firmly.

"All right *Boss*, whatever you say, but I think he ruffled more than your feathers."

~ * * * ~

Why couldn't I have met Julian *before* Derek entered the picture? I suppose I should have ignored Julian's advances, but I couldn't help myself. I can't say I regret our time together either; the last two months have been unforgettable and exhilarating.

"What am I doing," I whisper, as I enter my lonely condo.

As soon as I walk through the door, my greyhound dashes for me. What a great dog. Luke follows me to the couch and listens as I recount the evening's events. He agrees it's time to call off my engagement to Derek. The real question: how? Luke doesn't have an answer, but his brown eyes warm my heart.

I wish I hadn't allowed so much time to go by before ending this. What a complete and utter nightmare! I guess I could just explain to Derek how I'm not right for him...I feel rotten.

I wonder if Derek and Stacey would make a good couple. I could introduce them. No, that would be awkward.

I know. Julian and I can run away together. I'll leave a nice little note, and . . . . No, I'd miss Paige and the kids too much. Wait a minute! I could have Paige do it for me! She's so good with things like that.

Luke's reaction is nice. In fact, each time I say the words, "Goodbye, Derek. It was never meant to be," Luke licks my face! Next to my sister Paige, Luke is my best friend, except he knows about Julian. But the minute Derek walks in, Luke leaps up and bounds excitedly across the room. Derek quickly sets down his things, leans over, and scratches the anxious dog's back.

"Traitor," I mumble to myself. Did that dog even hear a word I just said? I'll need to remember to have Derek return his copy of my key. After all, this is *my* condo and *my* dog.

While I watch dog and man exchange greetings, I notice how disheveled Derek looks. His normally perfectly styled sandy-blonde hair is all over the place, and his work clothes are wrinkled. He has obviously had a rough day . . . poor guy.

After giving Luke his greeting, Derek looks my way. "Sorry about being late. I can't wait until this project's complete," he says, while scratching between Luke's ears.

"It's all right," I pause, trying to figure out what to say next. "Derek, do you think we could talk?" Concern floods his face, but he obliges and walks over to sit next to me.

Before I can even open my mouth, he interjects, "I'll save you the trouble of having to spell it out for me."

How could he know about Julian? Wait a minute, how much could he possibly be aware of? I feel sick. This isn't going like how I rehearsed.

"What do you think I'm going to say?" I question feebly.

"It won't always be like this. I realize I've been away at work a lot lately, but as soon as this project's finished, we can spend more time together. Perhaps even take a trip before the wedding," Derek suggests, grinning in his silly way.

"Oh," I say, glancing down at the ring, as I tensely spin it around and around.

"I know it has been difficult for you, having your fiancé away so much," Derek says sweetly, lifting my head. "I'm not blind. I can tell you've been distant, but I promise I'll make it up to you."

This is just great, now I'm tearing up. How am I supposed to call off our engagement, now? I can't crush this sweet guy. I know he would do anything to make me happy. And although I'm not the right woman for him, I wish I could be.

All right, so I'll break off the engagement another day. Right now, I can't bear to hurt him.

He reaches his hand for me and whispers, "Hailey, I don't mean to make things difficult for you."

"Derek . . . I um . . . please don't worry about it. You haven't done anything wrong. I'm just tired and need to go to bed. Thanks," I say and swiftly back away. At that moment, Luke jumps onto Derek. I leave the two behind and race for my bedroom.

I can barely hear Derek holler, "Don't worry; I'll lock the door when I leave!"

My breathing is jagged, cutting like a saw through the center of my chest. I shut my bedroom door and lean against it. "Tomorrow, I'll do it, tomorrow," I tell myself over and over.

~ * * * ~

Throughout the night, men wearing large gray masks with downward turning grins flood into my dreams. They surround me, swirling around and around! I am being judged! I beg for them to go, but they continue mocking me. I scream and cry and kick! Until suddenly, the floor beneath me is gone, and I begin to fall!

I awaken with a start, sitting upright! I'm in the safety of my own bed. Tears are streaming down my face.

"It was only a dream," I have to remind myself.

Desperately, I search for my cell. I don't want to wait any longer to tell Julian how I feel. I want to be with him and only him. After dialing his number, I wait anxiously to hear his voice.

There's no answer, and my call goes straight into his voicemail. Although his recorded greeting is cheerful and charming, I hang up.

"Last night was horrible," I sigh and rest back into my pillow. Luke is here with me, and I scratch behind his ears. "You like that, boy?" He licks my face and places his long front leg on top of me. Ah, a hug. "I'd love to stay here and cuddle you all day, but I better get ready for work."

~ * * * ~

When I arrive at my office building, I stand in the doorway and put on a happy face. This stinks; I don't like being fake, for any period of time. And I don't want to be rude, but I really can't be bothered by my coworkers' idle chit-chat . . . especially, Wanda. Okay, so nobody is even looking at me. Better play it safe though and dash straight for my office.

I'm almost there, but Stacey is standing in my way. I attempt to skirt around her, but she is literally blocking me.

"Good morning Hailey! Is there anything you want to share with me?" she asks, wearing an impish grin.

"Not really."

On a normal day, I don't mind swapping gossip with her. Only this is not a normal day, and she's irritating me. Stacey reaches behind her back and opens up the door.

Twelve long-stemmed red roses are sitting on my desk. The most beautiful roses I have ever seen.

"It's not every day a woman receives flowers at the office," Stacey says with a smile.

"Derek's been working a lot lately. He feels pretty guilty about it," I offer. "I'm sure he figures that sending me flowers is the only sensible thing to do."

"I see, and by the look of it he feels pretty terrible. You must have really laid it on thick. Nice going," Stacey says, gazing at the bouquet.

"I suppose."

After a few seconds of awkward silence, Stacey finally leaves. I continue staring at the little envelope. I resent it. I don't want to read about Derek's feelings. I don't want to feel worse than I already do.

Still, I wonder . . . . No, wait a minute, I don't care. I try glaring a hole through the card. It doesn't work. So I ignore it all together and shuffle through some papers.

After a few minutes, curiosity gnaws at me, and in a moment of weakness, I snatch the card. I tear it open and quickly scan over the words, but I have to read them again and again. I still don't understand. I read the words again, "I will always wait for you…just don't take too long. Love, Julian."

My weakened knees buckle, causing me to fall into my leather chair. I stare at my roses, all of a sudden, they look different. They've actually changed in appearance. Now, they're even more beautiful. I reach for one and hold it lovingly in my hand. I'm finally aware of its engaging fragrance, and I slowly fill my lungs with its sweet perfume.

Paige, Tuesday
Jewelry Counter

"Stunning, don't you think?" I hear a chipper voice inquire.

"Yes . . . they are lovely . . . and they smell so sweet," I say, still in a daze.

"The ring . . . smells sweet?" the woman questions.

Uh-oh, everything's coming back. I've just been somewhere else. How embarrassing, and this nice little jewelry person is looking so confused. It's Hilary, and I'm still trying on my sister's ring!

I must collect myself. I must come up with something clever to say. "Right, I'm sure Hailey will appreciate what you've done to make it fit perfectly."

I hand Hilary the ring, and she hesitates briefly before taking it. "I'll just place it in this box."

"Thanks," I say, but who really cares what I'm saying. What just happened? Did I just see what I think I saw? And who is this Julian person?

What's wrong with me? Am I losing my mind? I focus on my watch. After calculating the time, I realize only a few minutes have transpired. Strange, it feels like I've been gone much longer. The sales clerk gives me an odd look before handing me a cute little bag. It's tied at the top with a delicate ribbon. I scoff, as I am sure Hailey will appreciate that.

"Hopefully, we'll see you again, soon. Have a nice day," Hilary says, smiling.

I thank her and reach for the bag.

~ * * * ~

Just as I'm driving home, Hailey calls. I debate whether or not I want to answer. I'd love to tell her just how I feel about how she uses me all the time!

Probably best if I ignore the phone. It beeps, and I know I have a message from my sister. I don't care. I'm not going to listen to it.

Let's face it; I'm curious by nature, so it doesn't take long for me to listen. "Hello there, sis! I just want to know how the ring fits. I can't wait to see you later! Call me!" Hailey says cheerfully.

I delete her message and flip the phone around in my hand. If I'm being honest here, I don't want to return her call, but I dial her number anyway. After all, she is my sister.

Hailey answers on the first ring, "Hey there, Paige! How are you doing?"

After hearing her pleasant tone, I'm even more annoyed. "What do you need for me to do, now? Run another meaningless errand for the bride?"

"Whoa, take a chill pill. What happened in the jewelry store? Was Hilary rude to you or something?" inquires Hailey, and I am almost fooled by the sound of her innocent tone…not today.

"I think you're up to something," I say bluntly.

"Fine, you caught me. I mean, I hate to even ask this of you, but since the boutique is so close to the jewelry store, is there any chance you could do another tiny favor for me? I need to have my dress fitted one more time. Could you please go by there and do this one last thing for me, pretty please?"

"Why should I?"

"Paige, your taste in fashion is exquisite. After all, you were the one who picked out my dress, in the first place."

"Yeah, that's kind of strange. Don't you think? I mean, shouldn't you have picked out your own wedding dress?"

"Paige, don't be ridiculous. You're so good at shopping, and I trust you completely . . . with my life. Besides, you're the best big sister I could ever hope for," she says, and I soften.

"Fine," I say and realize that yes, I am a sucker.

"Thanks. And how did the ring fit?"

"Fine."

"Great, thanks again! Bye!" she trills and hangs up.

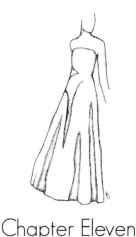

Chapter Eleven

I am so confused. Why am I doing this? I mean, why am I driving all the way over to the bridal shop, just to try on a dress she probably won't even wear? If I'm being honest here, I am so disgusted with Hailey, I don't think I should bother going.

I can't believe I am doing this for her. Abruptly, I leave my minivan and stomp off toward the storefront, ready to storm through . . . . That's strange. I hadn't noticed before just how charming the windows are. In fact, the etchings in the glass resemble my favorite fairytale castle. Hmm, how nice.

When I push open the doors, I hear sweet bells chime—welcoming me. There's a stunning chandelier dangling over my head, with crystals cascading down like water droplets. A little farther up ahead, a larger version of the same fixture hangs above the center of the circular room. I love it in here.

The walls are painted a powder blue and glossy white mannequins are strategically positioned around the area. Each one showcases a lovely gown: most are bright white, but a few resemble candlelight. I am surrounded by silk, chiffon, tulle, satin, and lace. Some gowns sparkle, while others shimmer with pearls. I feel like someone should wave a wand over my head, sprinkle glitter into my hair, and whisper a charm…may all of my wishes come true.

From a few feet away, a lady smiles before coming over to greet me. I've seen her many times. She is always so nice and patient when tackling everything Hailey throws at her, like sending me to try on the bridal dress.

"Hi, I'm here to be fitted for Hailey Smith's wedding dress," I offer.

"Why Hailey, you look remarkably like your sister Paige," the woman says pleasantly, but with an undertone of sarcasm.

"I know. Hailey couldn't make it, so I'm here instead. Will that be all right?"

"The bride would be better, but under the circumstances the maid of honor will have to do," the woman says and her lips curve up into a resigned smile.

She leads me to a dressing room at the back of the store. And there is Hailey's dress. Its design is elegantly simple and drapes straight to the floor. I reach for the gown and am immediately aware of how soft the white fabric is.

I can't wait to try it on, but not for Hailey's sake.

It fits perfectly. Actually, it looks great! I grin while twirling slightly from side-to-side. I don't normally wear strapless tops, but this looks nice. Maybe I should buy a strapless dress for myself. I could play princess with my daughter!

I am seriously considering my purchase, when the sales assistant interrupts, "I guess Hailey's a lucky bride, after all. This dress won't need a thing altered."

"Well, the dress is stunning. I'm sure Hailey will look beautiful on her big day." I look in the mirror and swirl—swish, swish.

You know, I bet after Hailey cancels her wedding I could talk her into giving me this dress . . . just a thought.

~ * * * ~

Just after dinner, I eagerly open a bottle of cabernet. It's red and smooth and pours easily into my glass. After all, Hailey will be here any minute, and I am wrecked. What am I going to say to her? I'm not entirely certain Julian even exists. What I "saw" and "felt" can't possibly be true. I mean, this is my problem, not hers . . . or is it? I'm so confused. I'll just focus on cleaning up dinner dishes and push Hailey out of my mind.

From the hall, I hear Elliott rattle some plates together. He rounds the corner and places them into the sink. He leans against the center island and crosses his arms tightly to his chest. He stares at me for another second before finally asking, "What's going on with you, Paige? I'm really beginning to worry. First, you're cooking these fantastic meals, and now you look different, good, but different. Don't get me wrong, I'm not complaining. I just don't understand the reason."

"So I'm wearing my hair down. It's not a big deal. I want to look good for my husband. Is there anything wrong with that?" I ask, while drying my hands on a dishtowel, and in the sexiest way I can manage, fling it back on the counter.

"That's what I'm talking about," he says, as I am sauntering in his direction. I pause and tilt my head so my hair caresses my shoulder. I run my hands up his chest and wrap them around his neck. His embrace tightens and his mouth is mere inches away from mine. I can barely hear him whisper, "Why don't you cancel on Hailey?"

"Ewww Mom, Dad do you mind? I have company here," Liam declares as he and his new girlfriend, Maggie, prance through the kitchen.

Wait a minute, are they holding hands? They're giggling about something Liam has just whispered into her long blonde hair. She looks at him adoringly before leaving the room. Puppy love, I remember it well.

Elliott and I grin, while slowly moving apart, and I return to my left-over food, packing it in plastic containers. I'm feeling kind of tingly and giddy. Wait a minute, would that be because of the wine or my husband? Not that I don't still adore Elliott, I do. I guess after having two children, our love life went from spicy to lightly-seasoned.

I submerge my hands back into the sink and watch the water stream down and over the dirty dishes, bubbles dancing and bobbing along. How calming.

Elliott is watching me. I don't even have to turn around to know he is looking back and forth between my almost empty wineglass and the back of my head.

"I'll agree to drop this for now, as long as you promise to let me help you," he says.

"All right, but please stop worrying. I'm sure I'm just out of sorts. You know, wedding stress and all," I say, searching under the sink for an S.O.S. pad.

"Except this isn't *your* wedding. It's Hailey's. You shouldn't be stressed over your sister's wedding."

"You have a good point there, but you know how much I've been helping her. She needs me. Now, where is it? It's a mess under here; I really must get rid of some of this stuff."

"What are you looking for?"

"I'm looking for something to get this bit of food off the casserole dish," I reply, shoving bottles of cleaner around the cabinet. "Ah, here it is."

I lather up my S.O.S. pad and scour the edges of a pan.

Elliott approaches me from behind and wraps his arms playfully around my body, squeezing me tight. I feel immobilized! After all, my hands are covered in soapy bubbles! I need to rinse my hands before I can hug him . . . except, maybe I don't have to. Strange, I find I am able to stop doing dishes and relax into his chest, bubbles and all.

"This is nice, you're not pushing me away to dry your hands," he says, nibbling on my neck and making me laugh.

"Who knew I was capable of something so spontaneous."

"Spontaneous, sounds interesting. What'd I miss?" inquires Hailey, rounding the corner. "Oh, am I interrupting a moment?"

"Don't worry about it. You didn't interrupt anything we can't pick up again later," Elliott says and releases me.

"We'll just have to see about that," I say, as he swiftly hugs Hailey and leaves the room.

"So Liam has himself a little girlfriend? I just met her in the hall. She's a cutie," Hailey says, peering over to my empty glass of wine and sticking out her lower lip. "I'm hurt. You started without me. And here I brought this bottle for us to share."

"Hailey, the way I feel tonight, I may need to open that one too."

"Rough day?" she asks and reaches into the cupboard for a glass.

"You have no idea."

"Well then, let me help you," she says and pours red nectar into both our glasses.

"Thanks," I say and watch as Hailey starts looking around the kitchen with her nose in the air.

"It smells yummy in here! Oh, did you hire a personal chef for tonight? What's the occasion?" she asks, still sniffing about.

"Funny one, but no. It may surprise you to hear, I am quite an accomplish cook. Don't look so shocked," I say. "There's plenty of food left. Or let me guess, you probably ate something on your way over, as usual."

"Yes, I did. No offense, but you're not exactly the best cook," she says, dragging a stool up to the counter top. "But, that smells so good I may actually have to try it."

"All right, and then you will have to eat your words," I say and pull out the containers of food.

"Paige, I really appreciate your helping me with all of the wedding plans. I hope it hasn't been too much of a burden," she pauses, looking almost sad. "I can't believe how strenuous it is to plan a wedding."

"Well, you know how I like to shop," I say. "I hope you're happy with *everything* on the big day. I mean, I hope you aren't just going along with what I want for you. Just trying to do what is sensible. By the way, aren't you curious about your ring?"

"Of course, I am! Where is it?"

"Here," I say, handing her the powder blue bag.

"Great, I'll try it on in a bit," Hailey says and shovels some food into her mouth.

Another glass of wine down, and I am still watching Hailey scarf food. She won't look me in the eyes or even speak, for that matter.

After clearing her second heaping plate of leftovers, we make ourselves comfortable in the living room. This is uncomfortable. I'm still not sure what to say to her about my latest vision. This is more difficult than I had imagined. I mean, we're close. Normally I can discuss just about anything with her, but how am I supposed to ask her if she's having an affair? I guess I could hint around and try to have her 'fess up.

Finally, I come up with something to say, "The strangest thing happened to me today, and I'm not sure how to shake it off."

"You are acting a little different. What happened?" Hailey inquires.

"Well, you can't get upset by what you hear. Okay?"

"You can't upset me *that* easily. Let me have it," she says, swirling wine around in her glass.

"I'm just wondering . . . that is, something has recently come to my attention," I pause, feeling a lot like a chicken.

"What? Come on, spit it out."

The wine in her glass is swirling around a bit too high for my liking, and it's going to spill on my floor. Is she as nervous as I am? I take another sip of liquid courage and fill my lungs with fresh air. Suddenly, I know exactly how to find out if she is having an affair.

"Um, I met someone recently. He said you knew each other. His name was Julian," I say in a garbled mess of words. She'll never buy it. I'm terrible at lying.

Now, I'm familiar with the phrase, 'white as a ghost.' Except, I've never seen someone's color fade like that, as if her very life is being drained.

"I do know him. He's one of my most recent clients. I'm designing the interiors for his restaurant," she responds and looks away, as if trying to connect the dots.

She basically just confirmed I'm on to something here, but how much of my vision is true. I'm actually pretty good at this detective work. I'll find out the truth, yet.

I'm considering what to say next, tapping my fingers on my knee. When finally, I come up with, "He's a very good looking guy, and the girl he was with was nice."

Suddenly, Hailey's face flares red! Yes, I've finally managed to get a reaction, except now I feel a twinge of guilt.

Before I am able to take back what I've just said, Hailey blurts, "He was with another woman? When did you say the two of you met?"

"Just the other day . . . I had lunch with a friend . . . and Julian was there," I say, and watch as Hailey stomps back and forth. I'm not sure if she wants to scream or cry or perhaps both. Maybe I wouldn't be such a great detective; this isn't fun anymore. Actually, I feel terrible. "Are you all right?"

"I'm fine!" she says with a shudder. She then looks down at her watch. "I'm fine. I probably need to head home."

"Is there anything you'd like to tell me?"

"I don't want to talk about it," she says, and I'm about to confess everything, when she snaps, "Where were you? How did you two meet? I mean, why did you two start talking in the first place?"

"Why do you care so much?"

"I don't care about Julian! I'm engaged to Derek, remember!"

"Ha, that's never stopped you before."

"What's that supposed to mean?"

"Let's see, I recall a pattern in your dating history. You always seem to think the grass is greener and quickly move on to someone else," I snap.

"That's not fair! Derek isn't a random boyfriend. Have you forgotten he and I are engaged right now?"

"I'm not the one who has forgotten. I remember every time you send me on another one of your stupid errands! And what exactly do you mean by *right now*?"

Hailey looks down towards the floor. She stands up and moves across the room. She reaches for the front door, and I notice her hand shaking.

"Thanks a lot, Paige. I guess I can always count on you to say it like you see it," she whispers.

What have I done? This wasn't how things were supposed to turn out! That was not what I meant to say! I feel terrible simply looking at her. It's pretty obvious I didn't handle this well.

"Wait a minute!" I holler. Hailey turns around and looks in my direction. "Don't leave like this. I need to explain."

Begrudgingly, she returns to the door and freezes on the front step. There's an invisible barrier between us.

"Look, I don't know why I said those things. Will you please come back inside, so we can talk?" I ask hopefully.

Without speaking, she skirts around me and sits awkwardly on the edge of a chair. I sit across from her and restart my story . . . my real story.

"I didn't actually meet Julian. I made it up so I could see how you felt about him," I say and watch as surprise washes over her already confused face.

"What! I don't understand. Why would you do that?" she asks, shaking her head.

How am I supposed to explain what I've seen? What I've "experienced" through Hailey's eyes.

I start by telling her about my visions with Delilah. Although it's unbelievable, I explain what I saw and heard.

And then, I describe what I witnessed through my second vision.

"Paige, you're crazy! That is horrible! How could you do such a thing! Are you actually telling me, you were living inside my head and saw me with Julian?"

"Actually, I wasn't literally in your head. I suppose I lived in a memory. Perhaps, it was projected from the ring. I don't know how it works exactly. I can only speculate," I explain.

"That is just weird. I'm not sure what to make of this. First, you feed me a bunch of lies. Second, you attack me for cheating on Derek; which by-the-way I'm not admitting to doing. Third, you inform me you are having visions, one of which involves you flying into my engagement ring and seeing a memory of mine. You have to admit, it sounds pretty farfetched. In fact, how can I be so sure you're not just making up this story about having visions? For a normally honest person, you are a pretty convincing liar."

"Ouch, I guess I deserve that, and I suppose all of this sounds completely unlikely. I'm asking you to open your mind to the possibility I'm telling you the truth. I didn't want to observe your life. Believe me, I wish I hadn't. I would rather not know you're cheating on Derek."

"Oh, so, we're back to accusations again! I thought this was about you and your little mental episodes!" she fires at me.

"Hey, wait a minute here! I just explained to you, I'm having visions and this is how you react? And whether or not you care to admit you're having an affair…let's face it, we both know you are! So just cut the innocent act! I know what I saw!" I fire back. "And for the record, cheating emotionally is even worse than cheating physically."

Hailey stares down at her restless hands. "Paige, I'm not sure how to respond. I need to figure things out."

She heads for the door, and as if in a dream, floats away. One last time, she turns towards me. Her eyes are hollow, ghost-like, and she says in a haunting tone, "Just for the record, you didn't really see Julian with another woman?"

"No, only you."

With that, Hailey is gone. I am frozen. This can't really be happening. Between my big mouth and crazy visions, I'm making a terrible mess of things. I'm not exactly sure why I'm so upset with her. I can't help feeling stung by her betrayal. After all, I'm her sister. She should be able to confide in me, especially something of this magnitude.

I just shared with her the biggest secret of my life! I have superpowers (at least that's what I've decided to call them). And how does Hailey react? By accusing me of lying! Just because I made up that whopper earlier doesn't mean I'm a serial liar.

Hailey's car has vanished from my view, so I return to my empty foyer. Elliott finds me, as I am leaning against the front door.

"I heard you and Hailey shouting at each other. Is everything all right?" he inquires, looking concerned. I've noticed this expression on his face a lot, lately.

"No, everything is not all right!" I say, shaking my head in disbelief. "Everything has fallen apart. I don't know how to pick up the pieces. In one evening, not only have I discovered my visions are real, but now I know Hailey is having an affair."

"Hailey's having an affair?" Elliott asks, rubbing his hand over his forehead. "That won't go over very well when Derek finds out."

"Derek can't find out. At least, not from us, Hailey needs to tell him."

"All right, whatever you say. You look terrible. What can I do?"

"Can we talk and figure out what's happening to me? Right now, I really need your help."

Chapter Twelve

"We have searched all over the Internet for a Delilah Jones. Perhaps she just doesn't exist," Elliott says, his fingertips rubbing his temples. "It's getting late, we should wrap this up."

"It's only 2:30 in the morning. We can sleep in! The kids can be late to school. Come on, we're so close. I need to know what's happening to me!" I exclaim.

"Honestly, we've come up with nothing. I have a feeling we could easily sit here all night and still not find anything," he says after pushing his chair away from the computer.

"We can't give up now. There has to be something out there that can help"

"Paige, the answers may not be on the Internet. Tomorrow morning, we should call a doctor and have you checked," Elliott says, placing his hand on my knee. I look down and am immediately irritated.

"What are you saying? Are you suggesting I'm crazy or something?" I exclaim, my cheeks beginning to redden.

"No, of course you're not crazy. We should, however, consider the possibility of some medical explanation. Perhaps you have something going on in your brain, an infection or maybe even a tumor," he says gently, like he's walking on thin ice, and right now, he is.

My mouth falls open in horror. I'm unable to respond. I can't believe he just said that. I'm angry, but deep down I'm also wondering if, on some level, he's right.

"Elliott, I do not have a tumor! I realize we haven't found Delilah, but that doesn't mean she doesn't exist! My vision with Hailey turned out to be real. Otherwise, how could I have known about Julian?"

Elliott slides his chair back to the computer and moves the mouse. "All right, you've won. Where do you suggest we look next?"

"We haven't looked hard enough for Delilah. She has to be out there somewhere," I say and bite my lip, trying hard to concentrate on the screen.

~ * * * ~

By the next day, although I won't admit it to Elliott, I'm exhausted. I've just returned from the grocery store. I am stumbling around my kitchen, when my phone rings. Maybe it's Hailey! I rush to the phone, but it's only my mom.

"Good morning, Mom. So you're back from your trip?" I ask, setting aside a bag full of lemons, garlic, and sprigs of rosemary.

"Yes, yes. I'm afraid our vacation was cut short. Tom had a business emergency and had to return home," says my mom, and I am absorbed by the comforting sound of her southern accent. I imagine she's waving her hand dismissively in the air, while flitting about her room.

"I'm sorry to hear that. Did you have a nice time?"

"Wonderful, dear, simply wonderful!" she pauses for a second before continuing, "Perhaps I should come down sooner than planned. I could help you with Hailey's shower."

"Sounds great, and the kids would love to see you!"

I'm excited about the prospect of having my mom here to help me. I almost forgot about Hailey's shower, and it's only a few short days away! I calculate Mom's possible arrival time from her home in Charleston, South Carolina down to Orlando.

"Great, I'm already packed...plan on my being there around 5:00," she chimes. "Oh, and I have a surprise! I'm bringing Emma's dressing table and mirror for you!"

"Really, why are you doing that?" I ask questioningly, although I am thrilled at the prospect of receiving my ancestor's treasure.

"It doesn't fit into my condo anymore . . . not with Tom's things there, too."

"So he's living with you now?" I say, trying to sound calm. "You've only been dating him for a few months."

"Yes, I'm very happy. Paige, he's a wonderful man. You'll grow to adore him, as I do."

Thank goodness for the Internet, because I'll be checking up on Tom the minute I hang up. I'll go through every search engine I can. I'll make sure he's not a bank robber or a serial killer.

"Mom, I don't understand. You've been in countless relationships. You didn't get so serious about any of the others. Why do you suddenly feel the need to move in with this guy?" I ask, feeling panicky.

"First of all, there were only two others. Honestly, you make me sound like a floozy! I didn't get serious about them, because I knew that both of those relationships weren't going anywhere. Tom is special."

"What's so special about Tom?"

"Paige, I realize the last time you saw him things didn't go very well. After you and Hailey interrogated the poor man...well, I'm surprised he was able to get a word in edgewise!"

"I don't know, Mom. He came across as a pretty shady character to me. What do you know about him?"

"Paige, you and your sister are going to have to accept that I am going to live with this man."

"Then, I guess congratulations are in order, but don't expect me to ever call him dad," I say begrudgingly.

"I suppose that will have to do. Actually, you're handling this better than your sister did."

"Hailey, you spoke with Hailey, already?" I ask anxiously.

"Yes, she called me earlier this morning. Strange really… she never did tell me the reason for her call. I guess she must have forgotten about it after hearing my news. I'm afraid she didn't take it very well. I didn't even have the chance to let her know I will be bringing her the grandfather clock she has always wanted."

"You're giving away the clock, too?"

"Yes, I have to get rid of some of my things to make room for Tom's furniture. It's called compromise."

"Let me guess, he needs room for his oversized moose head," I say, rolling my eyes.

"Now, that's enough out of you. You are going to give that man a chance!" Mom says sternly, and suddenly, I realize I'm losing this battle.

"Sorry, I just want you to be happy."

"I will be happy when I can comfortably sit in a room with you, Hailey, and Tom without having to worry about what snippy little comment will come out of one of your mouths."

"Yikes, was it that bad?" I ask, remembering our last encounter with Tom and feeling a twinge of guilt.

"Yes, it was that bad."

"I thought we were just watching out for you. I didn't realize how terrible we must have sounded," I say and cringe.

"You mean to tell me, you didn't find it rude to ask Tom to list off *all* of his prior arrests and number of previous marriages? With a note pad in hand! It's as if he were married five times!"

"Point taken, I promise to behave next time."

"I'll hold you to that, dear."

"Well, on a brighter note, I can't wait to see you! Drive safely, and I'll have a special dinner waiting for you."

"Oh, don't go through any trouble on my behalf. I can pick up something on my way," my mother informs me politely.

"I insist. I think you'll be impressed with my new cooking skills."

"All right, I'll be there for dinner. I can't wait to see you. Do you think you should invite your sister over?"

"Honestly, I'm not sure she would even come. We got into an argument." There, I've said it. It was bound to come out sooner or later.

"What are you two fighting about? I hope it's nothing serious!" Mom says, sounding sick with worry.

"It's not a big deal. We'll be fine. In fact, I'll call and invite her for dinner or maybe dessert," I reassure.

"That would nice. I don't want to hear about the two of you fighting, especially right before her wedding!"

"As if that is going to happen," I say under my breath and roll my eyes.

"What was that?"

"Oh, I'll see you soon. Love you, bye."

"That sounds good. Love you, too."

I can't believe she is bringing me the dressing table. I've coveted it for as long as I can remember. My great, great . . . grandmother, Emma, transformed the original Hepplewhite piece into a dressing table, and then hung a gilt framed mirror above it. The two pieces have remained in remarkable condition considering they're almost 200 years old and have been passed from generation to generation. There's a legend, about a secret compartment hidden somewhere inside the table. When I was young, I fantasized about what could've been hidden in there. I would have loved to have found a treasure from the past. And let's face it, I still would.

~ * * * ~

I'm so excited, I could burst! My mom will be here any minute. I can't wait for her to see how much better my cooking is. This natural talent has emerged from within me. A talent I didn't even realize was there.

While sampling the meal I've just prepared, I close my eyes and marvel at the succulent juices and spices from my roasted free-range chicken. Lemon, garlic, and rosemary have saturated the meat, making it tender, and the skin is slightly crispy and browned.

As I spread roasted garlic onto my potato wedges, I reflect about my earlier research on Tom. The Internet didn't reveal anything horrible. Most of the information was about the boards he's on and his other miscellaneous business dealings . . . blah, blah, blah. I did perk up when I came across a law suit that was brought against him. Only to discover, it was dropped before it went to trial. Something about its basis being frivolous and there wasn't enough significant evidence to support the claim. Truthfully, I'm not sure whether I'm relieved or disappointed. Believe me, I don't want to discover he's a bad guy, but if he is, I'd rather be able to inform my mother before she decides to marry him!

I squeeze lemon over the chicken and realize I still haven't called my sister. I'll do it after I finish making the salad dressing. It's unlike us to go even a day without talking. I miss her, but I'm also mad at her! I feel betrayed and used! Here, I've been running around like her personal servant, and she has no intention on even following through with the wedding! All of my hard work wasted!

All right, I realize this isn't about me. I just wish she hadn't pulled me into her mixed up life. It's gone so far, I've even lived in her thoughts! To tell the truth, I should have seen this coming. Maybe I shouldn't have encouraged her to pursue a relationship with Derek. It seemed like the sensible thing to do at the time.

Maybe I've been a little selfish. After all, Hailey and Derek spend a lot of time over at our house. I enjoy hanging out with them. Would Elliott and I even get along with Julian?

I'm not certain what the story is with that guy. I need to remember to do a little research on him, as well. Actually, Julian seems like a good guy and he treats Hailey well. Maybe she would be better off with him. Oh well, I'm glad I'm not in her shoes. From now on, I can't get mixed up with her affairs.

I've just sliced some avocado and am sprinkling feta cheese on the salad, when my children suddenly leap off the sofa and rush to the door. A loud roar erupts, as my mother gives Elle and Liam souvenirs from her trip. Elle has just received a fairy doll—I can hear her describe the glittery wings. And Liam must have just opened a new book—one with zombies and mummies.

By the time I'm able to leave the kitchen, the group has made their way into the family room. My kids clamor for their positions on either side of my mother. They are practically glued to her hips.

Elle is animatedly explaining a fantastical story. She has to catch her breath in between words. "I'm thinking, I'll fly like a fairy and change that light bulb up there, once and for all!"

"That is very thoughtful of you, dear," says my mother. "Don't you think so, Paige?"

"Yes, she is a child after my own heart!" I say, beaming at Elle.

"You should just have Dad get a ladder and change it for you," Liam adds helpfully.

"That's probably a more sensible solution. I'll mention it to your father," I say, marveling at how much Liam is like his father—practical. How sweet.

Mom is one of those people with the natural gift to charm just about everyone around her. She's wonderful with her grandchildren, and they adore her in return. When my children were babies, she'd hush them to sleep by whispering sweet lullabies.

I nudge Elle and Liam aside and give my mom a proper greeting.

"How was your trip?" I say, while still hugging her. Ah, she smells like a fresh bouquet of flowers.

"I barely managed to avoid rush hour traffic in Jacksonville, but I'd say it was a good drive," Mom says cheerfully.

"I hope you're hungry. Dinner will be ready in a few minutes!"

"I'm looking forward to it," she says half-heartedly and lavishes more of her attention onto her grandchildren. "Will Hailey be joining us?"

"Um, I couldn't get a hold of her. Sorry," I say, and this is sort of the truth.

After acknowledging my absence will go unnoticed, I return to the kitchen.

"Something smells good. Is this another one of Delilah's recipes?" inquires Elliott, finding me as I am carefully arranging each plate.

"Yes, but let's not talk about Delilah in front of my mom."

"Right, of course not," he says and then whispers silently in my ear, "Any new visions today?"

"No, I had a perfectly normal day," I say, but I must admit, I'd like to have another vision. I'm beginning to think they're fun. It's like watching a movie in 3D or being in a hologram. However, it's probably best to not reveal this bit of information to Elliott. He isn't exactly embracing my new gift like I am. He says it brings up too many questions about my health and that makes him uneasy.

My mother wanders into the kitchen. She raises her eyebrows up and throws a sly glance in my direction. "What are you cooking? I believe my mouth is starting to water!"

"Thanks, I'll take that as a compliment. You'll just have to wait and see," I chide.

"Mysterious. Have you been taking cooking classes?"

"The truth is, you wouldn't believe it if I told you."

"Hmm, we'll just have to see about that." My mother looks at me curiously then shifts her attention to Elliott, "Who is this handsome fella?"

"Good to see you, Mom," he says.

"Nobody mentioned that Paige has been learning how to cook," my mother says, as she flutters about the kitchen. "Elliott, how did you ever manage to nudge her in that direction?"

"I didn't have to. One day, she simply stopped burning our dinners," Elliott says. "Well, I'm sure you're thankful for that," my mother says.

"Hey, I can hear you," I say. "And for the record, I wasn't that bad of a cook."

~ * * * ~

My roasted chicken is a huge success! After dinner, Elliott helps unload the remaining items from my mom's car, most importantly, my new heirloom. Just as I had hoped, it looks fabulous in my bedroom. I hang the gilt mirror above the table, and then pull up one of my chairs. It looks amazing. I fall onto the chair and gaze into the old mirror, wondering how many women have stared in its cool surface. My mother joins me, sitting on my bed.

"You seem pleased," she sighs with contentment. "I'm glad this piece means something to you. This heirloom has been passed down from generation to generation. It was special to your great grandmother and her mother before. Are you going to search the table for the hidden treasure?"

"Please, if there was a secret treasure inside, it would've been found decades ago. There's really no point." Later, I'll probably search through the table thoroughly, however, I'm not about to admit that in front of my mother.

"You know, Paige, it's practically tradition to seek out the contents of the table. Your grandmother did, and so did I," my mother says and flashes a mischievous grin.

Not being able to stop myself, I pull out the drawer and rummage around. First, I feel along the right side, but don't find anything. I tap my fingers along the back, still nothing. Then, I run my hand along the left side and notice the wood feels loose. A box slips out of place, and I am able to pull it out of its confined space. With feverish anticipation, I investigate the object.

The box isn't a box at all, it looks like a simple little drawer . . . but sitting inside is a mysterious velvet bag. Before investigating further, I peer back at my mother. Curious, she doesn't seem surprised in the very least.

"What is it, dear?" my mother questions innocently.

"Do you know something about this?"

"How could you ask me such a thing? Why, I am as surprised as you are!" In a theatrical gesture, she places her hand over her heart.

I return my attention to the newly found item. I loosen the strings and the pouch falls open. I gasp in amazement! It is a treasure! A pair of cameo earrings is shimmering in my hand. I want to jump for joy…wait a minute, something isn't right here.

"You knew these were in there, didn't you?" I ask, feeling a little ridiculous at believing the stories.

"You figured it out. These too are part of the gift. They belonged to Emma. My great-grandmother added the fun treasure hunt. She was such a jokester. Paige, you would have absolutely adored her. She was there when my mother had me search the table."

I gaze down at the gorgeous earrings. Each has an oval band wrapped around a carved face of a beautiful woman set against a pale blue background.

"I couldn't wait to see the look on your face when you found them," my mother says.

"I don't remember ever seeing them on you."

"Oh no, they are lovely but not really my style. A bit old fashioned for my taste." She runs her hand along her clothes, as if proud of her modern fashion sense.

"Well, I'll wear them, maybe for the shower," I whisper, holding them next to my ears.

"I hope you do. They deserve to be worn and adored," she says, standing up from the bed and leaning over to kiss my forehead. "I'll leave you to it. Goodnight."

"Goodnight. Thanks!"

Left to admire my new things, I gently place the drawer back. I gaze into the mirror and carefully slip on my new earrings. I love them. Whoa, I feel weird. I stare into the mirror and watch as my bedroom begins to redefine itself. Everything is super clear: my new desk, my earrings, and my face in the mirror! I concentrate on my reflection and try to remain calm. I know what is happening. I'm being pulled back into another memory.

Calmly, I watch as the objects in my room start to fade. I hear a loud cracking sound, and the room stretches and reforms. I'm dizzy, this is too much. I close my eyes and focus on my breathing, inhale in and exhale out.

Glimmers

When it feels like the room has completed its transformation, I slowly reopen my eyes. Although I'm getting used to the effect of flashing around, I don't exactly know what to expect. I discover I am at the same dressing table, gazing into the mirror. However, the person staring back is from another time. Immediately, I recognize my great ancestor, Emma. She is sitting in front of the oval mirror, idly toying with her hair. At once, I am absorbed into her life. We are one and the same.

Emma's Story, May 1818
Heatherwood, England

Through my open bedroom windows, I can hear the river rushing just along the outskirts of town. The evening church bells echo throughout the vale. A cobblestone street cuts through the heart of town and horses with carriages travel along the road. The people of Heatherwood busy themselves by running errands and working their trade. Most mornings, I enjoy the scent of fresh bread as it wafts from the baker's open window. Heatherwood is a quaint village, not too far from London.

Rolling hills and grassy meadows surround my brick home. It is neither too large, nor too small. It serves our proud family well. At the moment, most of the household are diligently preparing for this evening's festivities. Doubtless, Papa is checking on this evening's libations; Mama will be supervising the kitchen staff to ensure every detail is perfect; and my younger sister, Victoria, will no doubt be primping. My older sister Mary and her husband live in London and cannot make it this evening. Sadly, my older brother Edmund is also away managing business for my father.

Papa is a good man with a pleasant disposition that has helped win him a reputation of the highest regard. His small fortune was earned through clever and insightful business dealings. The name Phillip Middleton is respected far beyond our town. Papa prefers to be in the middle of business dealings, rather than at either end; he is a factor, a matchmaker of sorts, although I believe my mother tries harder at making suitable matches for her daughters!

I am excited because in my father's most recent business endeavor, he has made the acquaintance of many of England's most prestigious fabric makers. I am delighted, as this means he frequently returns home with bolts of fabric in the latest fashions. I smile in delight upon receiving such lavish gifts. I have become quite accomplished in the art of designing and constructing gowns.

In fact, my dress planned for this evening is sculpted from blue silk. The sleeves caress my shoulders and tiny beads are stitched along the trim. It is one of my most recent designs. I am anxious to see if it generates any interest amongst our guests. I have very recently begun piecing together dresses for many of the young ladies in our humble town.

I realize I am humming softly; it is a melody I once heard played on a harp. I have forgotten myself, as I dreamily run a comb through my hair. My cameo earrings are already in place, and I observe their splendor.

My hair is hanging down, falling over my shoulders and down my back. I pull it up and attempt to tie it in place. I almost have it fastened, when my hair on the entire left side of my head comes loose and looks a mess. Honestly, how women manage pinning up their hair with ease everyday is beyond me. Fruitlessly, I try fashioning tiny ringlets.

Through the reflection in my mirror, I notice the smiling face of my younger sister Victoria. She is at the frivolous age of six-teen and delighted with the prospect of attending her first formal gala to be held at our home tonight.

"Why are you hiding, you silly girl?" I address her with a smile.

"I was only curious," the words from her delicate voice flow naturally into the air. Victoria moves across the room and sits closer to me.

"And may I ask, about what are you so curious?" I question, after turning my attention towards her.

"I wonder if you are at all nervous." She stares at my be-wildered expression and moves closer still towards where I am sitting. "You do realize a certain Mr. Percy Grant is downstairs speaking with father?"

"Is he . . . hmm?" I stare at my comb. "You don't suppose he is . . ."

It is unnecessary for me to continue, because my sister completes my sentence for me.

"Asking father for your hand? What else would he be doing?" She peers at me anxiously, before inquiring, "What will you say?"

How will I answer? I am not yet certain. I knew inevitably this day would come. After all, Mr. Grant and I have practically been betrothed since childhood. Besides, I am nineteen; our friends are beginning to think of me as a regular spinster. I do not wish to disappoint Mama, nor become a burden on Papa. "Of course, I will say yes. My marriage to him has been assumed since I was a baby! I am somewhat fond of him, he is a gentleman of sound reputation, and extraordinarily sensible. I will never have to worry about him leaving me to go off on some wild adventure."

"Oh Emma, this will be so very exciting! Think of the parties and celebrations!" Victoria giggles, as she wraps her arms around me in an embrace. "Here, I shall help you finish your hair. Honestly, can you not manage a simple ringlet on your own?"

Victoria swiftly situates herself behind me and hastily fastens my hair in place. With the motion of her hand, I glance at her reflection. Suddenly, she freezes; a strand of brown wavy hair is still wrapped around her finger. "I suppose you will design my bridesmaid dress. I should like it in a golden material that sparkles when I walk," she announces brightly.

"Do you have any other requests, dearest sister? Would you like for me to spin the golden threads by hand, as well?" I tease.

"I cannot keep myself from imagining what a joyous event your wedding shall be!"

"I am certain that in your vision of the event, all eyes will be on you instead of the bride," I say with a smile.

"I would not imagine it any other way," she says while laughing.

The weak streams of the last rays of the sun flicker past the heavy draperies. After noticing the sky has transformed into twilight, we rush in our efforts to become presentable for the party. Eagerly, we check our images in the mirror and anxiously exit the bedroom, ready to greet our friends waiting below.

Chapter Thirteen

Our guests are rejoicing in the festivities of the evening. They dance gaily about the room. As Victoria and I descend the staircase, music from stringed instruments glides up to my ears. Although I am anxious to join in the revelry, I try to slow down my pace and watch my shoes ease down one step at a time.

Once in view of the gathering, I smile. In the middle of the floor, some of the group has assembled into rows, facing in the direction of their dance partners. When the music begins to play, the couples wind and weave around in perfect unison. The ladies wear flowing gowns bedecked with lace and ruffles: blues, pinks, pale yellows, lavenders . . . and the men look stately in their formal attire. Most of our guests are long time familiar faces, and it makes me glad to see them having such a delightful time.

The party is held in a long and rectangular shaped room. A grand chandelier, filled with candles, illuminates the area below. Oil paintings, adorned with large golden frames, are hung on the lovely blue walls. In between the portraits are sconces where shielded candles also help dispel the dark.

My eyes dart over to the image of me, where I am wearing my very first Emma Middleton gown. I adore that ivory colored gown. I spent days sewing pearls into the top layer of sheer material, tedious really, but my efforts were well worth the trouble. Since Mama had not seen any of my designs, up to that point, she implored me to wear something sensible and restrained, preferably a dress she had purchased for me in London. Unbeknownst to her, I substituted her dress with one of my own. Thank goodness, both the artist and Mama were pleased with the outcome. I, however, cannot help being a little embarrassed by the portrait. The artist certainly did justice to the dress, but he also portrayed me to be far more poised and elegant than I feel.

Victoria, on the other hand, does not mind having our guests gaze adoringly up at her portrait. I suspect she would have more likenesses of herself in the house if our parents would permit. Personally, I prefer artwork that captures an interesting moment in time and has a fairytale-like setting along with mythical creatures. I should very much enjoy crawling inside my favorite painting and explore the fantastical world the artist has created.

"It is a festive event, indeed. Do you not agree, Emma?" Victoria whispers in hushed excitement.

"It is," I return her sentiment, taking in the opulence of the room.

"The only question remaining is with whom I shall dance, first."

I am entranced by the flow of people, watching them twirl across the floor . . . when someone sneaks up and startles me by giving my hair a gentle tug. After almost leaping into the air, I turn and see my older brother Edmund. He laughs heartily, obviously pleased with the results of his teasing. Victoria playfully swats at him, warning he had better never do that again.

"When did you arrive? We didn't expect you to return for yet another fortnight!" I declare, eagerly hugging him.

"My dearest sisters, how could I possibly stay away from a party with such an abundance of delight and amusement? Surely, you know me better than that," he says with a smile that warms my heart. "Although my time in London was necessarily spent attending many such frivolous functions, it was called short due to a business matter."

"Edmund, I wonder to hear of your change of heart, since I believe that, heretofore, your inclination toward business has been somewhat lacking. What is this manner of business of which you speak?" I ask.

"I must admit to being astounded by your lack of faith in my diligence in this regard," says Edmund, and we continue staring at each other for a few seconds. At last he reveals, "During my recent visit with our sister Mary, I made the acquaintance of a man from America. He resides in Charleston, South Carolina, where he possesses extensive fields of cotton. He has come to England to form a trade alliance with someone to whom he can sell his crops." Edmund pauses, looking quite pleased. "I have brought this man here to meet Father, who will easily recognize the potential for financial gain as being quite significant. The two of them can hammer out the remaining part of the transaction on their own. *I* am simply a match maker."

"Victoria, have you seen our brother, as of late? For this man standing before us is not he," I say in a playful manner.

I had not expected to see Edmund immerse himself in the work force with such uncontained enthusiasm, for his inclination runs much more to his leisure activities. He has not been known for his commitment to long hours of tedious contract negotiations. Although I frequently tease him in regard to his reputation as a carefree bachelor, I am proud of this recent change of direction.

"Where is this newly found acquaintance of yours?" questions Victoria.

"He is ensconcing himself in the guest quarters," replies Edmund.

Victoria stares speculatively at the dancing couples, appearing anxious to join them. "Edmund, it is grand to have you with us. Before evening's end, you must introduce me to your new acquaintance. For now, I shall not make our guests wait any longer," she says then whispers in my ear, "By the way; I simply adore your new gown. Perhaps you could make a similar one for me. Although, I would much prefer it in pink." She winks at me before flitting off into the crowd.

"I tend to worry about Victoria and her mastery in the art of flirting," I say. "She enjoys it far more than she ought. I pity any man who attempts to call upon her, for she usually tires of them quickly."

"Agreed, I wonder what we will ever do with her," says Edmund, and we quietly laugh together.

"It is so good to have you home. How long shall we expect you to be with us?"

"I am not entirely certain. I suppose that depends on how long I am needed here."

"I do hope you will be needed indefinitely. I miss you when you are away," I admit.

"You know I cannot endure living in the confines of a small town for very long. The city fascinates me so. What do you say if on my return, you accompany me back to London? Mary has been asking for you."

"The idea of going to London is an exciting prospect!" I say before remembering the impending engagement I am about to face. "I suppose we will just have to see how events of the evening unravel."

"To what do you refer?"

"I suspect Mr. Grant is at this moment asking father for my hand," I reply and watch as Edmund's amused expression immediately fades.

"My younger sister, engaged. Now that is unsettling. I thought for certain you would have more time."

"You appear concerned. Do you not approve of Mr. Grant's character?"

"No, no, he is a fine gentleman. Emma, I must be honest. This troubles me. You should wait before entering marriage. There is so much of the world for you to see. Once you are betrothed, your sovereignty is over."

"Edmund, in case you have forgotten, I am on the verge of becoming a spinster. How can I burden our parents? Mr. Grant is an admirable candidate for a husband. Besides, you know our mother has been planning this wedding since I was a child."

"Our mother would understand if you decide not to marry him. Do you have even the slightest inclination of love for Percy?" inquires Edmund.

"I do not dare ponder about such frivolous indulgences. Besides, I think even the notion of love is overrated. In time, I am quite certain Mr. Grant will be a good companion for me."

"Companion you say. Honestly Emma, you should seriously consider whether or not he has the same ambitions as you. I believe he is incapable of holding interests in anything unless his mother tells him he ought."

"What an unkind thing to say! For your information, Mr. Grant and I have much in common!"

"And what might that be?"

"Well, we both enjoy the country and parties," I say rather smugly. "Besides, he has many good qualities. For one, he is very punctual and for another, he is . . . sensible."

"I see; punctuality and sensibility are the most important qualities you seek in the man with whom you wish to spend the rest of your life. Is that the best you can muster? If that is the case, then I fear no woman will ever think I am a suitable husband." Edmund stretches his arms wide and fakes a loud yawn. "I think I am going to die from boredom, Emma. You have much too free a spirit to settle down with the likes of Percy Grant."

"Edmund, I have put off my marriage to Mr. Grant for long enough. Mother and Father will not be very pleased if I ruin their plans for me."

"Why must you marry at all? I do not understand the traditional mindset of having to marry at a certain age. In fact, you are still a child. You ought to travel and develop your own interests, not those defined for you by a husband, and that is exactly how it would be. I shudder at the thought of your likes and dislikes being formed for you by Percy, *or* his mother," says Edmund, muffling a chuckle.

"All of that is easy for you to say. You are a man, and as such, have an entirely different perspective of the world. You have freedom to do as you please."

"You could do the same," he retorts.

"Yes, in theory I could, but in reality the chances of my traveling is slight. In only a few short years, I would be seen as a 'poor old maid.' People would whisper cruel words behind my back. Besides, how would I afford to go on adventures? What little I have would dwindle away quickly, I fear."

"Fair enough, however, it would be nice if you found a husband with whom you could travel. You cannot allow your life to go by without going to Paris."

"Paris." I consider dreamily. "I am certain Mr. Percy would be more than willing to escort me to Paris, once we have married."

Edmund exhales loudly and says, "You act as though you are certain, but are you really? I sincerely doubt Percy Grant would be willing to leave his precious manor of Webshire."

"Edmund, I appreciate your concerns, but they really are not necessary. I am a grown woman and am perfectly able to make appropriate decisions in regard to my life."

"If marriage to this man is what you desire, then I am happy for you. For now, we shall dance in celebration of your impending doom, I mean betrothal," announces Edmund, flashing his mischievous smile.

"You are a loathsome creature! In spite of my disgust at your lack of tact, I shall dance with you in celebration of my upcoming wedding."

As children, Edmund and I were inseparable, and there have been many occasions when I have enjoyed having him as a dance partner. Upon his arrival this evening, I have found a familiar happiness sweep through me that I have not experienced for quite some time. That is until I am approached by Mr. Grant and my father.

My father's face brims with joy and he says in good cheer, "Good to have you home, Edmund! What brings you to the country?"

"Actually Father, I have a business proposition for you," says Edmund, and I cannot help but marvel at my brother's newly acquired confidence. Papa appears equally impressed.

"I am quite curious as to your newly found interest. It would appear we have much to discuss. Let us retire to my study," says Papa. "Please excuse us."

Before leaving, Edmund says, "Emma, I am afraid our dance will have to wait. I will make it up to you."

"I understand," I say and lean closer to whisper, "Good luck with Papa."

I am left standing alone with Mr. Grant, an awkward silence holds thick.

"How do you do this evening?" I inquire, graciously attempting to dislodge the uncomfortable tension.

"Very well, indeed," offers Mr. Grant before glancing back over his shoulder. Behind him stand his mother and my Mama. Both are watching us with an expression of keen interest.

"Mr. Grant, have you ever been to Paris?"

"I am not made for adventures over the high seas. I have a queasy stomach that would make the journey unbearable," he says and coughs into his hand. "Besides, it is more sensible to simply remain here in England. After all, there is much to see and do right here."

"Paris is merely a short jaunt over the waterway. High sea, indeed," I say, immediately regretting my lack of tact. Mr. Grant does not respond. He is still looking over at his mother.

After another awkward moment, he says, "My apology, I was distracted. You said something. What was it?"

"Oh, it was nothing important," I say, thankful for his temporary distraction.

Another immeasurable amount of time passes without a word between us. Desperately, I yearn for an outside source to intrude. A little gossip from Victoria would be greatly appreciated. Again, Mr. Grant glances over at his mother. He nods his head and returns his attention towards me.

"Miss. Emma, would you do me the courtesy of meeting me on the terrace, before the last dance?"

I do what is expected by obliging and give a curtsey. After this ridiculous display, I am able to take my leave of him. I imply I have obligations to fulfill in another room.

I race away, searching for the closest location for solitude. At last, an unoccupied room. I slither inside the dimly lit sitting parlor. Papa's study is located just on the other side of that wooden door. My father and Edmund are, at this very moment, discussing business. I can faintly hear their voices deep in conversation. I lean toward the door and become engrossed in their dialogue. It is difficult, but I am able to absorb a little of what they are saying.

I shuffle closer, when I am startled by a rustling sound from across the room. It is followed by a male's voice. "I do hope I am not interrupting anything." He may have said more, but I am too embarrassed to pay much attention. I do not want to turn around. I do not want to know who has just held witness my unladylike display of eavesdropping.

After an unsettling amount of time, I say, "Excuse me, sir. I was unaware this room was occupied."

At the very moment I complete my rotation, I behold a man sitting all too comfortably in my father's chair. I have never seen him before. I would have remembered his striking face.

He stands and moves closer to me. "I am truly sorry. It would appear I have alarmed you. I am here with Edmund Middleton, son of Mr. Philip Middleton. They are conversing in the other room. Of course, you must already be aware of that."

"Indeed, you are speaking of my brother and father. However, I am afraid I have not made your acquaintance, sir," my reply is polite, although tense, and I pray I am not blushing.

The stranger laughs under his breath and offers an enchanting smile. He continues moving closer to where I am standing.

"Please excuse my manners. My name is Andrew Stone. Although I feel I know your brother well, I have only just recently made his acquaintance. He has invited me to stay here," says Mr. Stone, now standing only a few feet away.

I am captivated by his foreign accent. It is proper like the King's English, but projects a casual ease.

"I am Edmund's younger sister, Emma Middleton. When I saw my brother earlier, he did mention he had brought a guest. Only, I had assumed you would be much . . ."

"You imagined I would be an old man? That is understandably your assumption. If it were a few months ago, you would have been conversing with my father, instead of me. With his recent passing, I have stepped in to take over the family affairs," offers Mr. Stone.

"I am sorry to hear of your recent loss."

"I thank you for that sentiment. My father was a good man. I am now running the plantations just as he would have." Again, a smile I find irresistible comes to Mr. Stone.

Suddenly, a light from the office floods into the dimly lit parlor, and its luminescence causes me to step away from Mr. Grant.

My brother stands motionless at the lintel, wearing a ridiculous grin. "Good-evening, this is a wonderful surprise, finding two of my favorite people within the confines of such a small area! Emma, what brings you so far from the festivities?"

"Um, well . . . Victoria sent me to look for Father. Are you still with him?" I say, deliberately turning my attention away from Mr. Stone, fearing he will suspect I was here to eavesdrop.

"I do hope everything is all right," says Edmund in alarm.

"Everything is fine. She has a concern that has probably already resolved itself. It is not important; please carry on with your business. It is a pleasure to have made your acquaintance, Mr. Stone. I look forward to our next meeting. Good-evening."

"I am quite certain the pleasure was all mine. Only in the future, please refer to me as Andrew. Mr. Stone sounds far too stuffy."

"Of course, Mr. Andrew," I say, swiftly rushing towards the door.

Following my departure, I overhear a brief conversation between the two men. It begins with Mr. Andrew's appraisal of me, "You neglected to tell me how fetching your sister is."

"Well, I am sorry, but I must inform you of her impending engagement," my brother responds, and my heart sinks.

"That is a shame. The night is young, and I say we carry on with our business matters expeditiously, so we may join in the party."

The two men's laughter fades, as they presumably enter into the study. I am left standing in the vacant hall, assessing the events of the evening. I am not sure what has come over me. It is disturbing to have been made aware of my recent addiction to eavesdropping. Normally, I am not the sort to meddle in the affairs of others, nor to gossip.

I also find it disconcerting that I am so undeniably charmed by the man I have just met. I question on what account he has enchanted me so. His casual accent lingers in my ears. I am be-guiled by Mr. Andrew's confident smile and bright green eyes. A budding desire has captured me, and I imagine running my hand through his golden-brown hair . . . . I am shocked to be having such unladylike thoughts! What has that man done to me?

Mr. Andrew's smile seemingly has an inappropriate affect on me. A pink blush spreads over my face. I raise my hand to cover my mouth and battle to suppress my nervous laughter. Our en-counter was but momentary, but I feel a brief wave of sorrow for dreams that could never be. I must remind myself of my impend-ing engagement to Mr. Grant.

After realizing I still linger in the darkened hallway, I place my hand on my stomach and inhale deeply. I must compose myself. It takes another minute before I feel ready to reenter the celebration, just a few steps away.

Chapter Fourteen

I draw closer to the merrymaking and am overcome by the sounds of laughter. I enter the warmth of candlelight, music, and happiness. The room has become magically enchanted, and our guests are having a grand time.

Dancing will wash away my cares.

I am wandering toward the music, when suddenly I realize I am sandwiched between my mother and Mrs. Primrose! How did I end up between these two cackling hens? Slowly, I try creeping backward. The two women have not noticed I am here, being they are in the midst of a heated exchange of gossip. Both women wear an expression of excitement and collusion.

I am almost away from them when my mother blocks my escape! I sigh with resignation. I am trapped.

"Emma, you have missed out on all of the evening's entertainment! Where have you been?" My mother affectionately nudges me, adding, "It has come to my attention that a certain daughter of mine will soon be betrothed!"

The two women look inquiringly in my direction for a response.

"Indeed, Mr. Grant has requested to meet with me on the terrace. I suppose he wishes to express his desire to marry me," I sigh. "Mama, I am not entirely certain Mr. Grant is the right man for me."

"Emma, I am curious as to the nature of the sort of young man that you would be inclined to marry. Besides, you and Percy have always gotten along so well together."

"Mama, we were children. Perhaps I should take a little time for myself, first. I could travel with Edmund for a little while. We could go to Paris!" I exclaim.

"Travel to Paris with Edmund? My dear girl, you panic your mother with talk of such nonsense. Why, Edmund would simply steer you right into trouble. You cannot possibly consider turning down poor little Percy's proposal, just to flit away on some silly holiday. Emma, stop pondering such ridiculous rubbish and be grateful for the opportunity God has granted you."

"You are right, Mama. I suppose I have allowed my nerves to overtake me. I would be foolish to deny Mr. Grant. He is a fine gentleman," I say with false confidence.

"Now, that is more like it. Oh dear, it is a joyous event! And Emma, you do realize, one day, you will become the Lady of the manor of Webshire!" Mama proclaims in delight, as if this were an accomplishment. "I only wish I could sit in to hear Percy's words of proposal."

"The very notion of your being there is preposterous! May it ease your mind to know, I will retell the whole event to you, word for word," I admonish in horror.

"I suppose that will have to do. I would not wish my future son-in-law to think of me as overbearing."

"Where would he ever derive a notion such as that?" I reply and can see my feigned attempt at sincerity has not been lost on the woman.

"I wonder, indeed!" says Mama.

"Good gracious, Emma is that one of your gowns?" inquires Mrs. Primrose.

"Why, yes it is," I offer, hoping to hear a positive appraisal of the dress.

"It is simply stunning! Do not you agree?" Mrs. Primrose says to my mother. "Your daughter has impeccable taste. I should very much like to commission Emma to design a new dress for both my daughter and me."

"Of course, I shall make a dress for the both of you. I cannot, however, expect you to pay for it. The simple fact you will wear one of my creations is more than enough recompense for me," I exclaim, still beaming from her compliment.

Mama peers over my shoulder, before interceding, "I do not wish to alarm you, but I do believe a young gentleman approaches."

For a fleeting instant, my heart leaps in the hope of it being Mr. Andrew and Edmund. I turn around and my smile fades; it is Mr. Grant who advances.

"Good-evening, ladies," he says.

Mama and Mrs. Primrose squeal with delight and greet him with high regard. He is smooth with his praise of them, and when they have finally concluded with their small talk, he acknowledges that I am here.

"Miss. Emma, will you permit me to escort you in a dance?" he inquires, boldly extending his clammy hand.

At his touch, I feel nothing. By this time, I should hope I would feel more. Why am I pondering such naive thoughts?

He escorts me to the dance floor, but all the while my smile is thin. We move smoothly through the crowd and find our positions. On cue, music begins to flow, and the dancers sway to the melody. I enjoy dancing, even if it is with the likes of Mr. Grant.

He continually pulls me out of my moment with his exasperating attentiveness and formal attempts at conversation. "Miss. Emma, are you enjoying the merriment of the evening?" he inquires.

"Yes, I tend to become quite swept away with dancing. Do you enjoy it, as well?" I return.

"I find it most invigorating. It is also much more preferable than being forced to listen to the drivel that comes from the minds of vacant people," he says flatly. *My* mind considers about whom in particular he is referring.

Although I would like to question him further on the subject, I remain mute. I return my attention to the music and attempt to find some enjoyment. It is common on such occasions to be passed from partner to partner, and I am thankful for this, as I spin with ease around the floor.

When the music comes to a halt, I give my regards to Mr. Grant and turn to leave.

"I will wait for you on the terrace!" he says rather loudly, before I am able to vacate the room.

"I would not miss it for the world," I reply, quickening my pace.

I weave through people, heading in the direction of the dessert table. As I observe the splendor, I am tempted to devour the entire display. Perhaps that will help feed the butterflies fluttering rampantly about my insides.

I am holding a tart, when I become jostled by Victoria. In contrast to me, she appears to be having the time of her life.

"I have just had a glimpse of Edmund's friend!" she exclaims, biting her lip. I have seen this look before. "Do you suppose I ought to approach Edmund for an introduction? Although, I am not certain our brother would be amenable to the idea."

I listen to her strategically dissect the situation, but am wondering about the tart I still hold. Perhaps she will not notice if I taste it.

"How delightful it is that Edmund has invited Mr. Stone to stay here!" Victoria looks overcome with anticipation.

"He seems nice, I met him outside father's study," I offer.

"How should you be so lucky as to stumble up on him, so? I am jealous!" She puffs out her lower lip. "I will just have to come up with something equally as clever."

"I wouldn't exercise too much thought on the matter," I say and indulge in the sweetness of the apple tart. "After all, he will be staying with us for at least a fortnight."

The tart is now completely gone, so I decide it would be rude to deny a macaroon my attention. After that, I treat myself to a variety of desserts, listening indifferently to Victoria's ramblings. She is in a tizzy, discussing the scandalous rumors circulating the room.

"Emma, I do hope you will not make a spectacle of yourself by gorging on the dessert table again," says Victoria.

"If you are referring to Mrs. Primrose's high tea, then I must inform you I did not make a spectacle of myself. I merely tasted some of the delicacies that were on display."

"Darling sister, if that is how you wish to remember the event then I shall leave you to your delusions." Victoria produces a handkerchief and wipes my chin with it. "You have some jam on your face."

I glimpse over at my brother and Mr. Andrew. They are speaking avidly to one another. I watch their faces light up with animated excitement. Their meeting with Papa must have gone well.

"There he is, now! Just over there, with Edmund!" Victoria exclaims, taking in the sight of him. "Mr. Stone has a certain distinctive air about him. Does he not?"

"Yes, he does," I reply.

"Oh and look, Edmund seems to be motioning for your future husband to join them," observes Victoria. "Why would our brother wish to introduce him to Mr. Stone? I thought Edmund found Mr. Grant to be a complete bore."

I stare unblinkingly, as my brother laughs while inviting an uncomfortable looking Mr. Grant closer into their conversation. Edmund looks pleased with himself. Why, he is grinning from ear to ear. What deviltry is he up to now?

Slowly, it occurs to me what Victoria has just said.

"What do you mean Edmund finds Mr. Grant boring? He has never mentioned his dislike of Mr. Grant to me," I say, still staring at the three men just beyond the threshold.

"Of course, he would not let you know how he truly feels about the man you are about to marry. That would be in poor taste, would it not? Now that you are aware of his feelings, I must let you hear some of the funny remarks he has made about Mr. Grant!" she offers with a large grin.

"No thank you, Victoria. I have a feeling I could guess some of them."

"You are no fun! Why, I laughed hysterically, when just earlier, Edmund referred to Mr. Grant as the most boring man in all of England!" She sniggers right in the midst of retelling the story.

I shake my head and continue watching Mr. Grant, as he wipes his nose with his handkerchief. His eyes keep shifting towards the other room. What has captured his interest so? I peer over to where he is looking. Why, he is watching his mother! I cannot believe it! I should think he would prefer to stare longingly towards me, not the woman who gave birth to him. And now, Mama is standing next to his mother. They appear anxious. They must be busy planning our firstborn's nursery.

Victoria interrupts my thoughts, "Join me in the other room. I would very much like to make Mr. Stone's acquaintance." Only, she does not wait for a response. She scampers off towards the three men, practically dragging me behind her.

"Go on without me, I will catch up with you later," I offer, removing my hand from her firm grasp.

Truthfully, the idea of being caught in a conversation between Mr. Andrew and Mr. Grant sounds mortifying. I restrict my attention back toward the dessert table and reach for another pastry.

From behind me, I hear a strange coughing noise. I turn around to see who it is. When I realize it is Mr. Grant, I feel my stomach tighten. I had naively assumed he was still in the other room. How did he manage to sneak up on me so quickly? I peer over his shoulder and see Victoria speaking with Mr. Andrew and Edmund.

I sigh, while trying to imitate Victoria's pleasing smile and pretend I am delighted. Although truthfully, I had believed I would be able to avoid Mr. Grant until our scheduled meeting on the terrace. What could he possibly want of me now?

"Miss. Emma, I must inform you that a most regrettable situation has occurred at my home in Webshire. It calls for my immediate return." He is speaking to me, but his attention is in the hall, where his mother and my Mama are still in heated discussion.

"Oh dear, I do hope it is nothing serious!" I say with genuine concern.

"I believe everything is well within my control. It is imperative, however, I be present. Unfortunately, I will not be able to meet with you as planned."

"How unfortunate; however, I can assure you there will be other opportunities for us to meet. Please, do not give it a second thought."

"You are ever so gracious. I thank you for your kind words of understanding," Mr. Grant says, gently taking my hand. "I will call upon you as soon as I can. Good-evening, Miss Emma."

After his departure, I return my undivided attention to the dessert table. There are a few colorful petit fours I have neglected. Reaching for one, I become aware of Mr. Andrew's stare. He must have witnessed the conversation between Mr. Grant and me. Why is Mr. Andrew watching me, when he has Victoria standing next to him?

Although it is entirely unladylike, I stuff a petit four into my mouth. I believe it to be my favorite and enjoy the vanilla icing. From the corner of my eye, I can barely see a smile spread across Mr. Andrew's face. Although it is a struggle, I pretend to pay little attention.

Victoria is close to Mr. Andrew's side. She appears to circle him as though she were a lioness stalking her prey. After a little while, he escorts her to the dance floor, at which point, I can scarcely focus on anything else. He moves his body effortlessly about the floor. My sister appears eager, as she follows his lead. An uninvited feeling of envy has crept into my heart.

Although I have wedged myself inconspicuously between some familiar faces, my brother has little trouble finding me and seems quite aware of my ungracious thoughts.

"Victoria has a way of attracting the attention of men. Do not you agree?" he says, edging his body between the surrounding people.

"She cannot help herself. Men are naturally drawn to her, as bees are to honey." I smile weakly.

"I understand Mr. Grant had to make a sudden departure. I am sorry if his leave taking has caused you any heartache," Edmund says sarcastically.

"I can assure you, it is of little consequence. In fact…may I speak freely, dear brother?"

"I hope you would feel comfortable enough with me to always speak freely."

"Oh Edmund, since we last spoke on the matter of Mr. Grant, I find myself feeling confused! I am not entirely certain I want to marry him!"

"Well, I am glad you have returned to your senses. I must say, I am not at all surprised by your lack of feeling for the man. Perhaps you can sneak away with me to London before he notices you are gone."

"We must not let him know or Mama and Papa, for that matter," I tease.

Edmund looks over at Victoria and says, "I suppose we ought to invite her along, as well."

"It would only be fair. I do fear, however, for the poor men of London and the trail of broken hearts that would undoubtedly strew the path behind her," I chide, and we begin to laugh.

"Agreed, but at the moment, she appears quite captivated by Andrew."

"Would you expect anything less from our younger sister?"

"It is unfortunate Andrew does not appear to share in her interest. I am very fond of the fellow and would like to see him with her. Shame really."

I peer down at my fidgeting hands. "Oh really, and why would he not be captivated by her?"

"Actually, I believe he has taken an interest in someone else. I am not entirely certain who she may be," says Edmund, shrugging his shoulders. "Well, we need to shake you out of this downtrodden-mood. Let us have a spin about the floor."

"Why Edmund, is it wise to keep you from all of the ladies here tonight?" I inquire playfully.

"The fair maidens will just have to wait. I wish to see your smile return, as you delight in my expert lead on the dance floor."

I smile brightly at him, as he leads me to where couples are already in the middle of a dance. We join them, as if we have been here all along.

Victoria grins from ear to ear and looks as though she is having the time of her life. Her partner; however, wear's an expression of feigned interest. It almost appears as if she is stepping on his toes.

Edmund must have noticed Mr. Andrew's discomfort, because he laughs before saying, "Hmm, as the events play out, this ought to be most entertaining. What a tangled web, indeed."

"I have not the slightest notions as to what you refer."

"We shall see about that!"

The night takes a turn I rather enjoy. Edmund and I spend most of our time laughing and dancing along with the assembly. The remaining portion of the night is frittered away in this playful manner, for which I am grateful.

Chapter Fifteen

The following morning, I awaken to the sound of birds singing sweetly outside of my window. The chime from our grandfather clock announces the hour is still early. If I hurry, I can walk into town and see the baker. I also need to purchase some ribbon and thread. Later, I shall visit a dear friend of mine; I am anxious to show her my latest sketches.

The party lasted into the late hours of the evening. In my haste for sleep, I had carelessly tossed my clothes about the room. I will have to deal with sorting through the mess later. For now, I have prior obligations in town. I leap out of my bed and dash, eagerly attempting to find something suitable to wear for my morning stroll.

I savor the solitude of my mornings, and after the merriment of just a few hours ago, the house is refreshingly still. Quietly, I tip toe the length of the hall and down the stairs. I dislike being sneaky in this way, but find it essential if I hope to leave the house alone. When I enter the kitchen, I continue peering over my shoulder.

"Good-morning," says a voice from behind me. I startle and tumble backward into a cabinet.

140

"What do you mean by frightening me like that?" I say, reaching for my pounding heart.

I turn more fully and see Mr. Andrew. He is sitting at the table, nibbling on pastries, and sipping coffee. A sun-beam filters through an open window, falling lightly over him, intensifying the gold in his hair.

"I am truly sorry for alarming you, but must you always recoil upon seeing me?" says Mr. Andrew, and his already perfect mouth moves into a charming grin.

I look toward the floor and concentrate on the grain of the wood. "I suppose, Mr. Andrew, while you are here I should pay more attention to my surroundings." Bravely, I lift my head and see he is smiling. "I wonder if perhaps you secretly enjoy scaring young women half to death."

Mr. Andrew raises his eyebrows and sets aside his book. "I confess it is rather amusing how you startle so easily, but it has never been my intention to cause you any unease," he says, shifting his body into a formal position. "Please, join me for breakfast. I have a feeling you will find the treacle tarts to be delightful."

"I am afraid I must leave you to it. I have prior obligations in town. Good-day," I reply and turn to leave.

Swiftly, he rises from the wooden chair and moves towards me.

"May I accompany you? I have seen so little of this part of England and would very much like to explore the area. Edmund has spoken highly of its charm."

Abruptly, I halt in the doorframe and stare at him in astonishment.

"Perhaps Edmund would like to show you around," I say, straightening out the wrinkles from my lavender dress.

"Perhaps I would prefer to have *you* as my guide," Mr. Andrew responds, slowly approaching me as if I were a timid deer. "You may even find you enjoy my company."

He is standing very near me. I can almost feel heat emanate from his body.

"Very well," I sigh and tighten my bonnet. "I plan on walking. You may find the journey tiresome."

"I doubt that very much. Besides, how far could it be?"

141

"I prefer walking across the meadows. Your boots may end up with mud on them," I say, motioning my hand towards his feet.

He looks from my head down to my shoes and says with a chuckle, "If it's all the same to you, I shall take my chances."

After my attempts at discouraging him have failed, we leave the confines of my home and set forth for town. Mist still holds to the dampened earth. A gossamer blanket covers the meadow, taking on characteristics of a fairytale. Our path veers left, leading us between ancient oaks.

It isn't long before my companion makes an effort at conversation, "Your brother was right in his description of the area. It is quite breathtaking. I can imagine you as a child, swinging under that large branch over there," says Mr. Andrew, as he finds a stick and swings it from side-to-side.

"Yes, it is beautiful here, and I have been known to swing from high branches," I inquire and watch lace from my dress as it gathers moisture from the grass, wishing I had worn something more suitable for our hike. "You grew up in Charleston, I presume?"

"Yes, I was born and raised there. My mother is originally from London and my father from South Carolina. It was an interesting union, to say the least," he says, laughing under his breath and looking down at the piece of tree branch he is holding.

"What amuses you so?"

"It is nothing, just remembering something." He runs his hand through his hair and it lightly rests just below his shirt collar. "Charleston is different from London in many regards."

"How so, may I ask?"

"For one, the weather in Charleston is much warmer. The clouds are scarce, rarely hiding the sun that reflects the cheerful yellow and pink buildings."

"I am attempting to imagine such a place. It sounds lovely. You must miss it when you travel."

"I do; however, I detest it in the summer. Unfortunately, it becomes unbearably hot in the South. The summer air in England is by far more agreeable."

"Do you plan on staying in England for the duration of summer?"

"Prior obligations require me to return home sooner than that," he says, and I am barely aware of our pace slowing.

"It is a pity you must return so quickly."

"I hope you don't mind my saying so, but I was under the impression you would rejoice in my absence," he says candidly.

"I am not entirely certain how you could have arrived at such an idea! How cruel you must think me!"

"I could be wrong; however, you seem ill at ease around me. I am still trying to figure out how I have fallen out of your favor."

"Whatever do you mean?"

"Please, do not feel offended, but your brother's description of his favorite sister does not hold an entirely true likeness of the person I see before me."

The air is listless. I have nothing to say to this man. He apparently notices he has stunned me to silence, because he then attempts to clarify his position. "Please do not take what I have said as an insult to your character; however, by his account, I had assumed that your nature would be more gregarious. If you do not mind my saying so, I have seen little of that in your regard toward me. If anything, I believe you have been avoiding me all together. I am not sure why really. Did I offend you in some way?"

"No, you have not." I shake my head wearily. "Under normal circumstances, I would accuse you of being too forthright with your remarks. I am afraid, I must agree with you. These past few days, I have not been myself."

"I see," he says, flinging his stick into the river. "Unfortunately, it is in my nature to speak too freely. I am sorry if I have offended you. You seem a delightful young lady." Half his lip turns upward in a smile.

"Actually…I do not mind."

"Do you suppose it is your impending engagement that has put you off?"

"How could you say something so wretched," I say, putting an abrupt halt to my walking and staring at him in disbelief.

"I am doing it again and am truly sorry. I will refrain from openly expressing my opinions in the future. It is none of my business with whom you become engaged."

"For your information, I am not yet engaged to Mr. Grant. I will, however, be soon," I say and begin walking again. I am a few steps away before I yell back, "You are right; it is none of your business!"

"Miss. Emma, please wait," says Mr. Andrew, and he reaches for my arm. A shiver passes through me. I have stopped walking, but refrain from looking at him. He then offers, "I did not mean to upset you. I would very much like it if we could be friendly with one another."

"Do you mean to call upon my sister?"

"I should think not. I hold her in high esteem, but am not interested in her that way."

I look back toward the river, and a faint smile spreads over my face. "I see. I am afraid she will be most disappointed by your lack of regard."

"I believe she will not suffer for too long. I am probably no more than a passing fancy."

"She appeared quite taken by you last evening," I reply just before the church bells ring.

"We must be close to town. Just over the bridge, I assume."

"Yes, it is not far now."

"After you, my lady," he says, extending his hand in the direction of our dirt path.

I trudge forward, leaving Mr. Andrew in my wake. I can hear the scuffling of tiny rocks, as his boots scurry forth. He quickly catches up to me and matches my hurried stride.

"What is it in town that has you so eager?" he inquires.

"I have many errands to which I must attend. For one, I must see the baker. He makes the most delicious loaves of fresh bread and the most flavorful tarts. In fact, if you inhale deeply you can smell their aroma from here."

"I assume they taste as good as they smell?"

"They taste even better!"

"And what of your second errand?" he inquires. I look at him quizzically. "You said you have many errands. I was wondering what else will occupy your time."

"If you must know, I will choose some ribbons and other accessories for a dress I am sewing. Nothing that would interest a gentleman, such as you," I offer, but have deliberately omitted information about my visit with Chelsea. I am certain with my bad fortune he would want to accompany me. How would I be able to divulge information about my distressing situation, if he were there to listen to my every word?

"That sounds interesting. Are you talented as a seamstress?" he inquires, pulling me away from my internal ramblings.

"No, it is not like that. I simply design dresses and piece them together. It is more of a hobby I have come to enjoy," I say shrugging my shoulders.

"Did you design the dress you were wearing last evening?"

"Mr. Andrew, do you even remember what I was wearing last evening?"

"It was pale blue, with delicate sleeves made of a sheer material. Beading must have been woven throughout, because it shimmered when you walked by the candlelight."

"That is an astute description of my gown. I am impressed by your accuracy. Most men would not be able to recall the color, much less notice the beadwork."

"I grow cotton and am surrounded by people who work with fabrics regularly. I suppose some of it has rubbed off on me. I might add how breathtaking you looked."

Why must he affect me like this?

We are silent for the remaining few steps into town. As we approach the main square, Mr. Andrew recognizes someone from across the way.

"I must speak with that gentleman, just over there. Would you care to join me?" requests Mr. Andrew, appearing hopeful.

I look over his shoulder and recognize the man; it is Mr. Henry Jones. He is also in the textile industry and spends much of his time in London. It is no wonder Mr. Andrew has become acquainted with him.

"I should leave you to your business. I will see you at our home later today," I say.

"Would you like for me to accompany you on your return?"

"I may be a while. I would not have you wait on my account. Thank you for escorting me, good-day."

"As you wish, good-day," he says, and I watch as my companion walks away. His stride is confident, and my mind is suddenly filled with a fantasy of him in Charleston. I envision him using that same stride on the streets there. Only instead of being surrounded by drab hues, he is encased by pastel colors.

I cannot pull my stare away from Mr. Andrew. He and the other man are deep in conversation. Mr. Andrew surprises me by gazing back in my direction. Appropriately, I look away and walk in the direction of the baker. I imagine Mr. Andrew's smile, and for some silly reason, I cannot wipe away the one I now wear. This is completely ridiculous.

After I purchase three loaves of bread, some jelly tarts, and a few spools of ribbon, I visit my dear friend, Chelsea. She lives just up the lane, a few paces from where I am standing. She is one of my oldest friends, with whom I share all of my most intimate thoughts.

Unfortunately, she missed the party last evening because of a recent injury she sustained in a horse riding accident. Thank goodness, the impact of the injury focused primarily on her leg and not her neck. The careless girl is often too swift with her riding. I have warned her many times to slow down. Perhaps now, she will listen to my words of wisdom.

After I round the corner of a large brick building, I can see her quaint cottage just up ahead. It is white with black shutters and is surrounded by a gorgeous garden. I move past the flowers, admiring their soft petals.

When I reach the door, I am greeted formally by one of her servants and led through the charming home. Chelsea is sitting in a chair upholstered in a soft butter cream fabric. She is draped with a wrap, concealing her injured leg. Her blonde hair is lovely as ever, pulled off her face and settled at the nape of her neck.

When she sees me her face lights up. She attempts to stand, but I motion for her to remain as she is.

"Please, do not stand on my account," I peer down toward her injured leg and grimace.

"Emma, please do not lecture me. I realize this accident could have been prevented if I had been riding at a slower pace, and if I had not insisted on taking that jump over the stream," admits Chelsea.

"It would seem there is little need of scolding you after all."

"Thank goodness for that! Emma, please do sit down. I am completely unprepared for a visit. What a wonderful surprise this is! I cannot begin to tell you how dull life has been these last few days," she says, placing aside her embroidery.

"I thought you might enjoy some fresh tarts," I say and set my basket on a table. "You might also like to hear about all you have missed."

"I would!"

I sit on my favorite chair and am engulfed in comfort. I have always adored this chair. In fact, I do not recall my ever sitting anywhere else in this room. The design on the cushion is extraordinary. Most of the surface is silky and of the palest honey color. There is a pattern stitched in a deeper shade of gold throughout.

I reach into my basket and retrieve my new finery.

Chelsea's face is bright with excitement, and a gasp escapes through my friend's lips. "I simply adore the color of that ribbon! You must show me the drawings for your latest gowns!"

I describe the ideas I have for adding a band of small ruffles and explain how I will use the ribbon to help enhance the figure.

"You are a visionary, but I wonder what Mr. Grant would say. After all, your enhancements are a little shocking," says Chelsea, blushing slightly.

"I recall our last conversation where you said you thought clothing should add to the allure of a woman and not hide it," I remind her.

"I suppose I did," she says and peers down at her hands, as they twiddle around some lace.

"You will be the very first to see my new dresses once I have completed them."

"I am certain they will be lovely. I should very much like one for myself, if you don't mind."

"Why Chelsea, what will your mother say once she sees you wearing such a dress?" I tease and a large smile spreads over my face.

I inform her of last evening's festivities and give detailed descriptions of the delicious desserts and dancing couples. After awhile, I run out of enthralling news and must inform her of my upcoming engagement to Mr. Grant.

"Well, you knew this day would eventually come," she says.

"It is of no consequence."

"How can you act as if it does not affect you? What are you not telling me?" Chelsea narrows her stare and leans forward.

"Edmund has returned home . . . and he arrived with an acquaintance, Mr. Andrew Stone from Charleston, South Carolina."

"He is actually from America? How exciting it must be to have a foreigner stay as your guest! And what else has you on edge?"

"I have told you everything," I say, but Chelsea does not respond. She is silent as if waiting for more information. I oblige by adding, "All right, if you insist. Mr. Andrew is moderately charming, he seems interested in my dress designing, and he often says exactly what is on his mind. I have never encountered such a man. Well, not including Edmund." I stare out the window at the tree branches blowing in the wind.

"I see. That would be cause for your current state, would it not? What sort of things does he say?"

"Well, he asked me why I acted so strangely around him. In my opinion, he has been speaking far too freely with me!"

If Chelsea is attempting to muffle her laughter, she has failed. Since this is no laughing matter, I give her a look of exasperation. After all, she should take me seriously.

"Perhaps, Emma, it is fortunate he is only here for a visit. I would not care for my dearest friend to suffer in any way because a man actually catches her attention," says Chelsea, tilting her head ever so slightly.

"Ha-ha, how amusing you are this morning. I am going to marry Mr. Grant. I cannot, in good conscience, fancy another man. Change of subject. Edmund has asked me to travel to London with him. I suppose that would give more time for . . ."

"You mean to say, more time to run away from your troubles? It is quite simple; if you do not wish to enter into matrimony with Mr. Grant, then you ought to say no to his offer of engagement. In fact, it would be best if you could find some way of discouraging him *before* he proposes. Actually, you were much better suited to marry Mr. Hamilton. He doted on you so. I believe *he* would be the sort to travel with you, although I agree he might have had a little gambling problem."

"Gambling problem aside, I could never have married Mr. Hamilton. Mama would not have allowed it! Besides, I am certain I could be quite content living in Webshire. I would have everything my heart desires right there for me. After all, it is the only sensible thing to do," I defend, and it does not go unnoticed by me that Chelsea is rolling her eyes in a most unladylike fashion.

"Emma, do you truly believe Mr. Grant is the most suitable man for you?"

"You know, as well as I do that Mr. Grant's mother and Mama have been planning our union for ages. Honestly, I could never consider a man other than Mr. Grant for a husband!"

"Besides, you feel safe with Mr. Grant. After all, you two were practically raised together."

"I do not see there being any harm in feeling safe with him."

"Agreed; however, I would like to see you open your heart to the possibility of actually finding someone who can match your zest for life. I am afraid Mr. Grant would cry to his mummy with even the smallest little scratch. Is that really the sort of man with whom you wish to spend your remaining days?"

"I suppose that is why I consider you a sister. Only a sister would be truly honest with her opinions, even if they are harsh," I say.

"My words may be harsh, but they ring true. I would not be able to call myself a true friend if I did not honestly air my thoughts on the matter. I only hope you follow your heart and not your head."

"I promise I shall take your words of advice. Thank you for speaking freely."

"My dear friend, I am here to offer unsolicited advice, any-time," Chelsea says, and we smile at each other. "What do you say to some tea and sharing in the treats you so kindly brought?"

~ * * * ~

Most of my morning is enjoyably spent in much the same way. Sometime after lunch, I notice Chelsea appears sleepy. Promptly, I take my leave of her and find my way back home.

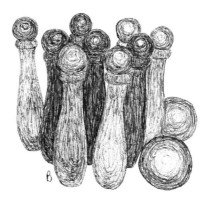

Chapter Sixteen

As I draw closer to my house, I hear laughter. A few steps more, and I am able to recognize the group ahead. Gathered on the lawn are Mr. Andrew and my family, playing a game of nine-pin. I quicken my steps, as I am eager to join them. What a grand way to spend the afternoon.

"I have been looking all over for you!" Victoria exclaims, as she swiftly glides over the grass. After reaching my side, she whispers, "Mr. Andrew and I have been set together as a team."

"It would appear everyone is caught up in the festivities," I say. "I notice you are in the middle of a break. Is it too late for me to join in the game?"

"Of course you may join us! Only, you will find Mr. Andrew and I are an unbeatable pair." She smiles and saunters back towards her teammate.

My father interrupts his conversation with Mr. Andrew to offer up his place as Edmund's partner. Swiftly, Papa is relaxing next to Mama, enjoying a cup of tea.

I find my place next to Edmund. He leans close to me, seemingly about to whisper. Only instead of coming out in a hush, he exclaims his sentiments loud enough for our rivals to hear. "All right Emma, it is time we show these two what they are up against! After all, they are no match for us!"

I announce with vigor equal to his, "I agree and am looking forward to reigning victorious in this tournament!"

Victoria is the first to throw the ball down the grassy lane and . . . she does moderately well. Edmund follows her turn and does even better than she. Victoria's voice becomes shrill with irritation. Edmund walks over to her, no doubt to gloat about his superior ability at the game. My brother beams with satisfaction while Victoria stands with her arms tensely crossed over her chest. There is a terse discussion about the rules, and I believe I hear Victoria mutter about how something is not fair. I cannot help but chuckle at the familiarity of the scene.

It is at this point, Mr. Andrew comes to stand at my side. "Did you have a nice day in town?" he inquires, still watching the drama between my brother and sister.

"I did, indeed. And what of your visit, did you accomplish your tasks?" My concentration narrows even closer on my siblings. They continue with their bantering, all the while, returning the pins to an upright position.

"I found my conversation with Mr. Jones most informative," says Mr. Andrew.

"That is good to hear," I reply and quickly shift our conversation. "Edmund and Victoria get on like this at every game. I am not entirely certain which I enjoy more; their ongoing debates over rules or the game itself."

"I can see the entertainment of it," says Mr. Andrew, peering down at me. "On my journey back, I came upon a most unsettling realization."

"Oh, and of what realization did you come by, Mr. Andrew?" I look up, returning his powerful gaze.

"Are you in love with him?"

I catch my breath and glare.

"I assume it is Mr. Grant to whom you are referring."

"If I may be so bold as to say, I do not believe you are," suggests Mr. Andrew, and my face grows hot. I am not sure how to respond. After an uncomfortable silence, it is Mr. Andrew who finally speaks, "I will take that as a confirmation of my assumption."

"You think me so shallow that I would become engaged to a man whom I am not in love! You are entirely too impertinent!" I say and am proud of the fierce intensity in my voice.

"You have not yet answered my question. That, in itself, speaks volumes."

I am ready to slap him, when my brother returns to my side. After looking at my reddened cheeks, he begins to laugh. "Emma, it would appear as if you have entered into the spirit of the game. It is your turn. Make your throw count," says Edmund, nudging me towards the end of the lane.

I am so completely outraged by Mr. Andrew, I can barely think straight. I take my hostility out on the ball and hurl it toward the pins. To my teammate's delight and my surprise, I mow down the entire lot!

In that moment, I have forgotten my rage and celebrate by raising my arms into the air with a shriek. Edmund bounds over to me, we embrace, and jump up and down.

"Good show, Emma!" says Edmund, and then he turns toward Mr. Andrew. "Let us see you follow that!"

I, in turn, scowl in Mr. Andrew's direction. Instead of appearing indignant by my outrage, the corners of his mouth turn up into an amused grin. This irritates me all the more. I stomp back to my previous position and wait for him to take his turn.

His eyes linger in my direction for longer than is necessary, and his twinkling smile makes me uncomfortable. I wish he would return his attention to the game. At last, he looks away from me and concentrates on the pins. He waits another moment before throwing. His strategy pays off, because he manages to hit all of the pins, as well. Surely, good fortune is with him. For a brief second, I see the joyful gleam in his eyes at his undeserved success. I wish, however, I were not aware of how brightly his eyes sparkle.

~ * * * ~

After dinner, my family retires to the library. The room is illuminated by light from the glowing fireplace, and all I can hear are crackling whispers from the hearth. Papa has pulled a book from the shelf and sits casually in his favorite chair. My siblings and I are eager for a spot close to him. It is quite common for our family to spend evenings in such a way. Most nights, my father will obligingly read a few pages from a book. I become carried away by his voice and am able to travel afar.

Edmund and Victoria are closest to Papa, and I find an empty place on the sofa. Thank goodness, Mr. Andrew has some business to which he must attend, and I will not have to endure his presence for the remainder of the evening. I sigh with contentment.

Beside me is a tray lined with sweet biscuits. I am easily able to ignore them and reach for my parchment. After showing Chelsea my latest drawings, I am anxious to design a new gown for her, and as I wait for Papa to begin his tale, I sketch my ideas.

My father's animated story is about faraway kingdoms, and I am immediately swept away. He is reading from the fifth page, when an unwelcome interruption creeps into the room. Without looking away from my drawing, I am aware Mr. Andrew has joined us. His unnerving presence, however, has failed to dissolve the web of Papa's story weaving, and I am grateful. The first available seat, of course, is situated next to me. Immediately, Mr. Andrew takes his place by my side. My body involuntarily edges away from him and I am pressed against the sofa's arm. I reach for a biscuit and nibble at it. My concentration is locked on my sketches, but I can sense Mr. Andrew's gaze on me.

"Ms. Emma, you seem to be out of sorts. Are you well?" he whispers in my direction.

"I am fine."

"Your drawings are quite nice. I did not realize you were an artist," he says, peering over my shoulder.

Protectively, I place my hand over my drawing. Again, I reach for a dessert. This time it is a raspberry tart, and juice from the berries sweetens my lips. I am lost for a moment in its splendor. In fact, I am barely aware that Mr. Andrew remains quiet for the rest of Papa's reading.

"That will be all for now. I must retire to my quarters," says my father, as he saves his page and shuts the book. I am utterly disappointed by the abrupt halt to his reading. I am quite certain I will not be able to rest my mind until I know the fate of the mighty heroine.

After the room clears, I find I am left alone. I approach the closed book and open it to the saved page. Secretively, I read what is to come. After flipping a few more pages, I am relieved to find the heroine will prevail through her hardships.

I return the book to its precise location and then pivot to leave the scene. All of a sudden, I notice Mr. Andrew. He is resting against the doorframe, obstructing my exit. I am aware that yet again, he is catching me at a most inconvenient moment.

"Goodness! You have managed to startle me once again. Is this your new favorite form of entertainment?" I sigh in exasperation.

"On my word, it has not been my intention to upset you. It would seem, however, I have been frequently doing just that," he says.

"It is of no consequence. The damage has already been done. Excuse me, for I wish to retire to my room." I attempt to slip through the doorway but am blocked by him. He is close, too close, but I am still able to mutter, "Excuse me, sir."

He reaches into his pocket and pulls out a handkerchief. He extends his hand towards my face, gently wiping the soft fabric over my chin.

"Here, this may be of better use to you than me," he offers, placing the cloth in my hand. I stare down at it and realize he must have just cleaned jam off my face!

"Excuse me, Mr. Andrew, I must get through."

"Emma, earlier today I spoke too freely and insulted your integrity. I am truly sorry for my poor behavior and promise to make amends," he says, and I glance up to see whether or not he is sincere. Perhaps he is . . . a little.

"I suppose I accept your apology, under the condition you will refrain from further insults. You may speak of the weather and little else."

"I suppose that will be more than acceptable. May I also remark, my odd behavior is not entirely my fault," says Mr. Andrew with a grin.

"Oh, and who is to share in the blame for your tactlessness?"

"You are, of course."

"How do you suppose I am responsible for your ill manners?" I ask in surprise.

"It is difficult for me to remain silent when I believe you are too good for that pompous Percy Grant," says Mr. Andrew, narrowing his stare. "Besides, I find your reactions unbelievably charming. My only regret is I anger you in the process. I suppose if only at our every encounter, I were not struck nearly witless by you, I might then be able to ponder my thoughts before speaking them."

I look away and try to comprehend the words he has just spoken. I cannot for the life of me think of a single thing with which to reply. I open and shut my mouth, hoping for something to fill the empty void. To no avail, I remain mute in my response.

"My sincerest hope is tomorrow we may start the day as friends, at least," he offers with a sigh.

I nod in agreement and begin to fan my face. He moves aside and allows for me to pass. My eyes are fixed on the floor, as I make my way down the long corridor.

When I am a few paces away, I turn and gaze upon his handsome face. "Mr. Andrew . . ."

"If we are to be friends, I sincerely hope you will drop the formality and call me Andrew."

"Good-evening, Andrew," I say in a hush.

"Good-evening, Emma," he says, and I stare at him another moment before making my way down the dimly lit hall, aware that his gaze has remained on me its entire length.

The walk back seemingly takes forever. When I finally reach my room, I notice my palms are perspiring, making it difficult to open the door.

"There you are!" I hear Victoria say, as she appears from behind the grandfather clock. "I was afraid you had lost your way. In another moment, I would have been forced to set out in search of you."

"Really Victoria, you should not worry on my behalf. I am perfectly able to care for myself," I reply, still trying in earnest to open the door.

"I am not entirely certain about that, dearest sister."

I turn and look at her in question to her remark.

"Whatever do you mean?" I inquire, feeling a rush of irritation.

"It is only . . . I think you to be a complete fool! There I have said it, do not be angry," she says, looking triumphant.

"How is it you perceive me a fool?"

"Can you not see what has been presented to you clear as day?" she inquires, leaning over to help me open the door, and I usher her inside.

"Have you gone mad and lost all of your senses? Whatever do you mean?" I inquire, perching uneasily in front of my dressing table.

"Is it not obvious that Mr. Andrew is utterly enamored with you?"

"That is complete rubbish. He is not enamored of me," I say, removing my cameo earrings.

"Are you blind? You cannot sit there and honestly say you have not noticed his eyes are set aflame by your mere presence. Why, he is totally besotted with you! Though why *you* and not *me*, I shall never fathom," she says with a grin.

I stop brushing my hair and tightly grasp the soft bristles in my hand. "You truly believe he has feelings for me?"

"One would have to be absolutely blind to not recognize the gleam in his eyes when he gazes your way. I suppose that leaves the question of what you are to do about Mr. Grant." Her eyes blaze excitedly.

"I suppose I shall do what any other rational person would . . . nothing," I say, and the expression on Victoria's face is one of astonishment. "First, Andrew has not indicated his intention of courting me. Second, I cannot in clear conscience insult Mr. Grant in that way. He has done nothing but to show me the utmost regard and deserves to be treated better. Third, I do not wish to upset Mama. Besides which, I must also consider your feelings for Andrew."

"That is a lot of hogwash! If you feel even the slightest inkling of affection for Mr. Andrew, then you should marry no other," says Victoria firmly. "And Emma, as far as you considering my feelings, although I appreciate the sentiment, I could very easily find someone other than the likes of Mr. Andrew. Good-evening and sleep well."

Promptly, Victoria leaves, practically giggling the entire way. I am left staring into the mirror. My poor hair, I realize I am brushing it far too roughly, but I do not care. When I am finished, I pace my room and rant under my breath. After much consideration, and many hours, I finally crawl into my bed and sleep on the matter.

Chapter Seventeen

The next day brings little in regard to resolving my inner conflict. I rush to my dresser drawer and withdraw my diary. Perhaps, through my writing, I shall find some inner peace.

21 May

I fear Andrew has stolen my heart. What am I to do? Perhaps my feelings for him will simply pass. After all, he is different from any other man I have ever met, and since he is a foreigner, that would be understandable. I am quite certain once I truly know him well, I would find him a little boring.

4 June

More than a fortnight has passed since Andrew's arrival... why is he still here? I thought he would have ventured back to London by now. I have spent much time with him and have come to understand him quite well. Unfortunately, I have not grown bored with him. In fact, I fear my feelings are growing beyond fondness. The urgency of my desire has stretched to the depths of my soul. It is torturous spending day after day beside him, with little more than flirtatious sentiments and longing eyes.

But Mama will have a fit if I tell her I cannot marry Mr. Grant . . .

~ * * * ~

My family has just been seated in the dining room, ready to enjoy our meal, when there is a harsh knock on our front door. A man is brought into the room by our servant. The stranger's hair is wet and clothes dirty. My father stands and greets the man, offering him a plate of food.

"I must see Mr. Andrew Stone. I carry an urgent message," says the man quickly.

"Please, let us retire to the other room," says Andrew, motioning to the door. He excuses himself and exits the room, leaving my family to stare at each other with wide eyes.

"Whatever do you suppose that was about? I do so hope everything is all right," my mother says.

Although everyone else is able to eat, I stare at the vacant door frame. I am flooded with concern and can feel my insides twist into knots. Andrew and the messenger are gone for an interminable length of time. When Andrew finally does reenter the dining room, his face is flushed.

"I am afraid I have been presented with terrible news. My mother has written me a letter. She is ill, and I need to return home. I am sorry, but I must make haste and return to London this evening," Andrew informs us.

"Of course, my dear boy, you must go where you are needed. I can see that your business affairs here are settled," my father offers.

"Many thanks, sir. I will return as quickly as I can," Andrew replies and turns his attention to me. "Emma, may I have a word?"

Without speaking, I rise from my chair and follow him into the next room. I am struck with emotion at his having to leave and am holding back tears. Before exiting the room, I can hear Victoria giggle and Mama's admonition to hush, reminding her it would be inappropriate to eavesdrop.

Andrew pauses in the center of the floor and takes my hands carefully into his. He gazes earnestly into my eyes.

"You must know, I would not entertain the idea of leaving if it were not a matter of dire importance," he says, and his stare deepens.

I nod and can feel a stream of water run down my face. I feel ridiculous at my open display of emotion.

"Please, do not be sad," he says sweetly.

When I finally manage to look at him, I realize he is smiling.

"How is it you are happy at a moment like this?" I question, becoming enraged.

"I am sorry, but until this moment you have been rather restrained about showing how you feel. I must admit it pleases me that my absence will sadden you a bit," he says, and my mouth hangs open a little.

"You enjoy watching me suffer?"

He shakes his head and holds his hand gently beneath my chin.

"No, of course not," he says, wiping a tear from under my eye. "It does please me that perhaps we share the same affections. Emma, I do not attempt to deny my feelings. If you can wait, I will return for you."

Tears continue streaming down my face, and I am unable to respond. I nod my head and place one of my hands over my mouth. I try to collect my emotions and manage to say, "Please, be careful on your journey home and give my regards to your mother. I do hope she recovers soon."

"I shall. She will be all right, but she cannot be expected to run the business on her own right now."

Abruptly, Papa walks into the room. I was not aware of how close my body was to Andrew's, until now, and we are forced to pull away.

"I am sorry for the intrusion. Is there anything I can help you with?" inquires Papa, appearing genuinely concerned.

"I thank you, but that will not be necessary. I believe I can pack my things quickly enough and be on my way," Andrew announces and returns his gaze on me. "I will see you again, sooner than you think."

He leaves and is escorted by my father, and I am left alone feeling terrible. I feel as if my insides have been rearranged, so my stomach is now in my throat and my heart now resides where my stomach used to be. I am not well enough to return to supper, so I sit and stare vacantly at my hands. I can hear someone enter the room but cannot lift my head. Instead, I stare despairingly downward.

"I am dreadfully sorry about Andrew's having to leave. Terrible luck that is," says Edmund sympathetically. "I have no doubt he will return. When he does, he will most likely rush to find you."

I say nothing in return. Edmund places his arm around me and gives a supportive hug. I feel comfort in his strength and lean my head on his shoulder. We sit like this for quite a long while, and when I am ready, I return to the dining table.

10 June

I have received a letter from Andrew! He must have mailed it before his departure from London. I have saved it in a hidden compartment of my dressing table. I reread the script over and over and have memorized its contents by now. I still cannot believe he referred to me as his "Little Sweetie" and included a handkerchief! I imagine he was hysterical with laughter when he wrote that.

14 June

Moments ago, I received a message from Mr. Grant. He will arrive here in the morning. I suspect he means to propose. Although, I knew this day would come, I had hoped I would have more time. Now, what should I say?

Since Andrew's departure, Mama commented on my surprisingly cheery disposition. After all, I have acted as though his absence has affected me little. I realize life must go on, but my heart still yearns to be with him. Mama knows about my feelings for Andrew and has released me from my prior arrangement with Mr. Grant. Although I was planning on releasing myself from the engagement, I was relieved to have her understand, none the less.

15 June

Mr. Grant is an admirable man. He apparently understood that he did not hold my affection. In fact, he almost seemed relieved. He mentioned something about how he and his mother did not understand the timing for my recent visit to Paris. I had no idea what he was talking about, but I did not question the sensibilities of the poor man. Obviously, his recent hardships have affected his sanity. I am grateful for the ease of our conversation and the end of it, for that matter.

16 June

I am going to kill Edmund! He has finally confessed to me the evil part he played in driving away Mr. Grant! Supposedly, Mr. Grant came and called upon me a few days ago. I was not home, as I was in town visiting Chelsea.

Today, however, Edmund explained to me that on the morning of Mr. Grant's arrival that he, Edmund, decided to take it upon himself to interrogate the man. My rotten brother then lied straight faced to Mr. Grant about my whereabouts! He told him, I had traveled to Paris. Honestly, I still cannot believe the nerve of my brother!

After admitting to his foul deed, he appeared smug, adding that his suspicions about Mr. Grant were correct. Edmund had asked Mr. Grant if he was fond of traveling and what of his interest in fashion. Of course, Mr. Grant's reaction was one of disinterest. Edmund decided that was the perfect opportunity for him to destroy any chance of Mr. Grant proposing to me. I am afraid that Mr. Grant's reaction upon hearing the news of my reckless traveling and carefree designs for gowns turned both him and his mother sour.

I suppose that helps explain the ease with which Mr. Grant allowed me to end our relationship. Most likely, he was incredibly relieved at not having to say the words himself. I, like a fool, said the words for him. He truly is a pathetic individual, allowing me to lavish false praise on him like he did.

16 August

Although I have been in good spirits, I find the days and weeks have begun to crawl. I spend my time as I normally would, but take little pleasure in these summer months. My thoughts are consumed by Andrew and our brief time together.

I think back to our open conversations; he always seemed interested in my ideas. Although I have not seen his perfect features for two months now, they have been imprinted indelibly on my memory. When I close my eyes, I pretend he is here, walking beside me in the twilight . . .

~ * * * ~

"Are you writing in that ridiculous diary again? I consider it a complete waste of time. You should be outdoors, enjoying the splendor of the afternoon sun." Victoria has found me hiding in the library, yet again.

"Perhaps you ought to indulge in your own advice," I say without looking up.

"If you do not mind my saying so, you really should go easy on the sweets. If you continue stuffing your face with treats, you will easily grow to the size of a house."

How dare my sister say such a thing to me? But when I peer over to the plate of sweeties nestled next to me, I wonder just how many of those I have eaten? Surely, they are not half gone, already.

Victoria sits beside me and peeks over at the page of my diary.

"My writing is personal," I declare, abruptly shutting my book and hiding it from her.

"Oh please, Emma. It is not as if I am not aware of what you write or whom you write about." She sighs and claps her hands loudly on her lap. "Come outside with me. It is a glorious day. We could take a walk into town."

"I suppose we could visit Chelsea, especially since she has recovered from her injury."

~ * * * ~

Victoria is correct; it does feel good to walk through the meadow and alongside the river's edge, its water lapping the bank. The air is fresh, and I am reminded of freshly washed white cotton linens.

I have taken to walking with a wooden stick. My hand involuntarily swings it from side-to-side, cutting through tall grass. It makes a swishing sound as it breaks across the blades.

Town is very near, and Victoria unrelentingly fills my lack of conversation with her lighthearted tales. She has trouble keeping my attention, as I notice how idly the baker's sign is influenced by the wind. It swings back and forth on the metal rod. Its movement is melodic, and I am captivated.

Hmm, that man sitting over by that statue resembles Andrew from behind. I wish he were here. As Victoria and I walk by, the man turns and smiles . . . . Wait, it is Andrew! Victoria nudges into me and giggles.

"Is it really him?" I say, staring wide-eyed at the man.

"Yes, you silly girl, it is Andrew! Now, go to him," Victoria replies, but all I can do is look at her. "Emma, it was meant to be a surprise. Only, I did not expect for you to appear so completely startled."

I close my eyes and shake my head. When I reopen my eyes, I see that it is in fact Andrew. I cannot believe he is actually here! I feel giddy at his sudden arrival and am overcome with laughter.

I race toward him. My feet barely even touch the ground. His pace quickens too, and we meet in the middle of the town square.

At last, we reach each other. I am so overcome with elation I literally throw myself into his arms! He lifts me into the air and spins around madly! I can feel my dress take to air, but I do not mind the spectacle. At this moment, all that matters is that he is here!

"You have returned!" I say enthusiastically, grinning from ear to ear.

"Yes, I have returned," he says, placing his forehead affectionately to mine. "I couldn't stay away from you any longer. I do not wish to be apart from you, ever again. You have affected my life in ways I never imagined possible. I do not expect for you to understand."

"I understand completely!" I say, with a silly expression plastered to my face.

A flock of small children at play forces us to step back.

"When I was home," Andrew resumes, "I discovered the most unique little building right in the heart of town. The owner informed me it was damaged a little in one of Charleston's most recent fires. I looked inside to see how much repair it required. The damage is merely superficial."

"I do not understand your reason for informing me of this," I say, shaking my head in bewilderment.

"I signed the deed just last week. I would like to transform the place into a clothing establishment. I will be in need of a top designer to help me with the fashions for its inventory."

"Andrew, what exactly are you saying? You just told me you did not want to leave me. This does not make sense. Are you returning home already?"

"I am good at expressing my opinions but terrible at expressing my emotions," he sighs and runs his hand through his glorious hair. "I am asking you if you would please join me on my return home . . . as my wife." He smiles, and I believe I can see a faint mist within his eyes.

I bounce like a little girl and again throw myself into his arms. I can hear a muffled laughter come from him.

"I hope this means you accept my offer," he says.

"Of course, yes! This time, I would not be so willing to allow you to sail across the sea without my being there to accompany you," I say in earnest.

"Emma," He catches his breath before continuing, "I love you and promise I always shall."

Paige, Wednesday
Dressing Table

I realize I am staring at *my* reflection in the mirror and am overcome with emotion. I can still feel Emma's love and joy.

Why am I not more like Edmund? I should support Hailey to do what will make *her* happy, not what I perceive to be responsible. She should marry for true love, not practicality. I feel wretched. My behavior has been horrible.

Suddenly, another memory sweeps over me, and I begin to search under the table. I root around and find another hidden compartment. I slide my hand into the space and can feel a dry piece of paper. Carefully, I pull out the yellowed and faded letter.

Gently, I unfold it and read out loud, "My Dear Little Sweetie."

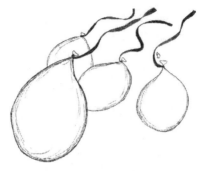

Chapter Eighteen

Desperately, I reach for my cell and punch in Hailey's number. The phone rings over and over. "Come on Hailey, answer it!" I say, but she doesn't, and it rings some more.

I'm sure she's ignoring me, not that I'm not surprised. I didn't exactly play the part of the understanding sister. If I were Hailey, I would ignore my calls, too.

"Where are my keys?" I reach for my purse and fumble around.

Elliott peers into the room and asks hesitantly, "Everything all right?"

"No!" I say and walk past him.

"Where are you going? It's after 10:00 at night." He follows me into the kitchen, watching my actions intently. "Paige, what are you doing?"

"I have to see Hailey. I'll explain everything to you later," I say, giving him a little kiss and gently rubbing my hand over his stubbly chin. "Love you. I'll be home in a bit."

~ * * * ~

"Her car isn't here!" I exclaim in frustration, as I drive in circles around my sister's carport.

Once more, I call Hailey. When she doesn't answer, I head directly towards Julian's place. For some reason, I know exactly where he lives. In fact, my car practically drives itself there, all on its own.

When I reach Julian's condo, I see a shiny black sports car off in the distance. I think it's her car! I was right, Hailey must be here! In relief, I pull into a spot and head for the elevators. I have no idea what I'm going to say. Maybe some divine inspiration will come to me.

Even if I flub this up, at least she will know I support her and am here to help. That's what sisters do for each other, right? I am aware these are not the actions of a rational person, however, after what has just happened, I am not thinking like a rational person.

The elevator doors open, and I stare down the hall. It's uncanny, I've never actually been here, but I recognize almost every detail: the intricate travertine floors, exotic wood paneling, and vibrant abstract paintings. The last painting stops me in my tracks, and I realize it is Hailey's favorite. This is really strange, I'm thinking, as I continue walking towards Julian's door. I can hear the sound of my boots resonating down the hall.

I take in a deep breath and contemplate my next move. I don't have one. I suppose I'll just wing it. Come on Paige, just one knock and face your fears. I stare at the wooden door with my hand suspended in air, frozen. Maybe this is a not such a great idea. Probably best if I return home.

I turn to leave, when suddenly, the door whisks open. Julian is standing there. He is half dressed, has one hand on the door and the other running through the back of his hair. He looks totally confused.

"You're not Hailey," he says with great disappointment.

"No, I guess I'm not. As a matter of fact, I was looking for her. I don't suppose she's here?" I ask, and my voice is shaky.

"You're her sister, Paige," he says, not really answering my question.

"Yes, I am," I say nervously biting my lip. This is so awkward.

"Your sister said she never wanted to see me again," he says, shaking his head. "I heard your footsteps and hoped she changed her mind."

"She left you?" I say unbelievingly and feel a slight twinge of guilt.

"Do you mind coming in? I don't want to wake up my neighbors."

Julian's place is nicely decorated, but a complete mess. Actually, Julian's a complete mess. I'm trying to explain that Hailey does love him and just needs time to think, but I doubt there is anything I can say to make him feel better. Poor guy, he's just sitting there with his head hanging down and his body slumping towards the floor.

After a little while, he appears to have cheered up, a little. I even feel pretty comfortable around him. In fact, I'm on a roll. I think Elliott will be proud of me . . . . Until, in one brief instant, I ruin everything.

"Julian, why don't you come to the party Friday night? Hailey will definitely be there. Maybe you, I mean I, I mean we, can take her aside and try talking some sense into her," I offer sweetly.

Wait one minute! I can't believe I said that! I don't know what just happened! I guess I felt so horrible for him that I went a little overboard. Unfortunately, there isn't a rewind button to life. The invitation's out there, I can't take it back.

"You think I should just show up to an event celebrating Hailey's and Derek's wedding? I'm not so sure about that," Julian says.

"You're probably right. You know, you should try going by her place and talk to her there," I agree wholeheartedly.

"That's just the problem. She's avoiding my calls and not exactly hanging around her place. She's probably spending her time over at Derek's house," Julian says and peers up at me with big weepy eyes. "It makes me sick."

"I'm sorry, I wish I could help," I offer as reassuringly as I can.

"Wait, if you're here, then Hailey must have told you about me. She said she wasn't going to tell anyone about us. I guess you two really are close."

"Well, I sort of only just recently found out."

"When you see Hailey, please let her know I'm thinking about her."

"I will," I say.

"You know, maybe I should come by Friday night. I have nothing more to lose. I'll do anything to get Hailey back," he says, making me stop in my tracks.

"Actually, why don't you just send her flowers? How about red roses?"

"No, I've already tried that. She had them returned. She didn't even look at the card."

"Okay, I'll tell you what; let me talk to her for you. At the very least, I'll have her call you. That way, you won't have to bother coming Friday night."

"Thanks, that sounds good," he says and walks me to the door.

~ * * * ~

I'm unable to concentrate on my ride home. In fact, I'm not entirely sure how I arrive in my driveway. I'm sitting in my garage, my head plunked down on the steering wheel, cringing inside. What was I thinking! What have I just done? Hailey is going to hate me more than she already does.

After a few minutes of self loathing, I wander into my kitchen and throw down my keys. There's a pale stream of yellow light seeping under my bedroom door. Elliott must be awake. Poor guy, just look what I've put him through. He has probably been worried sick. I have a lot of explaining to do. Maybe it can wait until morning. No, I'll face Elliott tonight and tell him anything he wants to know. Slowly, I drag my body down the hall.

~ * * * ~

Actually, when I pour my heart out to Elliott, I discover it's pretty therapeutic. In fact, I'm hoping he can make me feel better. Except, when I see Elliott is grinning slightly, I feel even more ridiculous. Again, I try explaining how, in just a few days, I managed to alienate my sister, had visions about my ancestors, and gave relationship advice to Julian. You bet I have a lot to be upset about! I express myself with even more angst, but by the look on Elliot's face I realize this is fruitless. Apparently, he sees my current plight as a funny little drama. I understand that he's tired and wants to go to bed, but I don't feel better yet.

At this point, I have little choice but to re-explain everything to him again, but I suppose I can wait until tomorrow.

~ * * * ~

When I open my eyes the next morning, I immediately remember what had transpired last night! Elliott is already out of bed, getting ready for work. I can hear him whistling. At least one of us must have slept well.

Elliott peeks into the room, chiming, "Good morning. Did you sleep well?"

"How can you act like you're okay with everything?" I ask while sitting up and leaning against my pillows.

"Why wouldn't I be okay?"

"Don't you realize that when I'm upset, you're supposed to be upset? Or at least pretend. Actually, I'd appreciate it if you could manage to not act so happy. What have I done? I need to tell Hailey what an idiot I am!" I exclaim, nervously fidgeting with my hands.

"All right, calm down. The party's tomorrow night, right?" Elliott asks, and I nod my head yes. "So, let's just wait and see what happens."

I stare at him blankly, I may blink a few times, but that's about the biggest reaction I can muster. Am I capable of just waiting? I suppose given my circumstance, I have no other choice.

"You're probably right," I say, pulling myself out of bed.

"I still don't understand how you knew exactly where to find Julian. This whole thing is getting stranger by the minute. In fact, *you're* getting stranger by the minute. I'm just trying to keep up," Elliott says with a grin.

His fingers button up his white shirt. He looks good. I walk over and pause in front of him.

"I appreciate that you're trying to understand," I say, wrapping my arms around his waist.

"No problem. Just do me a favor and try clearing up this mess with your sister, soon. I like Derek. It's not easy having to face him, knowing what I know."

"I hadn't really thought about how this might affect the both of you. Sorry." I hang my head and tug at my shirt bottom.

"You have no control over what your sister does. This isn't your fault," he reminds me, and I feel slightly better.

~ * * * ~

My morning is spent desperately trying to get Hailey on the phone, but she still won't answer. With every failed attempt, I feel more anxious. Perhaps I should stop by her work. I could ask her to lunch or something. Who am I kidding? She probably just wants some space. Hopefully, by tomorrow night, she will have gotten over everything, she'll forgive me, and we'll hug. I guess the only thing I can do is put on an amazing party and hope for the best.

~ * * * ~

It's Friday afternoon, and I'm in the dining room decorating for the big event. I've decided to suspend white balloons from the ceiling. They're attached to white satin ribbons, reaching down to different heights. I stand back and admire my work.

"It looks breathtaking in here! Hailey will simply adore it!" my mother says, as she enters the room. "You know, it looks just like something Hailey would design."

"Thanks. You could say I was *inspired* by her. I hope everything goes well, tonight."

My mother places her arm around my shoulder and says, "Paige, you've truly outdone yourself. Everything looks fantastic. The food is going to be wonderful, and Hailey will be surrounded by the people who love her."

"That's what I'm afraid of," I say accidentally.

"Whatever do you mean?" questions Mom.

"Oh nothing, I didn't mean anything by it," I say and smile brightly, in an overly reassuringly way. "You talked to Hailey. She said she was still coming, right?"

"Don't be ridiculous, of course she's still coming! It's her event, for heaven's sake!" My mother pauses, looking thoughtfully around the room. "I still don't understand why you and Hailey insist on having both males and females in attendance. It may seem a bit old fashioned to you, but I prefer traditional showers where only females are invited. I have a whole list of fun games we could play!"

"Well, I think it's a little too late. Besides, the shower is going to be fun! It will feel more like a cocktail party than an old stuffy frou-frou bridal shower."

"I happen to enjoy the frou-frou showers. In fact, the frou-frouier the better," she says with a smile. "Well, if you don't need my help, I'll just be off to pick up the children from school."

"Thanks, Mom. Do you have the directions to the sitter's house?" I ask for the hundredth time, not being able to help myself.

"Yes, her house is just down the street. Paige, I believe I can manage this," she says and smiles naturally.

"I know. I'm just wound up," I say, returning her smile. Only, my smile is tight and I'm gritting my teeth.

"You look a little pale. Why don't you eat a little something?"

"I just ate lunch and don't really like to eat a whole lot in between meals," I offer, but I have noticed that some of the desserts in the kitchen do look rather tasty.

"You've been working too hard. You need to take a nice, hot, bubble bath. Once you've put on that fun little outfit, you'll feel rejuvenated."

"You're right. I'll get ready and try to relax. Thanks again for helping me."

"No problem, dear. I'll see you in a bit," she says and walks out the door.

After everything is in place, I head for my room.

~ * * * ~

It is 5:30, and people will arrive soon. I'm dressed in a slinky black dress and strappy sandals (with two inch heels!). It's a little sexier than I would normally wear, but I feel edgy tonight. My mother was right, after taking a bath, I am rejuvenated. In fact, I feel like a whole new person. Actually, I look a little like Hailey. Funny, I never noticed that before.

The house is immaculate, but I still walk around in circles, just looking for something to do. I'll check out the dining room, surely there's something for me to do in there…except the room looks spectacular. Food is arranged on white platters, filling the entire length of the table. There are soft pink rose petals sprinkled over the tablecloth and twinkly white lights sparkle from their strategic locations. This is the nicest display I've ever created on my own. Yay, me!

Glimmers

The doorbell rings, and I nervously race for it. Our first guests are here…it is only Derek's parents. Eek, I feel a stab of guilt at seeing them. After all, they are holding a large stack of presents. I play hostess and lead them into the house.

A few more guests arrive, and the atmosphere is light and jubilant. People are talking loudly and nibbling on appetizers. I find my mother in the family room. She's having a conversation with Hailey's boss. I could be wrong, but I think I just heard my mother ask him what sort of maternity leave his company offers. Good thing I'm here to interrupt. Hailey may not realize it, but I am watching out for her.

"Mom, they're not here, yet," I whisper in her ear.

"Who, dear?" she asks in a booming voice.

"Hailey and Derek should have been here over an hour ago," I add quietly, so as not to alarm anyone.

My mother is about to respond, when a loud cheer comes from the front room. It sounds like the happy couple has finally arrived! I let out a long sigh and stand up straight. I walk toward the commotion and immediately see Hailey and Derek. A large smile is plastered on her face. Until she notices me, and her smile falters a little. Swiftly, she looks away and continues conversing with someone else.

If I'm being honest here, I'm a nervous wreck! I peer over toward the center island of my kitchen. Sitting next to the cake is a tower of delight, three glass tiers are adorned with puffed pastries. I saunter over and cannot control my hand from reaching for a mini chocolate creampuff. Wow, this is amazing! The center is filled with chocolate. I can feel it caress the inside of my mouth. Hmm, I wonder how the petit fours taste. I reach for the mini treat and indulge my senses with its sweetness. This is incredible!

~ * * * ~

Despite my reservations about the evening, everything is going very well. It's after 9:30, and I'm beginning to relax. And although we haven't spoken, Hailey almost smiled at me, once.

After a while, I find Elliott talking with a co-worker from FCH Engineering. "Sorry to interrupt, I need to speak with you for just a sec," I say, pulling Elliott's arm.

"See Paige, you worried for nothing," says Elliott, leaning in to kiss my cheek.

"You're right, everyone seems so happy!" I look around the room at the blissful scene. "Maybe Hailey will be happy with Derek after all."

"Who knows, but the good news is that it's not up to you," says Elliott with smile.

"Well, I do have control over when they cut the cake...and I say it's time!"

"Speaking of cake..." he dabs at my chin, "What have you been eating?"

I blush a little, when I realize I've been running around here with frosting on my chin! How embarrassing! "Thanks," I mumble and walk away.

After finding my mother, we rearrange the remaining spread of food on the dining table and create a new display—a dessert spectacular. I feel mighty proud at how good the transformation looks. Mom ushers the engaged couple towards the cake. A large group of people assemble and watch as the guests of honor beam at each other.

"Speech! Speech!" someone shouts from the crowd. Derek raises his hand and nods his head in recognition.

"First, I would like to say how grateful Hailey and I are that you all could be here with us tonight. I can assure you this is only the beginning of many fun wedding festivities." There are a few cheers from the group, and he continues, "We would also like to extend our thanks to both Elliott and Paige. Paige, you have truly outdone yourself, tonight."

Derek raises his glass in the air, for me! This is great! Everyone's staring at me, smiling and cheerful. I raise my glass and am about to . . . but suddenly, the night takes an unexpected turn, as the front door flies open. Everyone's attention shoots in that direction, and a gust of wind whips through the foyer and into the dining room, a few balloons swirl around in its wake. Standing in the doorframe is a disheveled Julian!

Immediately, I look over and see Hailey's reaction. She has lost color. Her gaze flits over to me and narrows. Derek watches her reaction and appears puzzled by the display. I panic! What do I do! What do I do! This is terrible!

"Glad you could make it! I never thought you'd arrive!" Elliott exclaims cheerfully, walking over to greet Julian. "Come on in, drinks are in the kitchen!" Elliott puts his hand casually on Julian's shoulder and escorts him out. I love my husband.

I gasp for air and look around the room. No one seems to be aware of anything. I take my napkin and fan my face with it. The group seems to have lost interest in the speech and have already dispersed around my house. Derek cuts into the cake, but Hailey continues staring vacantly at the door.

I slink out of the room, hoping to avoid Hailey, all together. I weave through clusters of people, as I make my escape. But just before I enter the kitchen, I feel a strong hand grasp my arm. I turn and see an irate Hailey glaring at me.

"What's going on here, Paige?" I can hear fury in her strained voice.

I look around, there are people everywhere. I scramble, trying to come up with someplace more private for us to talk.

"Hailey, you haven't seen my new vanity!" I declare loudly. "Come with me and I'll show it to you!" I take her hand and direct her away from the throngs of guests.

When we reach my bedroom, I shut the door and lock it. Hailey hasn't turned around yet, and I stare at her back, my hands still tightly clinched to the handle.

I clear my throat before saying, "Hailey, I'm so sorry about this. I didn't expect Julian to actually show up."

"You mean you *invited* him here? How could you!" She turns around, and I can see her eyes are becoming red.

"Let me explain. I went to his condo to find you . . ." I begin, but she cuts me off.

"Are you completely mad? What were you thinking?" She paces the floor, waving her hands in the air. "How did you even know where he lives?"

"I didn't know, I mean I knew, but that's not important right now. All right, I realize it was a bad idea to see him. It's just that you wouldn't answer your phone, and I was so desperate to talk with you."

"You went by Julian's place," Hailey states, shaking her head in obvious disbelief.

"In all fairness, before I knocked, I turned to leave. He must have heard me, because he opened the door anyway," I say, faltering a bit because her face is stricken with horror. I really don't want to say anymore, but I force myself to continue, "Julian and I only talked for an hour or so. I felt so terrible for what I did to you. I was only trying to help."

"You tried to help me what? Ruin my life? I had things handled. After you confronted me, I broke it off with Julian. I'm trying to do what is sensible here! Derek and I have been reconnecting. Only now, our relationship is going to be blown out of the water!" She throws herself dramatically onto the bed, sitting with her hands clasped in her lap.

"Not necessarily. Julian is with Elliott in the kitchen. I'll go in there and encourage Julian to leave. Derek won't notice a thing."

Hailey doesn't say anything. Her arms are now crossed over her chest. It's difficult, but I successfully keep my mouth shut.

"I don't know, Paige. Maybe it's time for me to confess to Derek. I can't keep living a lie," she says with a sigh.

"Hailey, who do you want to be with twenty, thirty, even forty years from now? Who do you see yourself growing old with? If you have any doubts about Derek, you shouldn't marry him."

"That's funny, because I recall you telling me I was a horrible person because I had betrayed Derek," she says, slowly shaking her head. "I'm not sure what to do anymore."

I sit beside Hailey and place my hand over hers. "I was wrong."

She looks at me, and I can see the tears welling up.

"That's great, Paige. When did you decide this?"

179

"Right after I had a vision about Emma and Andrew. Did you know she was engaged to someone else before she married our great grandfather?" I say excitedly.

"Paige, do you mean to tell me you actually believe in these 'visions'?"

"They were accurate about Julian. How else did I know you were with him? How did I find his condo? Wait, so that was how I found his condo," I suddenly realize. "Anyway, I think there's something to the visions. Perhaps I was meant to see Emma's life so I could help you."

Hailey stands from the bed and walks toward the door.

"Look, I realize you're trying to help me, but I think I need to figure this out on my own," she says, turning the handle.

"Wait Hailey, can't you please just give me another second? I have more I'd like to say."

"What now, Paige?" she asks in obvious frustration.

"It's just that . . . I know I was hard on you the other night. I judged you without giving you the benefit of the doubt. I shouldn't have done that."

"Let's just forget about the other night. I'm ready to move forward in my life and leave all of the negative things in the past."

"What are you going to do?"

"I'm not sure," she says, rubbing her hand roughly over her forehead.

"For whatever its worth, I hope you follow your heart and pursue a life with the man you believe will make you happy."

"Where did that come from? You don't sound anything like you. Normally, you lecture me about how I need to behave like a grownup and be more responsible." Her eyes narrow and she looks at me suspiciously.

"I know. I suppose I've gained a new perspective on life," I say, shrugging my shoulders.

"I'm still not sure what to make of this 'new Paige,' but I appreciate your understanding."

"Oh and another thing, when Mom and I refer to you as the 'creative one' it's not always meant as an insult. I admire your artistic side," I offer smiling.

"I don't get you. I'm not even sure how to respond, but thanks, I guess." Again, she reaches for the handle, "I'm going out there and I'm going to fix this mess."

"Good luck!" I exclaim, while crossing my fingers and arms. She smiles a little and opens the door. I'm still sitting on the bed, unsure what to do next. I've made a mess of things.

Wait a minute, I know what to do! Enthusiastically, I jump up and run out of the room. I enter the kitchen and see Hailey standing in front of Julian. Elliott has backed away from them and is inching out of the room. I rush over, and after seeing me, a hint of relief comes to my husband's face.

"What's happening?" I whisper. We're standing, somewhat obstructing the view from any potential onlookers.

"I'm not entirely sure. Hailey just stormed in here and started tearing into Julian," explains Elliott. "I feel bad for the guy. He seems to be decent and friendly enough."

"I need your help. Can you distract Derek for me? I've got to get Julian out of here!" I say anxiously.

"Paige, don't you think you've *helped* enough? Let Hailey handle this."

"Please, I need to correct my mistake," I say desperately. Elliott sighs, but doesn't answer. I begin to plead more, but he stops me.

"Fine, I'll just go and find Derek, but you owe me." Elliott winks and heads towards the dining room.

Chapter Nineteen

Hailey and Julian are really arguing. She yells at him, and for a moment even I'm scared, but then he fires right back. Although I'm frightened to death by them, I try to appear confident when I finally approach.

"Hey guys!" I say casually, placing a hand on both of their shoulders. They stop yelling but are still glaring at each other. All right, I know I can do this. "So Julian, I'm really glad you decided to come, but I'm thinking maybe you two should take this up another time," I say, showing them a huge grin.

After a few extremely awkward seconds, they look my way, but quickly return to their heated discussion. It's as if I'm not even here.

Julian says a little too loudly, "Hailey, you don't love that guy! You know you should be with me!"

"You think you know about everything, when you don't have a clue!" shoots back Hailey.

This isn't going well, not at all. Quickly, I interject, "I have a great idea! Why don't you both follow me, and I'll find a place you can talk."

I peer over my shoulder. I can't believe somebody hasn't noticed the fight taking place in the kitchen. These guests are oblivious.

Hailey may be looking at me, but Julian's eyes are dead set on her. I've never before seen such intensity in a stare. Ooh, it's kind of sexy. How can I get Elliott to look at me like that?

"Thanks Paige," Hailey acknowledges.

We are able to walk back to Elliott's office without running into anyone. I may actually get away with this! I show them the room and swiftly leave. After walking out, I quietly shut the door and slump against it. Before I am able to walk away, I hear more of their heated exchange. By the sound of it, they are really going at it. I'm guessing this will be the last I see of Julian. Such a shame, I was just beginning to like the guy.

Oh well, I nervously bite my lip and venture out to find Elliott.

Just as I'd hoped, Elliott and Derek are laughing it up with some fellow co-workers. It appears Elliott has produced his new laptop computer and is showing the gang its key features. What a nerd, I'm thinking. But then I see the small group of guys surround him and watch with keen interest.

"Nicely handled, Elliott," I say to myself and lean against the wall, watching Elliott's fellow nerds marvel at the technology.

Out of nowhere, my mother appears and is standing beside me. "I haven't seen your sister for a while. Not since that handsome stranger entered the scene. I don't suppose you know anything about what's going on?"

"Um, no, I'm not sure what you're talking about," I say, unconvincingly. I've never been good at lying, especially to my mom.

"That's what I thought. Come over here; I'd like a word with you, young lady." She takes me by the arm and leads me into the kitchen.

"Paige, I want you to tell me what is going on here," she says firmly, her eyes constricting to small slits. I hate it when she quizzes me. I keep my mouth shut in response. She leans closer towards me and says, "I will find out what Hailey is up to, with or without your help. I'm guessing it's probably better I hear it from you, than someone else. Or shall I go ask Derek?" She peers over in his direction.

Involuntarily, I look in the direction of Elliott's office. My mother's attention is drawn to that area. She peers back at me, appearing satisfied.

"I suppose I'll just have to see for myself," she says and heads down the hall.

"Mom!" I holler. What am I going to say? Quick, I must come up with something or it'll be too late, and she'll walk in on Hailey and Julian. "Mom, you're right! Let's go somewhere else to talk about this, okay?"

My mom doesn't pay attention to me. She's walking toward the office door. Instinctively, I jump and try to block her. She halts momentarily, and for a fleeting second, concentrates on me.

"Listen, please, don't go in that room!" I hang my head down in shame. "Hailey's in there with Julian. They're attempting to be a little more discrete."

"I see, and what do you know about this?"

"More than I want to. I think she's letting him have it, right now. Only I think she's making a mistake. Mom, she loves him. I know she does."

"Paige, I need to go in there. A bridal shower is not the proper place for Derek to find out about her having an affair!"

"All right, maybe you'll have some luck. I certainly haven't," I say and step aside.

My mother slithers past me and strides down the hall. Before she is able to knock on the door, we hear a loud crash! We look at each other, pure panic written across both our faces! I nudge her aside and throw open the door! My mother and I rush into the room . . . and our mouths just drop!

Julian and Hailey are half dressed, positioned awkwardly on Elliott's desk. Worst of all, their limbs are an entangled mess! Quickly, I haul my mother from the room. I slam the door shut, and we hurry down the hall. When we reach the kitchen, I think I can breathe, again.

Neither my mother nor I speak. All I can do is to stare at her. Finally, after a minute of stunned silence, my mother begins trembling. She's going into shock!

"Mom!" I yell. "Mom, are you all right?"

Surprisingly, a smile appears on her face and she snorts with laughter! I guess she'll be okay, after all. I join her and laugh hysterically.

My mom catches her breath and shrills, "Did you see the looks on their faces? Hailey's eyes were about to pop from their sockets!"

"Did you catch the looks on *our* faces?" I return, while still giggling.

Elliott enters the kitchen and sees us in a fit of laughter.

"What'd I miss?" He grins, and I motion for him to come closer.

"Let's just say, I'll never be able to work on a puzzle in your office again," I offer, still cringing at the vision of Hailey and Julian just as intertwined.

Elliott doesn't appear amused. In fact, he looks disgusted, rightfully so.

"Elliott darling, do be a dear and announce there is going to be a surprise bachelor party, and then usher everyone out of here," my mother says and calmly pats him on the back. "Go now and have fun!"

Elliott and I look at each other in complete disbelief. He shrugs his shoulders and leaves the kitchen. From the dining room, I can hear the guys ramble and plan. Derek declares something about how he can't leave without saying goodbye to Hailey. It is at this point, I believe the guys must have picked him up and hauled him out. Thank goodness for Elliott. He is doing exactly as my mother instructed and has the room cleared of the men in a matter of minutes.

"I must say, I'm impressed with Elliott this evening," I say more to myself, than my mother.

I look at my mother and notice she's frantically calculating something in her mind. "We've taken care of most of the party, but there are still some people in the family room. We must figure out how to politely ask the rest to leave."

185

Just then, Hailey's assistant Stacey enters the kitchen looking confused.

"Hey! I just arrived and everyone is leaving! What'd I miss?" Stacey asks, and my mother and I look at each other.

I know what to say. "Actually Stacey, I need your help. Hailey is suddenly not feeling so great. She's probably not in the best *position* to entertain guests right now. I'm not sure if what she has is contagious. I really hope it's not," I say and peer over at my mother with a grin, but she doesn't seem to find what I said funny.

Mom quickly interjects, "Would you be a dear and ask every-one to leave? Paige and I have our hands full at the moment."

"Of course I will! I can't believe Hailey's sick, and Derek just runs off to some bachelor party!" Stacey exclaims.

"It's just that . . . um, Hailey didn't want anyone to know, including Derek," I say. "She didn't want to ruin anyone's good time tonight. In fact, it was her idea to send Derek off to his bachelor party. You understand, right?"

"Okay, well, I'll go in there and make up some excuse to have everyone leave. Let her know I was here, and I hope she feels better soon," Stacey offers and leaves the room.

I can hear Stacey, as she ushers the rest of our guests out the door. I look at my mother, and wonder if she is feeling the same cocktail of emotions I am.

"I can't believe the lies I've had to tell, just to cover up for Hailey!" I say in irritation.

"It's for the best, I'm afraid. We wouldn't want everyone to know what Hailey is doing. She's in enough of a mess as it is," Mom says.

"What are we going to do, now?"

"*You're* not going to do a thing. Let *me* take care of your *sister*," she says with a frightening smile.

After everyone is gone, my mom grabs me by the hand and has me bring two chairs to the end of the hallway. We sit and watch the office door. There's a loud bang and some rants of profanity coming from the room. At last, an embarrassed looking Hailey and Julian open the door.

"I think we need to talk," my mother informs them.

To be honest, I'm surprised they were brave enough to come out and face her. I probably would have hidden under the desk or snuck out the window. Oh well, not my problem anymore, I'm thinking, as I begin to strut away from the awkward scene, but suddenly, my mother stops me in my place.

"And just where do you think *you're* heading off to?" she asks me, and I'm frozen to the spot.

I shrug my shoulders and look down. I peer over at my mother and mumble, "I just thought I'd give you some privacy."

"I don't think so. Now, I want you all to take a seat," instructs my mother.

In a matter of seconds, Mom has Hailey, Julian, and me lined up in a row. My mother paces the floor, with her hands grasped behind her back. I am reminded of a drill sergeant I saw on TV, only the one standing before me is much scarier.

Nervously, I pick at my nails. I glance over at Hailey's hands and see she is doing the same. I can't believe after all these years my mother still has the same effect on us. As much as we love her, and as old as we are, she can strike fear into our hearts like a viper.

I hear my mother's steps come to a halt and assume she is glaring angrily down at us. "The way you three have acted tonight is despicable! I am shocked by the adolescent behavior! What do you," she directs her booming voice toward Hailey, "have to say for yourself?"

"I'm sorry," mutters Hailey, swiftly looking back down towards her lap and proceeding to chew on the side of her nail.

"Hailey, that's pretty pathetic," my mother sighs and turns to Julian. "What about you? What in the world were you thinking, coming here tonight? Were you trying to completely destroy my daughter's reputation?"

"No ma'am," he pauses and glances at Hailey. "The truth is . . . I love your daughter, and I can't sit back and watch her marry another man." He looks at Hailey, and she appears to soften at his gaze.

"That's a very romantic notion. Funny thing, Hailey has failed to ever mention you to me. What was your name, again?" my mother asks, and I try to refrain from giggling.

"Julian," he says, his eyes still twinkling at the sight of Hailey.

"Julian, do you not agree perhaps another venue would have been more appropriate for you to declare your undying love to my daughter?" inquires my mother, raising her eyebrows.

"You're right, of course," he says. "I guess I panicked. When I met Paige the other night, she invited me to come and set things right. I felt I had to be here, or I'd lose Hailey forever."

Hailey and my mother look horrified, and my mom questions, "I see, and Paige, exactly why, may I ask, would you invite Hailey's lover to her bridal shower?"

Yikes, it sounds so horrible when put like that.

I rub the sides of my head and hope to disappear from this awful scene. When I return my attention to my mom, I see she is still waiting for my response.

"I guess . . . I panicked, too?" I'm biting my lip and trying to avoid the intense glare I'm receiving from Hailey. "Look, Hailey and I had a falling out. I said some things I wish I hadn't. I was only trying to help. I realize I shouldn't have asked for *him* to show up here tonight." Quickly, I shift my gaze toward Julian, who appears hurt. "Julian, I am so sorry. We should have arranged a better place for you and Hailey to reconcile. I really wanted to help you guys work things out. And you," I look at my sister, "weren't making things any easier by not accepting my calls." When I am finished, I sit back against the couch, hoping my interrogation is over.

"I see," says my mother, running her hand along her cheek. "Paige, I'd like to have a word in private."

"Great! I'll just head off into the bedroom. Take all the time you need out here," I say in delight, leaping from the couch and then boogying out of the room.

"Paige, not so fast, I would like a word with *you*," Mom explains, and my smile falters. She points a long finger toward the star crossed lovers, still sitting on the couch. "You two stay put. This is far from over. If I were you, I'd take the next few minutes and work out what you plan to do. *And* Julian, you may want to fix that button."

How embarrassing for them. I muffle a chuckle, as I am lead into my bedroom by my mother. I feel a lot like I did as a child after being caught doing something wrong. I'm an adult, and I shouldn't be scolded by my mother. Just when I get the nerve to leave the room, however, she nudges me in the direction of the bed. I am forced to sit, and she promptly joins me.

"Paige, what is happening with you? Do you want to talk about it?" Mom asks and reaches for my hand.

I look up and am surprised by her all-knowing expression. "What do you mean?"

"It's not like you, becoming wrapped up with such ridiculous nonsense. And lately, you've been different, somehow."

My mom *couldn't* know what is happening to me. That would be impossible.

"Paige, look at me," she says before I can answer. She lifts my face and holds it tenderly in her soft powdery hand. "I have a feeling I'll understand. In fact, maybe I can help shed a little light on your new *talent*." She places emphasis on the word talent, and I feel my body stiffen. Did Elliott or my sister say something?

I'm completely caught off guard and am dumbstruck on how to respond. Finally, after staring at her with my mouth wide open, I speak, "I'm not sure you would understand, Mom."

"Try me."

I take in a deep breath and then pour out my heart, "Okay, a few days ago, I'm standing in my kitchen and suddenly, it isn't *my* kitchen. I am looking in the mirror, but it's not *my* reflection I see. For months, I'm living Delilah's life and suddenly, *ZAP!* I'm back in my body and only half an hour passed." I pause, waiting for my mother's reaction.

"I see, but what does this have to do with Hailey?" she asks.

"Well, the day I went to pick up Hailey's wedding ring, I tried it on for size. But, when I looked down, I didn't see *my* hands, I saw Hailey's! But more importantly, I saw Julian. I saw Julian through Hailey's eyes, and I could actually feel her love for him!" I shake my head in dismay. "What was I to do?"

"What *did* you do?" Mom asks softly.

"Well, I confronted Hailey about it. Of course, she just denied everything, which made me really angry. We exchanged some rather heated words, and Hailey left. But then, I had a third vision. After you gave Emma's dresser to me, I flashed into her life."

I shift my position, beginning to relax a bit. "By the way, did you know Emma was practically engaged to another man before meeting our great-grandfather?" My mother's expression is difficult to read. She is sitting very still, so I continue, "Anyway, after watching Emma find her *true* love, I just knew I had to help Hailey, and that's when I went to see Julian."

After a few seconds of silence, my mother finally speaks, "Since the moment you were born, I wondered if this day would come, and how I would explain your talent to you…I'm still not sure what to say, but you are not going crazy. The things you have seen are real. They are memories of events that have truly taken place. In fact, your experience is not unique. A long line of women in our family have been blessed with a natural gift to see the lives of others. I wish I had been one of them."

"I don't understand. You knew this about me?"

"Not necessarily, no. I suspected, but I didn't know. I wondered when, as a child, you would tell me all about your imaginary friends. They changed from month to month. Do you recall your imaginary friend, Mr. Willis? He was your favorite. You began talking about him just after you discovered his set of gardening tools in the shed. It always struck me as funny how accurate you were in your description of the man, although you had never met him. After all, he passed away shortly after you were born. Nice old man."

"I do remember him!" I exclaim excitedly. "I thought I had made him up! I can't believe he was actually real . . . and you haven't told me he existed before now."

"What do you suppose I should have said? I wasn't certain you had inherited the gift. As far as I knew, you could have learned about Mr. Willis through a conversation you overheard between your father and me," my mother replies. "I decided to simply watch you. It was perfectly normal for a child of your age to have imaginary friends. You stopped talking about them when you were about nine years old, and I simply assumed perhaps your 'friends' *were* just imaginary and not real."

"I see," I say, still absorbing her words.

"Anyway, the gift bounces around the family, with no real rhyme or reason. What I do know is that *my* mother could do the same. She felt sorry for me that I had not been granted the same gift and she shared with me all of her fantastic tales. Most of them were extraordinary. I remember listening to her, as she described other people's lives." My mom looks at me and asks, "Is there anything else you'd like to know?"

"What causes the visions? Why am I starting to have them now? Will they stop coming eventually? Yeah, I guess I have a lot of questions for you."

"You call them 'visions.' That's cute. My mother called them 'glimmers.' She used to describe how everything became so sharp, the air would glimmer." Mom stares toward nowhere in particular. "Well, to answer your questions. They generally begin when you hold or wear something that was once important to someone else—an item that still carries 'emotional glimmer.' You were born with this talent, and I'm not sure why it has resurfaced now. My mother started when she was sixteen. The visions came and went for her, usually when she least expected it. Don't let it worry you, though, my mother lived a normal life and so will you. In fact, she said that eventually she enjoyed those moments. She loved seeing life from someone else's perspective."

"I understand that. After I got over the shock, I discovered they were kind of fun. Only, to be perfectly honest, I'd rather not see what is happening in Hailey's life, at least not first hand," I say, and we both laugh.

"I'll tell you what, let me go and deal with Romeo and Juliet. You and I can discuss this more tomorrow."

I smile at her comment and hesitate before asking, "So, just to be clear, I don't have to go out there with you?"

"No, you've had enough to deal with tonight," Mom says before standing and kissing my forehead. "Sleep tight."

"Thanks Mom. And you know what, I like the name 'glimmers.' I think I'll use that," I say with a smile still plastered on my face. "Goodnight."

"Goodnight, dear," she says, leaving the room. Before the door shuts behind her, I hear her lecture begin for my sister and Julian. "Now, as for the two of you . . ." and the door shuts mid-sentence. Darn, what was she about to say?

I debate about whether or not I should listen. Right now, I'd love to see the looks on their faces. That's probably not such a great idea, though. Instead, I'll take a hot bath and fall into bed.

~ * * * ~

Elliott drags into the bedroom around 3:00 in the morning. I guess he and the boys took Derek to an Irish pub in Winter Park. They spent the evening playing darts and drinking Black & Tans. Actually, it sounds like they had a great time.

I promise him the situation with my sister is under control, and my drill sergeant mother is on the case. I give him the play-by-play account on the lecture she gave us. I also tell him about what I learned from her about my little "condition." All in all, he seems to handle this information rather well.

~ * * * ~

As I awaken the next day, I snuggle closer to Elliott and discover I have a whole new appreciation for him. I stare at his sleeping face, when suddenly, his chest starts heaving erratically.

"She called them Romeo and Juliet?" he says, while laughing. "I would have loved to have heard her lay into them."

"Me too, I almost listened through the door!" I say embarrassedly.

"Do you have any idea how it went?"

"No, but I'm dying to find out. Let's go track down my mother and make her talk!" I leap out of bed and hurry to my closet. Just then, I realize Elliott is still under the covers and doesn't appear eager to move. I look at him curiously and ask, "Aren't you coming with me?"

"I'm thinking . . . no," he says and rubs his hand over my side of the bed. "Actually, I'm thinking, it's still early. We should stay here. The kids are at the neighbors' house, and I believe you owe me for my many acts of heroism, last night." He grins widely and slinks further under the sheets.

"Oh really," I say, making my way to his side of the bed. "And what exactly do you have in mind?"

When I'm close to the edge, he grabs my wrist and pulls me towards him. I land with a thud on his chest and begin to laugh.

"I guess you just answered that question," I tease, playfully landing kisses on his face.

~ * * * ~

An hour passes before we decide to emerge from the room. My anxiousness amplifies, as I hear hushed talking come from the next room. When I open the door, I see my mother is on the phone. I overhear her say goodbye with words of love, before hanging up.

"Mom, I have to know. What did you say to Hailey and Julian?" I eagerly wait for a response and plop down on the high back chair, leaning my elbows on the countertop.

"Paige, must you be involved in every aspect of your sister's life?" My mother looks up at me and shakes her head.

I sit back a little in surprise and say, "So you're not going to tell me? Come on, how did it end? What are they going to do?"

"They have a lot to think about and discuss with each other. I have serious doubts about the wedding with Derek ever taking place," Mom says, stopping long enough to stir cream into her coffee cup. "It's probably a good idea to hold onto the gifts. Perhaps you can put them in the office," she says, lifting one eyebrow.

We are laughing hysterically, as Elliott walks into the room.

"It seems there's a lot of humor in this house these days," he says, planting a kiss on my cheek. He stops by the coffee pot and puts his arm around my mother's shoulders. "Nicely handled, Sarge." He flashes a smile and pours his coffee.

"Whatever do you mean?" she says, fluttering her eyelashes innocently.

"I just hope this whole mess will be resolved soon, the sooner the better. I have to face Derek at work on Monday," Elliott says while sitting in the chair beside me. He places his hand on my knee and the other grasps his drink.

"Like I said, I am confident this will be resolved rather quickly," my mother reassures us.

Chapter Twenty

"**P**aige, hurry up; your sister's here waiting for us!" Elliott yells from the living room.

"I'll be right there! I just have to finish getting ready!" I run my hands through my hair and straighten my new dress. I still can't believe I managed to not only design, but sew my very own dress. It actually looks pretty darn good, if I do say so myself. It's tan with black embroidered designs dancing about the bottom. The top is styled with an empire waist and the fabric drapes nicely to just above my knees.

"Come on, Paige. We're going to be late. Wow, you look fantastic!" says Hailey, her head peeking through my bedroom door. "And I love your hair!"

"Thanks! I owe it all to Marcus! You were right about him—he is amazing!" I exclaim, spraying my hair in a light mist.

"I wonder if I should have seen him earlier today. He could have helped me with this heaping mess on top of my head." She motions to her beautiful hair with a look of disgust.

"Are you kidding me? You look gorgeous!" I say, rushing over to her. "And I love your little black dress. You know what, you are literally glowing."

"I suppose it's because a huge burden has been lifted from my soul. I can finally sleep at night. Paige, I can't believe I waited so long to choose between Derek and Julian. I should have known what was 'sensible,' a long time ago."

"Well, I know you made the right choice," I say, and we stare at each other with large smiles.

"What are we waiting for? Let's go!" she says, pushing me out the door.

Elliott and the sitter, Jenny, are standing in the family room. He is giving Jenny instructions on how to use the television remote.

"Hi!" I say cheerfully. "Honestly, Jenny, it took me days to fully understand how to use that remote control correctly."

"Hopefully, I won't have to call you later for remote trouble-shooting," she says and peers up smiling. "You look amazing! Where did you get that dress?"

"Thanks. I made it," I reply.

"You made *that* dress? You actually *sewed* it together?" Hailey asks, looking startled.

"Yes, I did," I say nonchalantly. Why is Hailey looking at me so oddly?

"Since when have you ever sewn anything?" Hailey asks.

"Since Mom taught me how," I say smugly.

"She taught you how when you were ten. You haven't sewn a thing since," counters Hailey.

"Sure I have. In fact, I made those pillows," I say, pointing towards the couch.

"Pillows are a little different than designing a dress," says Hailey, tugging at my hemline. "This isn't going to unravel later is it?"

"No, I think it'll be fine."

"Well, I'm impressed. Not only does it look fantastic, it may actually stay together. I want one too. Only, can you make it in violet?" she says, still admiring my work.

"I suppose so," I say. "So you really like it?"

"Yes, you have some serious talent!" Hailey exclaims.

"Thanks."

"Mommy, I want you to make a fairy dress for me, with wings and a wand!" Elle exclaims, appearing out of nowhere.

Liam is quick to chime, "Yeah Mom, could you make an alien costume for me? I want it to have big bulging eyes and lots of green slim!"

"Sure guys," I say, brushing my fingers through Liam's soft golden strands of hair. "Are you ready for these little characters tonight?" I say to Jenny.

"I think I can handle them," Jenny says, nudging Elle affectionately. Elle smiles adoringly up at her.

"We're going to watch the new fairy princess movie, right Jenny!" Elle exclaims.

"No, we're watching the new movie with those robotic aliens!" Liam counters.

"All right, it looks like we're having a movie marathon. How about if I get the popcorn ready," I hear Jenny say, as I begin to make my exit.

Hailey and I walk outside. Elliott is standing by the driver's side of the car with his hands rhythmically tapping the roof.

Hailey says quietly into my ear, "He appears to be more anxious about this than I am."

"I know; I think he is," I observe.

Hailey and I both enter the back seat.

"What am I, your chauffer tonight?" Elliott asks, sitting behind the wheel.

"That would be great! Thanks, you're the best!" I say and pat him lightly on the shoulder.

He shakes his head and starts the car.

"So are you nervous?" I ask Hailey.

"Yes. This is a huge event! I just hope everything goes well," she says, her knees shaking.

"After all of your hard work, I know everything will be perfect. It has to be," I offer.

We continue our drive down the highway towards the downtown area. It is a gorgeous May evening. The sun is setting brilliantly in the west, and there is a crescent moon overhead. For the first time in months, I feel like everything is right with our world.

I stare out my car window and sigh. Suddenly, I feel a nudge on my side. I look over toward Hailey and realize she is anxiously shifting around on her side of the seat.

"Are you going to be all right?" I ask.

"I guess so. I just wish he could have ridden with us. He's good at calming my nerves," says Hailey.

"You'll see him soon enough, don't worry," I offer.

Our car rolls around to the front of the restaurant. The place is already jammed with people. Everyone looks so elegant, too. Our doors are opened for us, and we step onto the sidewalk. I loop my arm through Hailey's and peer up at the sign. I have to shake my head and look again. Did I just see that correctly? The sign clearly reads *Desirez'* in red letters, curling over a shiny black surface.

I'm busy studying the sign and barely notice the trendy artwork lining the hallway. We reach the elevator at the end, and the sign to my left also reads *Desirez'*. How is that possible?

I'm still marveling at the coincidence of the name, when Elliott nudges me. "Paige, the elevator's here."

And Hailey adds, "You're planning on taking it, right? Otherwise, it's kind of a long hike up to the top."

Only, I can't move. Something begins to stir within me. It's as if I can sense a storm is coming. Hailey edges me into the elevator and suddenly, I realize she is staring at me.

"Are you paying attention to anything?" she says and raises her eyebrows.

"I don't recall you ever mentioning the name of the restaurant to me before. Where did it come from?" I ask Hailey.

"Why do you have that strange expression on your face? Are you okay?" she asks and places her hand on my shoulder.

"It's nothing. I was just wondering. It's not a very common name. It's asking, what you desire, in French," I say.

"I'm impressed. I didn't realize you understood the language of love," Hailey says, stepping out of the elevator. When we reach the main foyer, she peers anxiously around the room. "I don't see him, yet."

"He's probably just busy greeting people," I offer.

She lifts her body up to her tip-toes, searching over peoples' heads. Her eyes shift erratically around the area. On the other side of the foyer, four girls, each in trendy black shirts and pants, stand behind a dark-brown box. They wear headsets, and although they smile, their eyes are anxious. One of the girls is directing guests toward the bar.

The floors are a mixture of travertine and wood. I'm taking in the pattern of the carefully arranged boards beneath my feet, when I bump into someone. I glance up and realize it is Hailey's assistant.

"Sorry, Stacey, I wasn't watching where I was going. There is so much to take in here," I say, still peering around the room.

"Don't worry about it. I've been here a million times and I'm still taking it all in. It turned out pretty fantastic! I mean, I saw the sketches before, but I still had no idea it would be this cool!" Stacey offers excitedly.

"Hi Stacey, what do you think?" Hailey asks, moving closer towards us.

"You truly outdid yourself. I can see a mixture of the original plans along with your subtle flair for detail sprinkled throughout. Gee, I wonder what inspired you to create a space like this," Stacey says, nudging Hailey lightly.

Hailey nudges her back, and when she looks up her smile brightens. About a hundred feet away stands Julian, talking with a petite woman.

"There he is! I can actually feel butterflies in my stomach!" she exclaims. "I suppose in time I won't feel them anymore."

"That's not always true," I say, peering over to where Elliott is standing; he's having a conversation with a co-worker of Hailey's. Do I still have flutters when I see him . . . yeah, there they are. Perhaps they aren't as noticeable as when we first met, but they're still there. "They may not be there all the time, but hopefully, they never go away."

"Come on, let me show you around!" Hailey says, eagerly tugging at my arm.

She leads me into the fashionable dining area. There are tables arranged throughout, partitions made of etched glass and dark wood divide them. I hear a loud whoosh come from the kitchen area and look over in that direction. Discretely hidden between the guests and the chefs are walls of glass. I can see people wearing white aprons and hats, busily preparing gourmet meals. I'm actually beginning to feel a little hungry and would love to see a menu. Suddenly, I feel a strong arm around my shoulder.

"Good evening, ladies." I hear from behind us.

I turn around and see Julian, lightly placing a kiss onto Hailey's cheek.

"Julian this place is amazing! Hailey told me the desserts are exquisite. I can't wait to sample some of them," I say, pulling Julian's gaze away from my sister. Lately, I seem to be interrupting a lot of their lovey-dovey moments.

"Would you like for me to have a plate made for you?" he offers.

"No, you're busy enough, but I'd love to see a menu," I say peering over to where I believe the food is located.

"No problem. I'll be right back," Julian says and runs off in the direction of the hostess.

"Oops, I could have gotten it myself," I say, feeling slightly guilty.

"Don't worry about it," says Hailey.

"Here you are," he says, wearing a proud grin on his face.

"Thanks," I say and look down at the menu. It's made of black leather with the name *Desirez'* scrolled across the front in red. "Julian, where did you come up with the name for the restaurant?" I ask, running my fingers over the surface.

"My business partner came up with it years ago. It's the same name as the Palm Beach site," he explains. "By the way, she's here. In fact Hailey, she was asking to see you earlier."

"Paige, you'll just love Mrs. B! I only just met her a few weeks ago, but I feel as if I've known her for years," says Hailey.

"She's over by the bar; I was just talking with her," says Julian.

"Oh, let's go!" squeals Hailey.

"Right this way," Julian says and escorts us to another section of the restaurant.

It doesn't take long for me to see my husband. "Hailey, I'll catch up with you. I need to speak with Elliott for a sec."

"All right, we'll see you in a bit," Hailey says.

"Hello there stranger," Elliott says after seeing me.

"Hey, are you having a good time?" I ask.

"I'm having a great time. I was just talking with Roger; he's a riot."

"Do you mean the president of Hailey's company?" I cringe while imagining all of the 'funny' things Elliott must have said to him.

"Yeah, great guy."

"Listen Elliott, something strange is going on here."

"Uh-oh, are you about to *go* somewhere?" he asks, sounding concerned.

"Not at the moment. It's probably just a coincidence, but the name of this place is the same name Delilah chose for *her* restaurant." I wait for Elliott's reaction.

"You didn't mention that before."

"It didn't think to mention it before. Besides, I just found out what this place is called. Don't you think that's kind of weird?"

"I don't know. I mean, everyone has desires," he says, appearing thoughtful. "By the way, who *is* Julian's partner?"

"Her name is Mrs. B."

Elliott and I both stare wide-eyed at each other.

"So you don't really know her name?" he asks.

"Not yet, but she's with Hailey. Just over there."

"Well, I say we need to meet her. Maybe Mrs. B knows Delilah or something. Although, it is highly unlikely."

Anxiously, I grab Elliott's arm and glide through clusters of people. I'm almost to my sister, when I hear someone from my right side holler, "Delilah, you're needed in the kitchen ASAP!"

The woman talking with Julian and my sister turns toward the voice.

I gasp when I see her! It's her! It's Delilah Jones, only 24 years older! The space between us seems to stretch, appearing like a transparent tunnel. My throat tightens and my breathing is strained. I reach for Elliott's arm.

"Darlin', are you all right, you look like you've seen a ghost?" I hear a familiar southern accent say to me.

It's Delilah and her strawberry-blonde hair, she's staring down at me, concern on her face.

"Can you speak?" Delilah asks, motioning towards her throat. "Do this if you're choking?"

"I'm fine . . . thanks," I force my reply.

"Good thing, I can't have someone choke opening night." She smiles brightly and taps my shoulder. "I hope you enjoy the rest of your evening."

"I will, thanks," I respond weakly.

She smiles again and walks away.

My sister is the first to reach me. "What was that? Are you all right? I thought for sure, at any moment, Mrs. B was going to give you the Heimlich!" says Hailey, sounding both concerned and amused.

This is embarrassing! I have to pull myself together!

"What's going on, Paige?" Elliott asks, rubbing his hand over my back.

I peer up and can feel tears prickling my eyes. "That was Delilah!" I exclaim.

Elliott understands, but Hailey appears confused. I look over toward Julian; he is leaning over the bar explaining something to the bartender.

"What are you talking about? Who are you talking about?" Hailey asks.

Elliott interjects, "Hailey, Julian's partner happens to be the same Delilah from Paige's vision."

"No, it can't be!" Hailey exclaims.

"Delilah is from Lewisburg, West Virginia, and she used to dream about opening up her own restaurant," I say peering around the room. "And it looks like she did just that."

"I thought Mrs. B was from somewhere close to D.C. Hold on a sec," says Hailey. She scurries over to Julian and says something into his ear. He responds, before running his hand affectionately along her arm, and she smiles brightly up at him. Another cutesy moment passes before she shakes her head and her eyes widen. She pulls away from him and rushes back to me.

"She *is* from West Virginia. How did you know? You're sort of freaking me out," Hailey says.

"You're freaking out! How do you think I feel? I saw that woman less than a month ago, only she was only seventeen years old. Now, I find her here opening a restaurant with your boyfriend!" I exclaim; my breathing is frantic. In fact, my head feels light. "I need to sit down."

Elliott and Hailey find a nice leather chair for me. I use the oversized menu to fan my face. I realize I look ridiculous, but at the moment I don't care.

Chapter Twenty-One

Glasses clink, and laughter erupts sporadically from all around me. Hailey and Elliott are still trying to figure out what to do next. I can hear what they are saying, but in my mind, I'm replaying my interaction with Delilah over and over.

I glance up, and watch as Hailey's and Elliott's lips move. I'm having trouble understanding what they are saying because of their muffled voices. Hailey paces back and forth, while Elliott's hand fiercely rubs over his red and blotchy forehead.

Geesh, they really appear worried about me. I lean in a little closer and can finally hear what they are saying. I think maybe I can finally speak, too. "You know what will make me feel better, some of those yummy looking desserts. Do you think we could have someone load up a plate for me?" I ask Hailey, wearing my nicest grin.

"Oh, so basically you have been sitting there comatose for 15 minutes, and the first words out of your mouth are that you fancy a plate of pastries," states Hailey, giving me a stern look. "Do you realize how worried we've been? What's the matter with you?"

"Sorry. I didn't realize I was quiet for so long. I guess I've been shell shocked by meeting Delilah. Boy, that was a complete surprise," I say.

"Well, pull yourself together. We still have a long night ahead," Hailey says. "And Paige, I want to help you with your problems, really I do. Only, can we deal with them later?"

"Sorry, of course we can. After pretty much ruining your shower, I definitely don't want to upset this night for you," I say.

"Look, you didn't ruin my shower. In fact, if it weren't for you, I could very possibly have married Derek and let the true love of my life go. I'm happy now. Julian is perfect for me. It just took me a while to see that," she offers.

"Well, that's a relief. I promise to behave at your and Julian's wedding," I say, smiling.

"Good thing. I wouldn't want Derek to show up and cause a scene," she says and smiles back.

"Does that mean you and Julian have talked about getting married?" I prod.

"Sort of, I mean, the subject has been alluded to," she says while blushing. She then stammers, "You know, it's not like I'm wearing a ring or anything. I just have to wait until he's ready. I wouldn't want to push him or anything."

"Hailey, don't worry. Julian isn't going anywhere," I offer, trying to calm her.

"Why do you say that? I mean, what makes you so sure?" she asks.

"I can see it in his eyes every time he looks at you. It's very sweet, actually," I say and can hear Hailey sigh.

"All right, I'll get you a plate of desserts. Can I offer you anything else, my dear?"

"No, that will be all for the moment," I tease back.

Hailey gives an unconvincing scowl before leaving. I peer up at Elliott. I don't believe I've ever seen him wear that sort of expression before.

"Paige, are you going to be all right?" he asks, kneeling down to my eyelevel.

"I suppose so, but I'm still a little light headed. I think my blood sugar level just dropped or something."

"Well, I'm relatively certain the sugary desserts will help with that," he says with a half-grin.

"You think? I like the sound of that," I begin and realize he was just kidding. "Not funny. Unlike you, I do believe desserts will help me. I can feel it deep inside. I know they will do the trick."

Elliott's face suddenly doesn't appear as amused. It has reverted back into looking serious. I don't really like the transformation. I can only guess at what he is about to say, but I'm pretty sure I'd much rather discuss something fun, like pastries.

"Paige, you must understand this situation is very bizarre. Honestly, Hailey and I don't know what to do with all of this," he says, running his hand affectionately over my cheek. "It was one thing for you to tell us you were having visions; now, we're in a completely different league. To me, Delilah didn't *really* exist before, now she does. She is here in the flesh. I'm sorry, but I'm just having trouble grasping this."

"Elliott, I appreciate that you're trying to," I sigh. "How do you think I feel? I just made a complete fool of myself in front of Delilah! How am I supposed to show my face to her again?"

"Let me get this straight. Your visions have basically just been confirmed, and all you care about is that you choked a little in front of her?" he says exasperatedly.

"Well, yes," I say, running my hand soothingly over his back. "I accepted my new talent a long time ago, and although I enjoy my new gift, I never expected to actually meet Delilah."

"Here's your plate of goodies," Hailey has reappeared and sets the plate on my lap. "You're looking better. Do you think you're up to socializing?"

"Wow, this is delicious! You must try one of these!" I exclaim and shove a second mini pecan pie into my mouth.

Hailey lets out a loud sigh and stares at Elliott. The two seem to have a private conversation through their eyes.

"All right guys, remember me? I'm sitting right here. What's the plan?" I ask and pop in a chocolate truffle. "Seriously, you have to try this."

They look down at me and stare as if I'm from another planet. Elliott reaches for a cocktail napkin and swipes it across my chin. "If you keep plastering your chin with chocolate cream, I'll have to start carrying a roll of paper towels," he says with a smile.

"Ha-ha, very funny. Really, what should I do about Delilah? I'm thinking, I should probably run out of here and wait for you two in the car," I say.

Hailey is quick to offer, "Paige, you can't run away from this. You need to face her. It would be better if you didn't have food on your face and try not to choke this time."

I can't believe my sister's actually wearing a serious expression. I quickly exclaim in horror, "Hailey, I can't talk to her! Didn't you see my reaction last time? It was mortifying, really it was."

"Paige, I think Hailey is right. You can't run away from this. We'll be with you. Just act natural," Elliott says in an overly soothing tone.

"No, don't act natural. Just keep quiet and let me do the talking," Hailey says, and Elliott narrows his eyes at her. "What?"

"Paige will be fine. In fact, I think we should just explain to Delilah why Paige acted like that. Delilah seems nice enough. Maybe she'll understand, *and* she can help us fill in the gaps of Paige's glimmers," Elliott says. He quickly notices Hailey and I share an expression of pure shock, mouths hanging open and all. "What's wrong with telling the truth?"

"Oh, only that Paige will look like a complete psycho. Have you even considered that Delilah is Julian's business partner? I can't have her thinking my sister is crazy. Believe me, that is a very bad idea. Paige has been rambling on about this new special gift of hers to me for a month, and I'm only just now starting to believe it!"

"Gee, thanks Hailey," I say in between bites of chocolate mousse and Crème Brule.

"Sorry, I didn't mean it like that. I am supportive of you. I just don't understand what exactly is happening here," she offers, reaching down and plucking the raspberry tart. "Mmmm, this really is good."

"I know. Try the chocolate one there," I say, pointing to the yummiest looking dessert on the plate.

"Can we focus a little more here?" Elliott chimes. "I say we walk over to the bar, get a drink, and enjoy ourselves."

Hailey and I look at each other and shrug our shoulders.

"Okay, but if Delilah returns, you can't leave my side," I say and turn toward Elliott. "See, I told you a few desserts would make me feel better. I just needed a little sugar."

There's a band in the corner playing some fun jazz. From what I can see, this place is a real hit! I'm beaming with excitement for Hailey and Julian.

"Where have you three been hiding?" Julian asks and offers me a napkin. "Oh, I see you've been at the dessert table."

"Honestly sis, can't you keep your face clean for even a minute?" Hailey asks.

"Julian, this restaurant is unbelievable. In fact, I think it's my new favorite!" I exclaim.

"Thanks, Paige. I'm glad you like it. Hailey did a phenomenal job creating just the right atmosphere. It wouldn't be the same without you, babe," he says and winks at Hailey, who appears to blush slightly. I rub my eyes, because I know I must be imagining things. Hailey never blushes!

"Julian, we haven't seen the terrace, yet. I hear it has a nice view of the town," Elliott exclaims, smiling peculiarly.

"Right, well then, let me show it to you," Julian says just as awkwardly.

Julian extends his hand in the direction of the glass doors. Hailey and I walk ahead of the men, and she loops her arm through mine.

"The terrace overlooks the lake, has a gorgeous view, and is one hundred percent my design! It's my pride and joy!" she exclaims in my ear. "You could say the terrace has somewhat of an Asian influence. I ran my ideas through with the architect, and he loved them."

I turn around and realize that Elliott and Julian have fallen behind. I watch as they are having a serious discussion about something. I can't quite make out what they are saying, but Elliott is nudging Julian forward, as if reassuring him of something. What are they talking about?

"Paige, are you coming?" Hailey asks anxiously.

"Look at the guys; there's something going on here. Have you noticed they are acting a little strange?" I ask, still trying to read their lips.

"Paige, the only person acting strange tonight is you. Now, come on!" she says and tugs on my arm.

We walk through the double doors. A breeze is rustling sheer white curtains; stars sparkle in the sky; white paper lanterns glow and appear as if they are floating magically in the air. Tables are divided by delicate fabrics and bamboo clusters. Each booth is its own oasis, set apart from the rest of the world. How romantic. Elliott and I must have a date here sometime soon.

Aside from soft music playing, I can barely hear a sound.

"Oh Hailey, it's gorgeous. The best part of the restaurant," I say admiringly.

"Thanks. Julian gave me free reign out here," she says, brimming with pride. "You still haven't seen the view."

She leads me to the far side of the patio. A reflecting pool cascades over the building's ledge. When I stand closer, I peer over the side, and I see water is streaming down the building for an entire story. The wall has chiseled blocks that sporadically project out and the interesting design creates a path for the water to follow. Down below, clusters of chairs are surrounded by decorations mirroring the ones from up above. People are down there, how did they get there? I look around and discover that hidden along the sculpted blocks is a staircase leading to the oasis below.

"Wow, Hailey. This is really astounding. Everything in here is absolutely fantastic. You must be incredibly proud," I say.

"I am. The designs came together pretty easily. It doesn't hurt to fall in love while working on a massive project," she says, glowing.

Just then, Elliott and Julian appear out of nowhere.

"Did I just hear you say something about my divine presence inspiring you?" Julian asks, wrapping his arms around her body.

"Ha-ha, something like that," Hailey says and nuzzles into Julian's shoulder.

"Everything is perfect," I say quietly.

"Actually, it's not perfect, yet. Give me a sec," Julian says and runs off.

Abruptly, Elliott begins asking Hailey questions about her inspiration for her designs. Since when has he ever been interested in fabric swatches and mood lighting?

"Elliott, what are you and Julian up to?" I ask.

"What do you mean? Nothing, nothing at all," he says guiltily.

I'm watching him skeptically, when Julian returns.

Julian's standing with one arm behind his back, watching Hailey with keen interest. It seems as if he's waiting for something. Hailey's consumed by her conversation with Elliott and hasn't noticed. That's strange. Why did Julian rush over to the bar, if he wasn't planning to return with a round of drinks or bottle of champagne? I assumed we were going to have our own little celebration; a toast to wish good luck for a successful opening night.

All of a sudden, a woman joins the string quartet and begins to sing *At Last*, by Ella Fitzgerald. Oh, how nice.

As if on cue, Julian approaches Hailey, a red rose in his hand. Ah, that is sooo sweet. Wait a minute! Is there something shiny in there? What is that? Julian's face is consumed by a huge grin. What's going on here?

Actually, I think he's about to . . . he's about to . . .

"Hailey," he says and reaches for her hand.

She stops talking with Elliott and shifts her attention toward Julian. Elliott is wearing a goofy grin. He must be in on this little scene.

"For a while there, I was scared to death of losing you forever to someone else. I'm fortunate that I've been given a second chance. I don't want a day to go by that I don't get to spend at least a moment with you in my arms. I love you and want to spend the rest of my life with you," he says, handing her the red rose. "Please tell me you feel the same. Will you do me the honor of marrying me?"

I look up from the rose and watch Hailey's reaction. Are those actual tears in her eyes? Now I think *I'm* going to cry. She reaches for the rose and peers down. From the petals, she retrieves the most gorgeous ring I've ever seen.

Julian goes down onto one knee and places the ring on her finger. Hailey nods her head vigorously, up and down, while covering her mouth with her right hand.

"Hailey, you haven't actually answered yet. I'm not going to take my knee off of your foot until you say yes," he says and his smile is so large I can see his teeth sparkle.

"Yes, Julian! Of course, yes!" she exclaims and wipes a tear from her cheek.

He stands, and the two circle their arms around each other. I try to give them a moment before rushing over. I wait and wait. They are still hugging. How long are they going to embrace? I can't wait any longer and am ready to leap towards Hailey, but Elliott grabs my arm and steadies me in my place.

"Give them another minute, Paige," Elliott whispers.

I may narrow my eyes at him, but I agree and wait some more. After what seems like forever, the happy couple move away from each other. I lunge forward and squeeze my sister for all I'm worth. When I pull away, we bounce like little girls!

"Hailey let me see the ring!"

Proudly, she dangles her fingers, showing off her new finery. There's a round diamond, with the most unusual design in platinum, wrapping itself around the setting. It's very stylish and modern, just like my sister. And this time around, I'm *not* going to try it on for size.

Elliott approaches Julian, pats him on the back, and shakes his hand. "Welcome to the family. Good luck. You'll need it with these women."

I want to send Elliott a dirty look, but I can't stop beaming. Everyone seems so happy!

"Don't tell me I missed it," I hear that same southern voice appear out of nowhere, and my chest tightens.

"Sorry, I couldn't wait any longer," Julian says and hugs Delilah.

"Congratulations to you both!" Delilah says, reaching for Hailey's hand and admiring the ring. "It's beautiful, and this is so exciting! When Julian told me how he was gonna pop the question at the opening of the restaurant, I said I just had to witness it for myself. I can't believe I was held up in the kitchen. Enjoy the moment, darlin'. You'll remember this day for the rest of your life."

"What was it like for you on the day Mr. B proposed?" Hailey asks.

"Well," Delilah says with a sigh. "William proposed to me as we were sitting on a picnic blanket, right underneath the Washington Monument. It was very sweet, but I could tell he was rattled with nerves."

"You married William Berringer!" I shout a little too overzealously.

Delilah is wearing the oddest expression of confusion, and Hailey has her hand on her face, shaking her head.

"Yes, we married some time ago. Let's see, it's been about fifteen years now. Only, we met quiet some time before that," Delilah offers with a gleam in her eyes.

"You met while you worked at The Greenbrier Resort!" I say excitedly.

"Yes, we did. It started off as a summer romance. Thank goodness, he found me a few years later and swept me off my feet. In fact, he was instrumental in my opening up the first restaurant. He encouraged me to do it, he even drew up the designs," she says, smiling sweetly.

"He became an architect?" I ask, realizing I should settle down, only I can't control myself.

"Yes, he is an architect. How do you know so much about us?" she asks suspiciously.

Hailey quickly interjects, "Oh, you know, Julian can't stop talking about Mr. B, you, and the restaurant."

"Is Mr. B here tonight?" I ask anxiously.

"Not yet, but he will be. He had to drive in from Palm Beach tonight. He had an important meeting he just couldn't miss," Delilah offers.

Hailey exclaims over-eagerly, "I can't wait to finally meet him in person! I love his designs. I studied some of them in college!"

"Well darlin', I'll most certainly introduce you to him when he arrives. If you'll excuse me, I have to make sure the kitchen hasn't burned down to the ground yet," Delilah says and heads across the restaurant.

Hailey and I are left staring at each other. Simultaneously we burst out in laughter. Elliott and Julian peer over and see us keeling over, clenching our stomachs.

"See what I mean? These two are tough to read, and their mother—forget it," Elliott offers, and I swat his arm. "What?"

"You love me and you know it," I say playfully.

Elliott inches closer and softly touches his lips to mine. "I love everything about you, Paige. Even the nutty parts," he says sweetly (I think). "I saw you talking with Delilah. How'd it go?"

"It was fine. I may have appeared a little clairvoyant though. Hailey helped me out a bit," I offer.

Hailey interrupts, "A bit? If you had continued rambling nonsense to Mrs. B, she would have thought you were a stalker or something."

"That I'm a stalker? What about your obsessive need to meet her architect husband?" I shoot back.

"You're right. She probably thinks we're both completely mad," Hailey says, rubbing her hand on the side of her cheek.

"I can't imagine either one of you could possibly say anything that bad. I'm sure she adores you both," Julian says, sliding his arm around Hailey's back and squeezing her closer to him.

"I wouldn't be so sure about that," Elliott mumbles, barely holding back a chuckle.

"You think you are so funny, don't you," I say and narrow my eyes.

"Hailey, here's your chance to meet William for yourself," Julian says, peering behind me.

Swiftly, Hailey, Elliott, and I search for William. I don't see him yet. Where is he? All of a sudden, I realize a very illustrious looking man is approaching.

"Julian, there you are. I was just in the kitchen greeting my lovely wife. She mentioned you were over here," William says, shaking Julian's hand.

When Julian introduces William to Hailey, she beams from ear-to-ear. William's features are just as striking as I remember; his dark hair has begun to grey, making him look even more distinguished. In a way, he resembles his father. I wonder what ever happened to his parents. How does Delilah get along with his ice-queen mother? I'm just dying to ask, but decide to keep my mouth shut.

"Paige, Elliott, this is William Berringer, part owner and architect," Julian says and turns to William. "Paige is Hailey's sister."

"It's great to meet you both. I just heard the good news about Hailey accepting Julian's proposal. I suppose that makes us practically family," William offers.

Did he just say family? Heat rushes to my head. I'm dizzy. The thought of sitting across the Thanksgiving table from him and Delilah is overwhelming. Thank goodness Elliott is now chatting with Mr. Berringer, I mean William.

After a few minutes of listening to Elliott and William's conversation, I begin to feel confident enough to join in. Actually, it's as if I've known William for years (in a way, I suppose I have). It's strange to see how William and Delilah have aged. I remember them as teens. Today, they are only a about ten years older than I am. I wonder if we could be friends. What do we have in common? I know Delilah likes to cook, as do I. Maybe Elliott and I could have a dinner party and invite them over. Maybe they have kids. Our kids could play together. That would be so sweet.

I'm imagining all of the good times we'll have together, when I notice Elliott is staring at me. He winks playfully then returns back to his conversation with William.

I shift my attention away long enough to take in the surrounding atmosphere. The quartet is playing a sweet melody. I am surrounded by people sipping their cocktails, their voices rising and falling spontaneously. Elliott and Julian are laughing about something or another. My sister is explaining to William an idea she has for one of her new clients. He is staring thoughtfully at the floor, with his hand resting on his chin. I've seen him do that before, he must be interested in her ideas.

A loud sigh of contentment escapes from my mouth and a smile plasters my face. All of a sudden, I feel a hand rest carefully on my shoulder. I glance to my right and see Delilah looking ahead at the group.

"I hope you aren't sighing from boredom," she says.

"No, I'm enjoying this moment more than you'll ever know," I say and lift my glass to offer her a toast. "Here's to following your heart, doing what you love, and overflowing with success."

"I'll definitely drink to that!" she says excitedly and our glasses meet.

Epilogue

"**M**om, can we take Maggie to Magic Kingdom, please?" Liam asks, joining me in our kitchen.

"Sure. Elle and I would really enjoy that," I respond, flipping over a grilled cheese sandwich and appreciating the golden surface of the buttered bread.

"You know, maybe you guys could go to a different park. How about Animal Kingdom?" he offers hopefully, raising his eyebrows up and down.

"I'll tell you what, we'll stay far away from you little love birds. Besides, don't you think you're a little too young to go on dates?"

"Mom, Maggie and I are just friends! And don't you remember that I just turned eight?"

"Sorry, I forgot," I say while stirring a pinch of oregano into the tomato bisque. "Make sure Maggie asks her mom if it's okay."

He nods his head in agreement and walks away, punching numbers into the phone.

Thank goodness for theme parks. Since we have annual passes, much of our summer vacation will be spent there. Before the kids were finished with the school year, I filled my calendar with fun activities for us to do. Most of my brilliant ideas are working out great; however, I had to scratch 'Mom's Art Projects' after a little incident involving some handmade play dough. I may have many new talents, but arts and crafts are not one of them.

My children's laughter comes at me from all directions of my house, and I'll miss it when they're at camp next week. At least there, they'll be challenged creatively, unlike with me, where I'm just creatively challenged. I'm not sure what I'll do with myself while they're away. I'll probably use that time to catch up around the house. Oh who am I kidding, I'll waste away in front of the computer shopping on eBay.

Last week, I bid on a gorgeous Marc Jacobs bag. I watched my computer screen eagerly, waiting to see if the bag would be mine. In the end, I am delighted to say I reigned victorious!

"Liam just said we're going to Disney!" Elle exclaims, bounding into the kitchen, wearing her new homemade fairy outfit.

"It looks that way," I pause and watch as the tulle of her dress swishes. "How do you like your new costume?"

"I love it! Thanks, Mom. Can you make me another one? Maybe in white, I can be a snow fairy," she says, waving her wand.

"Sure, maybe we can stop by the fabric store tomorrow."

"That would be great! I want sparkly glitter on it, too," she says and dances out of the room.

"Elle, please change into something more comfortable, before we leave!" I holler in her direction, but with her selective hearing, I doubt she will.

I watch as she leaves, still admiring my handiwork. I'm pretty good at this sewing thing. Who knew? I surely had no idea I could make anything look that good. Strange, I have been doing a lot of things better lately.

Maybe I've gotten my new flair for cooking and sewing through my glimmers. Maybe they unleashed a hidden potential from deep within me. I can't believe I didn't realize this before! Now I *really* want to have another glimmer. I'd love to learn how to paint, or play an instrument, or fly a plane! If only I could find just the right object to help me leap into the life of a musician. I should buy a used piano! Maybe if I touch just the right key, I could have another glimmer! It would be so cool to find myself playing a concerto in front of an adoring crowd.

I may not have a piano or an airplane handy, but I know I have a paintbrush somewhere.

"There you are," I say to the fuzzy little tool.

All right, bring on another glimmer. I pull out some paints and paper. I'm going to paint like Picasso . . . . All right, this looks more like preschool art. This is ridiculous. I begin to rinse off the bristles, feeling a little silly. Even with the help of having a glimmer, I doubt I could ever learn how to paint *or* play an instrument. It's absurd to think I've gained a talent through having a glimmer. I could cook and sew all along; I must have just chosen not to until now.

Suddenly, I hear our doorbell ring. I make my way to the front of the house and peer through the window. It's our mailman. He's holding a package and some envelopes. A little thrill passes through me. I swing open the door and stare eagerly at the brown parcel.

"Here you are. I just need you to sign this for me," he says.

"Thank you for saving me a trip to the mailbox," I say and smile widely.

"No problem. Have a nice day," he says and returns to his vehicle.

Anxiously, I rush to the kitchen and set down the mail. I tear open the package, lean against the counter, and admire my new bag. Its black leather appears buttery soft. There are vertical zippers at the sides and the handle at the top is adorable.

My hands can't remain at my sides any longer. I reach over and grab the bag off the counter. They run over the surface and slowly pull open the magnetic-snap closure, exposing the inside. I peer down and rummage around. Inside a pocket, I feel a little card. After removing it, I read its contents. The name on it says Chloe . . . there's a phone number and email address, but there isn't a last name. I suppose this person doesn't need one. Maybe she's a pop star, like Prince or Madonna.

All of a sudden, the bag looks clearer. I stare at the little leather wormhole. Come on, come on. All right, this is it! At last, I'm having another glimmer! My eyes begin to water, but I don't dare blink. After what seems like five minutes, I look around and sigh in disappointment. Nothing has changed.

"Oh well, maybe later," I mutter and shrug my shoulders.

I set down the bag and shift through the pile of mail. An oversized envelope pops out onto the counter. I recognize the golden handwriting. It's Hailey's. I rip open the envelope and stare at the contents. Scrolling letters in glistening gold announce the upcoming wedding between my sister and Julian.

Finally, as Hailey often says, she is doing what is sensible. I look forward to the big day. This time around, she is actively participating in the plans. The only concern I have is all of the items she wants to borrow of mine. In fact, just the other day, she asked if she could use Emma's cameo earrings. Now, I don't have a problem with her wearing the earrings. It's all of the other things she wants to borrow, but that is another story all together.

The End

Look for Book Two:

Beyond Glimmers

Recipes

Delilah's Shrimp Etouffee

- 6 TBL unsalted butter
- 6 TBL olive oil
- 1/2 cup all-purpose flour
- 4 cups chopped onions
- 2 cups chopped yellow or orange bell peppers
- 2 cups chopped celery
- 2 TBL minced garlic
- 3 (14.5-ounce) can diced tomatoes
- 2 bay leaves
- 2 tsp salt
- 1/2 tsp cayenne pepper
- 1 tsp each of the following: thyme, oregano, pepper, paprika
- 1 quart chicken broth (I use Better than Bouillon—chicken flavor)
- 1-1/2 to 2 lbs medium shrimp, peeled and deveined
- 2 Andouille sausage links cut
- 1/4 cup chopped parsley leaves (I use dry)
- Steamed white rice

Directions

Heat olive oil in a medium pot set over medium heat. Add the flour and stir continuously to make a roux. Mix the roux over medium heat until the color of peanut butter, 8 to 10 minutes. In a separate large pot melt butter and sauté the onions, yellow bell pepper, and celery. Stir often for 10 minutes (add the garlic at the last minute so it doesn't burn). Mix roux in with the sautéed vegetables. Add tomatoes and season with the bay leaves, salt, and cayenne. Cook for 2 to 3 minutes and then whisk in the chicken broth. (I also add Tabasco, but you don't have to).

Bring the mixture to a boil then reduce to a simmer. Stir occasionally, for 45 minutes. Season the shrimp and sausage with salt, pepper, and paprika and add them to the pot, stirring to evenly distribute. Cook the shrimp in with etouffee for 5 to 7 minutes, or until they are cooked through. Add the chopped parsley to the pot and stir.

Serve immediately over steamed white rice.

Delilah's 'Bite of Delight'

Cake Instructions
- 1-1/2 tsp baking soda
- 2 cups sugar
- 1-3/4 cup sifted cake flour
- 1 tsp salt
- 3/4 cup cocoa powder
- 1 cup buttermilk
- 1/2 cup Mazola oil
- 1/2 cup buttermilk
- 2 unbeaten eggs
- 2 tsp vanilla

Preheat oven to 350. Grease and flour two 9" round tins. Sift together dry ingredients. Add 2/3 cup buttermilk and Mazola oil. Mix together. Then add ½ cup buttermilk, 2 unbeaten eggs, and vanilla. Mix again until well blended. Pour into round metal tins. Cook for 30 minutes at 350.

Filling Instructions
- 2 cups sugar
- 1/2 cup butter
- 1/2 cup milk
- 1/3 cup cocoa powder
- 2 cups instant oats
- 1 cup peanut butter cups (crushed)
- 1 cup peanut butter (smooth or nutty)
- 2 tsp vanilla

Over medium heat, combine sugar, butter, milk, and cocoa. Stir until mixture comes to a rolling boil. Remove from heat. Add peanut butter, blend together. Add oats, crushed peanut butter cups, and vanilla. Mix well and set aside.

Frosting Instructions
- 2-1/4 cups cocoa powder
- 2 cups softened butter
- 8 TBL cream
- 9 cups powdered sugar

- 1/2 tsp salt
- 2 tsp vanilla

Over low heat, melt cocoa and butter together. Add cream, salt, vanilla, and enough powdered sugar to spread. Blend together.

Once cakes have cooled, pop them out onto a clean surface. Spread peanut butter filling over the surface of one cake and place the other cake on top. Cover the outside of both cakes with chocolate frosting. Enjoy!

Paige's Roasted Rosemary Chicken

- 1 whole chicken
- 3 sprigs rosemary
- 6 cloves garlic
- 2 lemons
- 1/4 cup olive oil
- 1 tsp salt
- 1/2 tsp pepper

In a bowl, add rosemary, squeezed lemon juice, dice 2 garlic cloves, salt, pepper, and olive oil. Put the chicken in a sealable plastic bag and add the marinade. Seal the bag and refrigerate overnight.

Preheat oven to 350.

Remove chicken from marinade and place in a casserole dish or roasting pan, legs up and back down. Stuff 4 garlic cloves (whole), extra rosemary sprigs, and lemon wedges. Pour remaining marinade over, inside, and under chicken's skin.

Very loosely, place some tinfoil over top of the chicken. The amount of cooking time will vary, depending on size of chicken (usually, about one hour to one pound—check the bag the chicken came in).

When the chicken is done, transfer it to a cutting board, cover loosely with aluminum foil and let rest for 10 minutes. Remove the rosemary sprigs, lemon, and garlic from chicken. Carve and serve!

Paige's Roasted Garlic Potatoes

- 1 small (about 5 lbs) bag of red potatoes
- 3 TBL olive oil
- 1 tsp pepper
- 1 tsp salt
- 7 garlic cloves
- 3 TBL chives
- 2 TBL white wine vinegar
- 2 tsp Dijon mustard

Preheat oven to 375.

Slice potatoes into thin pieces and place in a bowl. Mix all of the ingredients together and spread evenly into a casserole dish.

Cook for about 35 minutes and check. Once potatoes are lightly browned, remove from oven. Squish the garlic cloves and spread over potatoes.

If you like, add parmesan cheese and return to oven for about 5 minutes. Enjoy!

About the Author

Currently, Barbara Brooke resides in sunny Florida with her supportive husband, two adorable children, gorgeous greyhounds, and scruffy mutt. She is actively creating new worlds and interesting characters for the next book in one of her series. Shhhh, can you keep a secret? Not only does she write spell-binding, heart-pounding women's fiction, but she also writes books for the young-at-heart, adventurous sort, who yearn to dive into a good young adult fantasy story. These particular books are written under the name H.B. Bolton, but that is another story all together.

Check out her websites
http://www.barbarabrookeglimmers.com
http://www.hbbolton.com

Follow her blog
http://www.barbarabrooke.wordpress.com

Become a fan on facebook:
http://www.facebook.com/#!/BarbaraBrookeAuthor
http://www.facebook.com/#!/GlimmersNovel

Acknowledgments

This book is dedicated to Brad, Lauren, and Wade. We have held together through the worst of storms, and through it all have remained strong. I love you and appreciate you more than any word in our extensive dictionary could ever express. Thank you, Mom and Dad for encouraging me to daydream and aim for the stars. Thanks, to all of my close friends and family who endure my endless babbling about my parallel realities and multiple personalities. I am truly blessed to have surrounded myself by so many wonderful people: Uncle George, Kathy Butler, Aida Campbell, and so many others. Of course, I would not be the writer I am today if it were not for my close friend and writing guru, Erica Michaels.